THE
WOWZER

Presented By:

Friends Of The Library
YORK, NEBRASKA

THE
WOWZER

Frank Wheeler Jr.

THOMAS & MERCER

Published by Thomas & Mercer
P.O. Box 400818
Las Vegas, NV 89140

ISBN-13: 9781612182124
ISBN-10: 1612182127

ACKNOWLEDGEMENTS:

I'd like to express my thanks to the following people:

My mother, grandfather, and uncles from Arkansas and Oklahoma for instilling in me a great love of storytelling.

Vance Randolph, Ozarks linguist and folklorist, without whose research (especially in his book *Down in the Holler: A Gallery of Ozark Folk Speech*) this book would not have been possible.

Jonis Agee and Brent Spencer, for their confidence in my work and pointing my manuscript in the right direction. And Jonis, again, for more than a decade of advice and patience, and for making me finish a draft before revising.

My agent, Stacia Decker, for reading it, getting it, and selling it.

CHAPTER ONE

Jerry sets the fur.

I'VE TRIED SEVERAL different types of gloves. Them leather ones is great for this kinda work, but get real expensive when you gotta throw 'em away ever' time. Them disposable ones—the latex, vinyl, an' nitrile—they's real cheap for a box, but that baits another problem. Say you got somebody by the hair, an' they start a clawin' up at your hands, them fingernails can tear through pretty quick. I figure the best gloves is just the regular ol' dishwarshin' kind. Cheap an' sturdy. I buy the smallest size I can find, 'cause I want 'em real tight over my skin. That way there's no messin' with the trigger guard.

The woods all 'round Ronnie's house are thick'n tangled. Lotsa choked undergrowth, lotsa dead felled branches Grandma used to call widow-makers back when she still spoke. I stand 'hind a patch of cedars that's a little taller'n me an' fish my pocket for that plastic packet with the gloves. Trampin' through this mess of briars an' Ozark kudzu scratched an' stained my uniform a little, an' I'm kinda pissed. But I reckoned the best thing was to park the patrol car a ways up the road an' come in from the back.

After my gloves is on real tight, these ones is yellow, I take out my 'lectric tape. I keep it with a half inch folded back over so's it's easy to start with gloves on. Tape's important to me, too. Scotch tape's too damn restrictive. Duck tape don't never wanna get started at all. But 'lectric tape, it stretches real nice an' accommodates the circulation when I wrap it 'round the open side of my gloves to seal 'em up. Tears good, too, if'n you give it a hard tug.

Tom called me this mornin' right after I left the house an' said I gotta give Ronnie a talkin' to. Said he's goin' off the reservation again, sellin' his own shit on the side. Tom's rules are real simple: keep your head down, keep close to the willows. Ronnie cain't seem to do neither. If'n he asked me, I'd tell Tom that Ronnie's more trouble than he's worth. But Tom don't ask me my opinion that much, nor do I care to give it. Even so, when he asks a favor, I do it for two good reasons: he's the best boss, an' also the best friend I ever did have.

Ronnie lives north of Huntsville, up off Highway 23, near where them hills turn to mountains. He bought a little house off a dirt road with no neighbors visible from any place in his yard. That's part of how he got permission from them Fayetteville folks to sell their shit in the county. He started out as one them college dropouts they hire on to watch the crops, harvest, then package an' ship back to Fayetteville. Funny thing, for all the shit they grow up in them hills, hardly any gets sold here in Madison County. Less'n he knows Ronnie, or one or two others, a feller might have to drive all the way into Fayetteville to buy a dime bag, when half a mile away, on the other side of the mountain, there's a whole crop a growin'.

Hain't no lights on in the house, yet. 'Course it's only seven in the mornin', an' Ronnie usually stays up till five a.m. Cain't hear no TV or no music a playin'. There's a little charcoal grill on the patio. Some paper plates scattered on the concrete an' grass. A few cans an' bottles here'n there. I flex my hands a few times, pop the snap on my sidearm holster, an' walk outta the trees into the backyard.

The grill's still warm as I pass by. There's all this wrought-iron furniture 'round. Chairs, table, a reclinin' somethin' or other. I cain't see nobody inside through the patio door. When I get right up to the glass an' look through his dinin' room an' back into the livin' room, I can see the TV light reflectin' offa the picture frames on the wall.

I decide not to fuck 'round with it, pick up one of them chairs, an' throw it through the glass. Ronald Mayfield, white male, 25, 5'10", 135 lbs, blue eyes an' curly brown hair, jumps offa the couch, trips backward over the coffee table, an' stumbles toward the front door. I walk in through the hole, a crunchin' glass under my shoes, an' he don't take his eyes off me the whole time. He reaches for the door, an' I pull my weapon, tell him to set still. He turns sheet white an' bolts down the side hallway. There's three boys, maybe fifteen or sixteen, all in ratty jeans an' stained T-shirts, eyes bloodshot, jaws a hangin', all starin' at me from the couches as I head into the livin' room an' down the hallway after Ronnie.

He's locked himself in the bathroom an' I can hear him tryin' to get open the window. The door ain't nothin' but cardboard in the middle, so I kick it in no problem, an' sure enough, Ronnie's got his head an' both arms out the window. I holster my weapon an' pull out the collapsed steel baton, my favorite toy. I clack it out to twenty-six inches an' slap him 'cross the backs of his knees. He loses his footin', an' I grab his shoulders an' let him fall backward. I shift him to land right in the tub.

"Ever had the fur set on you, Ronnie?" I yell. I hate havin' to yell.

"I didn't do shit, man, I fuckin' swear!" he screams an' puts his left arm on the side of the tub to pull himself up. I slap his forearm hard with the baton. He shrieks an' falls back in, a clutchin' at it.

"That ain't what I asked," I say, turnin' to look at the countertop over the sink. Then I open the doors to the medicine cabinet. "I asked if you'd ever had the fur set on you. 'Cause the way you been actin' lately, you need some of that."

Ronnie's a grindin' his teeth, tears startin' to come down his pocked, bone-skinny face. He looks up at me an' groans, tryin' not to scream again from the pain in his arm. Now I got his attention.

A coupl'a them boys from the livin' room take a quick peek 'round the door, then disappear. I yell for 'em to come back. I want 'em to see this.

"You smell somethin' awful, buddy," I say. "Hain't takin' proper hygiene."

I take the big plastic bottle of green mouthwarsh, twist off the cap, an' dump it all over his head. Drop the empty bottle in the tub with him. Then I take the cologne. The spray nozzle won't come off, so I smash the whole thing on the tile a few inches from his face. Grab a can of deodorant. I spray it all up an' down his body till the can starts gettin' cold in my hand. There's that big white bottle a shampoo in

the basket hangin' from the showerhead. I unscrew the cap
an' squeeze it out over his head an' sling it in his face some.
Last, I take his tube of toothpaste an' empty it over top of
the shampoo.

I take his arm, red an' swellin' right up, an' he screams
'cause of my grip. I see a tattoo on his bicep peekin' out
from under his left sleeve. It's this tiger, 'bout the size of
my thumbprint, all made outta stripes. Ronnie tries to twist
away again an' I clamp down harder.

"You fuckin' fight me, boy, an' I'll have your friends dig
a hole for you 'bout a hundred yards back in them woods.
Now shut up," I say. He does, still cryin', an' groans when I
move his hand up to the top of his head. I start scrubbin'
the mess with his hand. Ronnie twists his head away from
me an' begs me to stop it. I keep at the scrubbin' till he's
got a blue-white foam on his head an' it's drippin' down
his neck an' chest. There's little spots of red in it, too,
probably from where the cologne bottle cut him. I yell for
them boys to come an' take a look. One peeks 'round the
door again, an' I grab Ronnie by his shirt an' pull him out
enough for the kid to see the mess. He takes off like he's a
cuttin' mud.

"There you go, buddy-boy," I say. "Now you had the fur
set on you."

"Please," Ronnie sobs. He's rubbin' at his eyes 'cause
that mess is a stingin' now.

"You gonna quit sellin' shit on the side?" I ask.

He nods. "Uh-huh, yeah. I fuckin' promise, okay?"

I stand back an' look at him. Weepin' foamy bleedin'
curled-up little thing. Like a new calf that just dropped out.
I turn on the showerhead an' walk out in the hallway.

Too God-damn noisy in there. I lean against the wall by the doorframe an' light a cigarette. That's a trick with them dishwarshin' gloves still on. I look over to the livin' room an' see them kids is all gone now. This with Ronnie's been gettin' worse an' worse. It's a delicate operation we got runnin', an' it seems like lately, he's been doin' his best to fuck it up. There's other folks 'round that'd like a shot at it, an' all it'd take is one major mistake to give 'em that. Flick my ash on Ronnie's carpet. Look down to see if any got on my shoe. I'm startin' to pull at the end of that 'lectric tape when somethin' catches my eye. There's these small spots on the light-blue carpet leadin' from the bathroom 'cross the hall to another door. They're brown, some a them's darker an' some's lighter. Hain't wet an' looks stained in. I open the door 'cross the hall an' look inside.

It's a spare bedroom, an' there's a couch opposite the bed with somebody a layin' on it. I walk on in an' go up to the couch. I know her.

"Damn, Ronnie," I yell to the bathroom, "is this Pam Hillman?"

He don't say nothin', but I recognize her. She was a year ahead of me in high school. She's facedown an' naked under a shawl. Breathin', but passed out. I squat down an' look at the bruises an' sores on her arms. She been mainlinin' God knows what. Them spot-stains on the carpet lead to the couch. Pam used to be Ronnie's girlfriend, but nobody's seen her 'round for a while. Afore that she used to work up at Miss Suzie's place, a sellin' her ass, like lotsa girls from these parts end up doin'.

I wanna get a closer look an' see if I can figure when them stains come from, but I'd have to touch her. I don't never care to touch a whore. My stomach twists right up just thinkin' 'bout it. Still got them gloves on, though. That oughtta be all right. I give a small retch reachin' out to take her ankle, then it passes when I feel the glove 'tween me an' her.

I pick up her leg an' turn it to look at the sole of her foot. I count seven small weepin' blisters, even-spaced. Some's scabbin' up, an' others ain't got the skin broke off. I reach for the other foot an' find nine more there. I set back on my heels an' take a drag, thinkin' 'bout where the blisters come from. I look at the cigarette in my fingers. The size of them looks about right. I stand up an' pull back the shawl. Turn her over on her back, careful to touch only with the gloves. Her belly an' tits got them blisters all over.

"I guess Pam's workin' from home, now, huh?" I yell.

Ronnie don't say shit.

Drivin' south down Highway 23 I can hear Ronnie groanin' in the backseat, damn near bawlin' after ever' pothole I hit. After passin' some of them long chicken barns, I cross Highway 412 an' then glance back at Ronnie. He's nursin' his arm pretty careful. He been screamin' that it's broke, so I said I'd drop him off at the ER.

"Passin' the sewer plant now, kid," I say, "so shut your nose up."

I coulda just taken regular 412 on down to Business 412, an' that's where Huntsville Memorial Hospital is. But I need some more cigarettes, an' I want Ronnie to set in the backseat awhile an' see how it feels, starin' through that mesh-metal barrier.

A ways further down, right when the highway turns to Parrot Drive, we pass the concrete company, an' I look out over them big white mixers an' open-top trailers parked along the fence by the road. This here's where the town starts as far as I'm concerned, all the rest is just suburb that built up over the years. Folks been movin' out here from Fayetteville, wantin' to get quiet country life, what with all the changes been happenin' in the city.

Where Parrot Drive splits, I take the right onto War Eagle an' drive half a block. Cut through Abbie Reynold's vacant lot an' cross Main Street into the Sonic parkin' lot. Pull into the Shell station an' park. Ronnie's pissed somethin' awful from all the bouncin'. Run in an' buy my cigarettes. Get a stick of beef jerky from the jar at the counter for Schnitzel.

Get back in the patrol car an' head down War Eagle, the strip with the courthouse an' the sheriff's station where my desk is, city police on the other side of the square. Then get onto Main to head back up 412, up to the hospital. Park outside the ER, get out an' open the back door for Ronnie. Then, on the way inside, I realize I shoulda checked my hair in the mirror, 'cause I know she's workin' this mornin'.

"You gonna keep that rat-dog in here the whole time?" Bobby asks. Schnitzel's down at my feet, settin' real quiet an' patient. That's my wiener dog, Schnitzel. He's lickin' his chops from the smell of corned beef hash on the stove. He's maybe four years old now. Got him when he was just a coupl'a months from a Mexican feller in Fayetteville who breeds 'em.

"Kindly refrain, sir," I say, "from talkin' thataway 'bout a law-enforcement dog."

"That ain't no law dog, dumb-ass," Bobby says. He can talk to me like that 'cause he's on the bowlin' team with me an' Tom an' Conrad. This is his diner, too. That's how come it's called Fat Bobby's. Bobby's one of maybe a dozen black folk in a county of thirteen thousand. He come up here from Nawlins after them levees gave an' bought this place. At first I wasn't sure how good a black bowler'd be, but when I seen his scores on that board, Bobby made me a believer.

"Well, I'm a lawman, an' he's my dog. That oughtta count," I say. Robert Hamilton, black male, 41, 6'2", 310 lbs, brown eyes, shaved head an' goatee, starts to chuckle, an' then I chuckle a bit a watchin' all that jigglin' under his T-shirt.

Most black folk leave here pretty quick when they see there's hardly any others. But Bobby, he loves the idea of bein' one of only a handful of eligible black men in a sea of white country women. An' if Maggie wasn't seein' me, I know she'd be on his list, too.

"It counts for dog shit, Jer," he says, tossin' my dog a piece of bacon. I laugh, 'cause I know he likes havin' Schnitzel in here much as I do.

"He don't mean that," I say to my dog. "Bobby, watch this," I say, an' snap my fingers over Schnitzel's head. "C'mon, buddy," I say, "who's ya boss? Who's ya boss?" He rolls over for me, an' comes back up a beggin'. I take a little piece of Bobby's bacon an' toss it down to him. Bobby's got bacon around a lot, especially in the mornin'. Often he'll just carry it with him in a little red basket like the kind he uses for the fries, an' just chew on it.

"I thought you wasn't s'posed to bring that critter to work with ya," Bobby says.

"Takin' him up to the hospital later. I told you 'bout that, right? Tom's got everybody on his staff doin' some kinda service for the community. I picked them kids in the hospital."

"You dress him up? Is that right?"

"He got a little vest with two toy six-guns on the sides, an' a tiny cowboy hat that's hell to get to stay on him. Likes doin' it, though. Tail wags the whole damn time."

"You dress up too, Jer, don't ya?"

"Got a matchin' vest an' hat. Hell, I don't mind bein' a clown now'n then."

Bobby laughs again as he heads back into the kitchen. I look down at Schnitzel. I don't like big dogs. Never have. They make me nervous somethin' awful. But as far as I'm concerned, Schnitzel's my huntin' dog. Tom got a retriever, an' Conrad got himself a large spaniel of some kind, an' I always like to go huntin' with 'em. Don't mind *their* two dogs long as they keep 'em under close watch. But not havin' no dog to bring along made me feel a little left out, I guess. So when I's watchin' the animal channel a few years back, I seen them dachshunds. That show said they was bred for huntin'. Real damn killers. Could take down a badger, even, an' badgers is pretty mean. That's what I tried to tell Tom an' Conrad when I brought Schnitzel along. They just laughed the whole time. I told 'em he's bred for it. What do they know anyhow?

Mostly, I brought Schnitzel with me today 'cause Maggie's meetin' me here, an' she likes him a awful lot. Maggie's the reason I'm still a little hung over now. I don't never drink as much as I do when I'm out with her. Been seein' her for a coupl'a years now, an' I never knowed a woman could put it away like she does. Even I cain't keep up.

Bobby comes back from the kitchen to the front counter an' pours me some more coffee. He looks down at Schnitzel an' says, "I seen Nawlins nutria bigger'n him."

So that's when she walks in. Margaret Gordon, white female, 33, 5'5", 150 lbs (though she don't want me to know), curly red hair an' olive-green eyes. Pale skin with freckles on her face. She's still in her blue-green scrubs an' got her hair tied up in back. One untied shoelace. I just watch her walk over. I like doin' that. As looks go, she's mighty far from the cullin' list. She sets on the stool next to me an' says hi to Bobby. I can hear him grin. Then she looks right at me like I'm her life raft in freezin' water.

You're probably thinkin' right now, what the hell's this God-damn beauty, this fuckin' med school graduate who operates on people in the ER an' saves folk ever' day, doin' with a peon deputy who didn't wear shoes regular till high school? The bit about the life raft just now, it ain't afar off. Three years ago I pulled her out of a burnin' car.

Tied a rolled-up towel on her leg to slow the bleedin' an' drove her to her own emergency room. She was five months along with her ex-husband's baby. She lost the kid an' damn near bled out.

I knew I shouldn'ta moved her, but all that blood made me anxious. Neck braces don't do shit if you already gone. I 'member walkin' in with her in my arms, she was mumblin' somethin' I couldn't understand, bleedin' on my uniform an' the floor from her head, from the gash in her thigh, an' from 'tween her legs. After, I sent her a get-well card. Some stupid little bear diggin' in a honey pot on the front, sayin' feel better "beary soon." I figured, if'n I was her, I'd get sick of all them sympathy cards an' want a chuckle.

That's how she met Schnitzel. When I's up at the kids' wing, I figured I'd just as well bring him down to her room. She didn't say much, but I could tell she liked him a waggin' his tail an' lickin' her face. I 'member her smilin' at me then, real shy. I 'member she thanked me for the card.

Took her a whole year 'fore she'd talk to me about the accident. I don't blame her. I reckon she got a idea 'bout who I was. Like I was the kinda guy'd be good for her to be 'round. I hain't contradicted it yet.

So Maggie asks Bobby if he still has that spinach lasagna in the cooler from yesterday. Bobby says he'll get it quick, an' asks if she wants her glass of tomato juice. She nods yes, then looks over at me.

"What are you starin' at?" she asks.

"Them freckles make me hungry," I say. She laughs. Actually, I haven't stopped lookin' at her since she come in. I put my hand up on her shoulder to rub it.

"That's good," she says, "both hands, please." She turns away so's I can rub both shoulders.

"You know you got a undid shoelace?" I ask.

"Gee, *Dad*," she says, "thanks a *whole* bunch."

She lowers her head an' I look at them little orange hairs on the back a her neck.

"Rough mornin', then?" I chuckle as she lets out a groan.

"Three criticals in a drunk accident on four-twelve. I was the only attending, of course, and Mike took his sweet time gettin' there. Then some stupid kid tries to fix a lawn mower and gets his arm torn up. Then you bring in that

Ronnie kid with the broken arm, and he was a pain in the ass, too. Cussin' the whole time, screamin' like a little child when we set it, even though I'd numbed it."

"So it was broken after all, huh?"

"Yeah. The left ulna." She reaches back over her shoulder to my left arm, finds my pinky finger without lookin', then traces her fingers down along the outside edge a my arm. She pinches a little over 'round the bone. "This one here. And it was a clean break, too."

"Should you be tellin' me this?" I ask, jokin'. "I mean, ain't there HIPPA or somethin'?"

"Well, technically, since you brought him in, you'd be workin' on his case."

"What case, hon? Detectives have cases, I'm just a deputy. An' anyhow, I thought he fell down his stairs."

"I said it was a clean break, Jerry. No bone fragments. That'd be consistent with a fall like that, except for the skin. No cuts or abrasions that you'd usually find. Plus he kept mumblin' how he was gonna get the bastard. Made me think somebody did it to him."

"How 'bout that," I say, leanin' into her shoulder with a little more pressure.

"Jesus, that's good," she says. "Mike said he heard that Ronnie sold drugs. You think maybe he owed money, or somethin' like that?"

"Could be. I heard that 'bout Ronnie too."

Bobby sets her glass of tomato juice in fronta her, then the lasagna. She thanks me for the rub an' starts a cuttin' up the food. She glances back to see if I'm still lookin' at her. By then I'm lookin' at my own plate of corned beef hash an' scrambled eggs. She offers Schnitzel, who's a waitin' with true hunter's patience at her feet, a small piece of melted cheese.

"Tell me if you heard this one already," Bobby says, leanin' on the counter opposite me'n Maggie. "I heard this'n from a old Cajun boy my first cookin' job in the Quarter."

"This ain't about Arkansas, is it?" Maggie asks. Last time he told her a joke it was somethin' like what do you have when you got thirty-two Arkansawyers in a room: a full set a teeth. Although I know she liked that one 'cause Maggie's dad's a dentist in Fayetteville.

"Strictly Acadian, my dear," Bobby says.

"Then proceed, sir," she says, grinnin' at the botha us.

"Little Joey brings hisself home a fiancée, young Mattie from down by the river. Daddy sees his little Joey and that Mattie sittin' on the couch, an' he calls for Joey to come on outside for a word. 'Boy,' Daddy say, 'what you doin' with that girl in there?'"

Maggie bumps her knee against mine without lookin' away from Bobby.

"So little Joey, he say, 'Why Daddy, I asked Mattie to marry me, she my fiancée.' Daddy rubs his temples an' stare down at the ground an' get red in the face. Daddy say, 'Boy, you cain't marry that girl. You just cain't.' 'How come, Daddy? I sure do love her,' little Joey say. ''Cause, boy,' Daddy say, 'she your sister, only she don't know.'"

She'n me both laugh a little, an' I throw Schnitzel a piece of my breakfast. I sneak a peek at them tiny little freckles 'round her nose. I'm fonda lookin' at her when she ain't aware.

"Well, this takes the wind outta little Joey's sails for quite awhile. He's got hisself a broken heart for all of two whole months. Then he find hisself that nice Carol Ann from up the road. So he get hisself a new fiancée, and he bring her home to show off his new woman. Then Daddy see little Joey an' that Carol Ann sittin' on the couch together, an' he call his Joey outside for a word. 'Boy,' Daddy say, 'what you doin' with that girl in there? You cain't marry her.' 'But how come, Daddy?' Joey asks, 'I sure love her awful.' "'Cause, boy,' Daddy say, 'she your sister, only she don't know.'"

"Damn, I guess Daddy gets around," Maggie laughs.

Bobby just nods an' keeps at it. "Well, don't this just beat all. Now little Joey's twice heartbroken. He just sit 'round the house all day a mopin' and a poutin'. 'Fore long, Momma see him draggin' his feet, an' she step in. 'Joey, what's a matter with you, boy? What happened to them girls you had 'round here a bit ago? Why don't you marry that young Mattie from down by the river, or that nice Carol Ann from up the road?' Joey don't say nothin' at first, but Momma keeps at him till he give it up. 'I cain't, Momma,' little Joey say, "'cause Daddy, he say they my sisters, only they don't know.' Well, Momma, she take a deep breath, an' her face get all red, an' she look up at the ceilin' for a minute. 'Look here, boy,' Momma says, 'you go an' you marry whichever one of them girls you want to.' 'But Momma,' Joey say, 'Daddy said that—' 'Hush now, boy,' Momma says, 'Listen here. He ain't your daddy, only he don't know.'"

All three of us bust up laughin'. Bobby slaps the counter good, an' I just 'bout fall offa my stool. I watch Maggie turn bright red an' lean over the counter shakin' with the chuckles.

After a minute more, Bobby goes back in the kitchen to start the prep work for lunch. Maggie picks at a piece of lasagna an' turns to look at me 'fore she speaks.

"So you think that's why Ronnie didn't say anything about who did it? 'Cause he's involved in the drug business somehow?" she asks, takin' her first bite.

"I'd say that's probably a fair enough guess."

She chews her bite of food, takes a gulp of juice, then looks down at her plate. Maggie turns, leans in to kiss me. Her lips are clean an' warm an' taste like tomato.

"You know you cain't bring that dog in here, Jerry," Harold yells at me as I walk in the sheriff's station.

"Kill ya own snakes, Harold," I shout back down the hallway. I walk over to my desk in the middle of the room an' look for any messages on them little yellow slips that dispatch leaves. I plop down in my chair an' tell Schnitzel to set.

"This is gonna mean a write-up, Jerry," Harold says, comin' in closer to me. He ain't my superior. Just a prick in a deputy uniform.

"I'm just checkin' messages, an' I gotta get mine an' his vests," I say, pointin' down at my dog. "I'm on my way to the hospital right now."

Harold walks, grumblin', back over toward the holdin' area, an' I hear Tom's office door open.

"Jer," Tom says, "go on an' bring him in here."

I cain't find any messages in my inbox, under my keyboard, or stuck behind my framed picture of me an' Maggie on a beach in Puerto Vallarta last summer. I snap my fingers an' Schnitzel follows me on into Tom's office.

Thomas Haskell, white male, 58, 6'0", 285 lbs, grayin' black hair with a full white beard, points to the seat in fron-ta his desk. I set an' wait for him while he gets a piece of jerky for my dog from his desk.

"So Ronnie went all right this mornin'," he says, motionin' for me to close the door. I push it enough to click an' look back at Tom.

"I didn't mean to break his arm, but he was fightin' me," I say. "You know how he gets."

"Maybe he'll get it through his skull this time."

"He'll get somethin' through his skull if'n he keeps it up," I say, an' right away wish I hadn't. Tom wrinkles up his brow an' shakes his head.

"The board up in Fayetteville wouldn't take too kindly to that."

Them's the folks that set up the whole thing. Dependin' on his mood, which is fair today, Tom calls 'em either the board or the Sanhedrin—on account, he says, of how they're all a buncha backstabbin' Jews.

"You know I's just bullshittin', Tom," I say. He nods an' scratches at his beard.

"When you go into town next, do me a favor an' ask Big Cal where's the fire at?" he says. I don't know what he means, but they got lotsa inside jokes. Tom an' Cal used to be city cops in Fayetteville 'fore Tom got hisself the job as sheriff of Madison County. 'Tween the two of them, they run a pretty tight ship.

"You bet," I say, an' get up to leave. When I open the door, Tom looks up again at me.

"Oh, hey. Almost forgot," he says. "Take a stroll down by the drunk tank. See what we got in there 'bout five this mornin'."

"Holeeee shit!" I say. "Nappy Freddie! When they catch up with you?"

"Fuck if I know, Jer," he says. Frederick MacDonald, white male, 26, 5'8", 130 lbs, an' long blond hair bunched up in dreadlocks, which is how come he got his nickname, looks back at me from his bunk bed in the drunk tank. He's got bad bruises on his face an' arms. I reckon he didn't come voluntarily.

"Where the Christ ya been, Freddie? We been lookin' for you the last ten months."

"Around, you know?"

Freddie was in custody, last year, in a holdin' cell in Fayetteville. He was one of them crop boys like Ronnie, an' then went an' shot a few folks on a PCP binge. They caught him but couldn't hold him for long. Before he could talk to a lawyer even, he escaped. Damndest thing.

"You look like you been a livin' back in them woods, Freddie," I say.

"Yeah, I done some of that."

I ask him if he wants a smoke, an' he says he does. When he gets up from his bunk to take it from my hand, I notice the tattoo on his bicep.

It's that thumbprint tiger, all made of stripes.

It's all good at the kids' wing. They love Schnitzel an' me clownin' around. I walk 'round bowlegged, like John Wayne, an' say How-Dee-Pardner. I hand out these little toy silver six-guns an' let the kids take turns a shootin' caps at me whilst I fake fallin' over dead. Then I take Schnitzel 'round to each one an' let him go to work.

This part of my job I really do like. I know how bad it sucks to be a kid in the hospital for a long stretch.

After the hospital, I go back to work. My shift ends at eight tonight, an' so does Maggie's, so 'bout then I'm gonna meet her at the sandwich place she likes. Till then I got time to kill while I'm technically still on the clock. I drive back to my house an' drop off Schnitzel.

Me an' Grandma live out in the woods a ways south of Huntsville. She's lived here since she was born. She's ninety now, so that'd be 1918. When she got married at sixteen, her husband, my grandpa, just moved in with her an' her folks. He died a piece back, afore I was born.

Grandma's out in the garden when I show up, on her hands an' knees a workin' in the dirt with the trowel. She can still grow vegetables an' weed it real good. She can still cook on the stove, an' clean the house, an' do the warsh. She can even tend her still back in them woods. She just cain't talk no more. Not the last five years anyhow.

I walk out on the back porch an' call to her. She stands up to look at me. Evelyn Bowden, white female, 5'7", 140 lbs, white hair that used to be blonde, faded blue eyes. She shoves her trowel in the front pocket of her apron an' heads up to the house.

I'm a true bush colt. That is, I never knew my father. Didn't hardly see my momma, neither. Maybe that makes me a double bush colt, if there is such a thing. Don't matter a damn, though, 'cause Grandma took care of everythin'.

I check to make sure she got her medicine out on the counter for the night. I write a note that I'm gonna be at Maggie's tonight, an' tell her, too. I don't know how much she understands. She might think I'm my Uncle Ray. She might think this is 1962 for all I know. Long as she takes her pills an' don't burn the house down, there ain't no problem.

I walk up the stairs to my room, an' Schnitzel follows me. It's near two in the afternoon now, an' I won't have time to clean up when I get off work. I got the dispatch radio on my uniform an' ain't s'posed to be away from it, so I cain't get in the shower. So I settle on clippin' my fingernails an' toenails an' givin' myself a good shave again.

I clean the rest of the foam from my face an' look in the mirror. Jeremiah Bowden, white male, 32, 5'9", 165 lbs. Blond hair an' blue eyes like my grandma used to have in pictures of her I seen from the 1950s.

I look down at the bruise on my collarbone. Maggie done that last week. She's gettin' into games. Them sex games, I mean. She had me show up at her house in my uniform an' make like I was gonna arrest her for solicitation of a sex act. Handcuffs an' everythin'. The idea was, she'd barter her way out. I told her I didn't like hookers, an' she said that's fine, we could both pretend. Anyhow, she can get pretty wild sometimes, an' that's where that bruise come from. As far as her fondness for them games, I don't particularly like *it* much, but I like her, an' *it* don't hurt me none.

When I leave, Grandma's out in the garden again, bent over the dirt, workin' at the carrots. I don't think they's ready yet, but I hain't gonna tell her that.

Busy time in July's from four p.m. to six. That's when the shift change starts down at the mine. When school's in, the rush starts at three. Today's borin' as shit—no speeders, no accidents or overturned hog trucks—so I just set in the patrol car in the parkin' lot of the sandwich store, smoke cigarettes, an' listen to the dispatch while I read the paper.

I think 'bout them tattoos on Ronnie an' Nappy Freddie. Hain't never seen them kind before. Cain't be jail tats 'cause Ronnie ain't never been arrested, an' Freddie only been in that holdin' cell for maybe a day afore he bust out.

Startin' to get dark now. Freddie looked like he ain't been fed in months. Used to lift weights, an' now he looks skinnier'n Ronnie. Eyes looked like they's dead. Like how a fish's pop out when ya step on it. He'd been livin' up in them woods, he said. I wonder if he seen that Wowzer that lives back in there. That's how I reckon a feller'd look if he did.

Freddie lived in Madison County for a few years 'fore he went off a shootin' folks. First one he done in, though, that was close to home. Killed his wife, on accident he says. That dust got him paranoid somebody was a comin' after him, so he took his SKS carbine an' hid 'hind his couch. Then when his wife come home from workin' as a waitress at the bowlin' alley, he started unloadin' rounds right through the door soon's the key hit the lock. Out of a thirty-round banana clip, she only caught three or four. Anyhow, it was enough. Woods or no woods, I figure he seen the Wowzer all right.

Thing is, he mighta been right 'bout somebody comin' for him. I heard things here'n there. Nothin' I can say for sure, though. Trails like them'ns go cold all the time.

Maggie shows up at 'bout ten past eight. We go in an' get our sandwiches together. She's changed into her jeans an' that low-cut black blouse I like. Since I got tomorrow off, I gotta drop off the patrol car at the station, so she follows me there an' waits out front on the street while I take in the keys.

Tom, Rhianna, Bill, an' Harold are all in the office area, bullshittin' 'bout somethin' or other. I go over to my desk an' unlock the bottom left drawer. The little black box is still inside, like I left it a week ago. I cain't leave items of value in drawers up at the house, 'cause Grandma'll go through 'em from time to time an' forget to put things back where she found 'em.

"This here's for you," I say as I get into Maggie's car.

"What's this?" she asks. She opens up the little black box an' looks up at me a tad confused. "Jerry, how can you afford this? This must have cost like a grand."

"Just put it on an' don't ask no questions."

"Jerry, I'm serious. I doubt your salary, not to be rude, but..."

I take the necklace outta her hand an' undo the clasp myself. It's a light gold chain with them diamonds, like the kind I seen her lookin' at in the mall in Fayetteville a few months back. Feller in the store called it a journey necklace. I fasten it 'hind her neck an' look at it on her.

"We'll get a better look at it inside, but I just couldn't wait," I say. "But don't worry 'bout my salary, hon, I saved up. 'Sides, today's a special occasion."

"How's that?" she asks.

"Two years, Maggie, since you done took the cuss offa me."

"Oh. That," she says an' grins.

"Okay, I got somethin' for you, too," she says when we park in her driveway. "But you gotta stay in the car while I get it."

She gets out an' hurries up the back steps into the house she rents. She only takes a minute, comes right back out to the car, an' knocks on my window. I roll it down an' she hands me a small paper sack.

"See what's inside," Maggie says.

I open it an' take out a black ski mask.

"Well, it's nice, but what am I gonna do with this in July?" I ask.

She leans in the window an' bites my ear just hard enough to leave a mark.

"You'll figure it out," she says, an' turns to go back up the porch steps.

I look down at the mask in my hands.

"Gimme a minute to get the shower runnin', okay?" she says 'fore she steps back inside.

I look back down at the mask. I think 'bout throwin' that chair through Ronnie's door this mornin', 'bout all that glass everywhere an' how scared he looked when I walked into his home.

The water starts runnin' in Maggie's bathroom.

I bust out laughin'.

CHAPTER TWO:

Maggie takes the cuss off.

WHEN MY GUARD unit got activated regular army, I used to could run five miles ever' mornin'. I'm down to three now, so I got a deal made with myself. If I cain't make three miles ever' mornin', I'ma quit smokin'. So I work extra hard to make them three.

Since her house is out on the edge of town, I run up into the hills a ways, 'bout a mile an' a half afore I head back. I always start out at a quarter of six. 'Bout six or so the dark turns gray, an' I can make out them tree branches up above me. I can see the broken yellow line on the blacktop. There's crickets out 'hind the trees. A woodpecker knockin' back up the road. I can smell cedar, some honeysuckle, an' the kudzu the county's been clearin' back from the road. My head's poundin', but not too bad. Must be the only time I ever get mad at Maggie is when I jog hungover from drinkin' with her the night before.

She still ain't up when I get back to her house so I figure on makin' breakfast. Hain't hardly nothin' in her fridge but a few eggs an' some chunks of cheese, so I start me a omelet. I never was taught proper how to cook, I learnt by doin' it myself. When I's five, Grandma started a new kinda punishment 'cause, she said, I's too damn ornery. If'n I broke one of her rules, she wouldn't feed me the whole next day. Anythin' I et was my own doin's. If I wanted cereal, or bread, I's outta luck. Any vegetables I had to take from her garden when she wasn't lookin', or the neighbor's. If'n I wanted meat, I had to kill somethin' from the woods with the .22, or catch it in the creek with a pole. I had to clean an' cook it myself, an' if I forgot 'bout pickin' up after myself, then it'd be the next day as well. First time I reached for the refrigerator while she was cookin' on a punishment day, she slapped my hand away with that spatula she's turnin' her bacon with. So I learnt to cook real quick.

I've already got the coffee a goin' when Maggie shuffles into the kitchen, eyes half-shut. She don't want breakfast, just coffee. An' she says we gotta go to the grocery store 'cause there ain't nothin' for lunch.

Usually it works like this. I push the grocery cart with her purse set in it. She walks in fronta the cart, a pullin' things from the shelf while I stare at her ass in them jeans. I do believe I enjoy ever' minute I spend with her.

"You wanna go to Willie's later on?" I ask. Tuesday's our day off together, an' sometimes we'll go out to Tree-Dog Willie's for a drink an' shoot some pool.

"Can't. Remember, my brother's comin' in. He wanted to meet you."

"Which brother?" I ask. She's got five. An' two sisters. She's the baby of her family.

"John. He's the one that works outta Fayetteville for that rural mental health outreach program. He's the shrink."

"Oh, sure," I say, watchin' her bend down to pick out a bag of onion rolls. "Willie's serves food. Maybe he'd like to go there?"

"Not his kind of place, Jerry. An' he already made reservations, he said."

"Shit. You mean a tie."

Tree-Dog Willie's is where Maggie first come up to talk to me after her accident. She'd been outta the hospital for maybe a month. Me an' Bobby go out to Willie's ever' Friday night for the bluegrass jam. Hollis, he's the owner, gets a whole mess of local bands to come on Fridays an' do a few songs each. Just the local good ol' boys, nothin' fancy. Bobby didn't think he'd like bluegrass when he first come out here. But sure enough, he got sold on it when he dug the knee-slappin' rhythm. Same went for me when Bobby made me listen to John Lee Hooker. I didn't care for it none till he played "Bad Like Jesse James." Then I got it.

That first time I seen her there, she just walked right on up while we was shootin' pool an' said she'd play winner. Bobby said he's surprised to see a doc at a place like Willie's. She just swallowed her beer an' said it's like where she used to hang out in college. Then she blushed an' said, I 'member, high school too.

An' I 'member she laughed when I spilled my drink. Hollis's dog, Willie the sixteenth, come right up to me while I's sippin' my beer, put his paw up on my leg, an' when I looked down I liketa shit an' spit out my beer. I don't like that blue-tick hound, an' the little fucker knows it. I won't hit him 'cause Hollis wouldn't never let me back, but I shooed him away. Maggie laughed at me an' that grin caught me off my guard.

Maggie's pickin' out ground beef for lunch. She likes the way I make sloppy joes, but don't want the fat that come with it. So she picks through the packages, lookin' for the 96, 97 percent lean.

"What do you need to make the sauce?" she asks me.

"Just a can of that Hormel. Some 'basco, an' some Wooster sauce to throw in."

She puts one package back an' reaches to the next shelf up.

"You wanna run an' get that?" she asks.

"If you hadn't worn that tank top, maybe," I say. "But seein' things is how they is, I'ma stay put." She gives me that funny-but-seriously-Jerry look, so I go an' get the rest. While I'm walkin' past, I check the price on dishwarshin' gloves.

I know the looks she gives now. I learnt 'em pretty well over the last two an' a half years. Startin' with that night at Willie's. Had wide eyes that night. Like she was a little nervous an' wanted me to think she was interested.

I didn't go home with her right away. That took me a coupl'a weeks. Not that I didn't want to. I didn't think there'd be any point. Finally, I give in an' went an' sat on her couch an' let her scoot over to me an' lean in. I knew what'd happen, so I didn't want to ruin nothin', but I figured she'd get pissed off worse if I didn't do nothin' at all.

Kissin' her that first night was awful nice. She figured me for a shy one, an' didn't move it along too quick. It musta been difficult for Maggie, 'cause she's never been shy when she wants somethin'. After a few nights, she put my hands on her. An' that was somethin' real nice too, got my blood rushin' good. Then she slid her hand down 'tween my legs an' seen I hain't got nothin' up. Nor did I when she kep' it there a while.

I 'member feelin' bad, thinkin' she was gonna get pissed like happens most times in this particular situation. The look on her face then was wrinkled forehead an' narrow eyes an' said what's-the-problem-here-Jerry?

"Everything okay?" she asked. I nodded.

"Don't work," I said.

"How long has it been like that?" she asked.

"Long time. Somethin' cussed it good."

Much to my surprise, Maggie didn't back off, like some others had. What she done was put on her doctorin' hat an' go to work a figurin'.

Ever' time I look at her I'm a little surprised by it. It's somethin' new for me. Delight. I reckon that's the name for it. Hain't known that in a long time.

Watchin' her a waitin' in line at the checkout, readin' a magazine from the stand, I feel warm in my stomach. Like after a swallow of my grandma's farm liquor, how it spreads from the bottom right on up. Only this don't burn none.

"I'm thinkin' about cuttin' my hair short," she says without lookin' up from the magazine. "Like hers," she points to some scrawny actress on the page with short hair.

"Don't do that, hon," I say. She looks up.

"Why not?"

"'Cause my world might end."

Tearin' open the hamburger package spills some black blood into the sink. After warshin' my hands, I knead the meat some 'fore settin' it in the skillet to brown. I warsh the little bits of meat off my fingers under the faucet an' watch the water pick up them little blood spots. First step was the blood.

After I'd told Maggie 'bout my problem, she asked me some more questions.

No, it wasn't total. I could still get it up sometimes.

But not 'round somebody else. Magazines an' Internet was what worked.

I reckoned that it started when I's seventeen. I got a bad case of gonorrhea from one of Miss Suzie's girls. Got cured up with one shot of antibiotics, but when you're seventeen, an' you don't know to go in right away, you set around for two weeks, scared to shit your pecker's gonna rot right off. You don't know why. Don't know nothin' at all.

After that, ever' time a girl tried touchin' it, it went right dead.

So Maggie had me come into the hospital after a couple weeks. She brought me back into the lab. Set me down at the counter where she'd arranged a tray. Glass tubes with black stoppers. Cotton balls an' white tape. Iodine wipes.

She took my left arm an' rolled up my shirtsleeve. Tied a rubber tube 'round it below the bicep. Took the iodine packet, tore it open, an' wiped the inside of my elbow.

"I need you to trust me, Jerry," she said. "This is just the first step, okay?"

I 'member I nodded but didn't say nothin'. If'n she wanted my blood, I didn't mind.

She tore open another packet that had a needle in it an' put it mosta the way into the black stopper on one of them tubes.

"This is a vacuum tube, so it'll draw it by itself. Just hold your arm still while I find a good vein."

I knew what a vacuum tube was. I'd seen 'em when they took my blood when I got tested for the Guards. She held my arm while she worked the needle through the skin into the vein. Once it was in, she gripped the needle an' worked it all the way back through the stopper. I watched my blood fill that tube up right quick. Then she undid that rubber tourniquet on my arm, put a cotton ball over the puncture, an' pulled that needle outta the vein. She worked the needle outta the stopper an' set the tube back on the tray. Put that white tape over the cotton ball.

"Now you do me," she said.

"I hain't had no trainin' on that," I said. She shook her head at me.

"All you gotta do is hold it firm an' I'll guide it in. Don't worry 'bout hurtin' me. ER docs get so many inoculations, I don't even flinch anymore."

I done what she asked. Tied her arm. Wiped the iodine. She set the needle in the stopper an' handed the new tube to me.

"This one here's the median cubital," she said, guidin' my hand, "that usually works good on me." She touched the needle to her skin an' looked up at me. "I conferred with a colleague. He says it sounds like an arousal disorder, and psychologically based, not biological."

"You told somebody 'bout me?"

"As an anonymous case study. That okay?"

"Sure, I guess."

She pushed the needle through the skin an' found the vein.

"The trauma of your infection, Jerry, is what brought this on. Your body's put up a defense mechanism. You developed an association between sexual contact and infection. Sometimes it happens that way."

"So you want me to know you ain't infected? That what this is about?" I asked.

"It's just a first step."

She worked the needle back through the stopper, an' I watched her blood fill the tube.

"This has to do with trust," she said. "I'm just settin' a baseline."

After untyin' the tourniquet, she had me pull out the needle an' tape the cotton ball in place. I saw her set the tube next to mine on the tray.

Probably, I haven't moved in an hour. Maggie an' I are settin' up in her bed watchin' TV, been smokin' grass, she's layin' over my lap, an' we're just still. I seen two episodes of some cartoon I don't understand come'n go, an' I hadn't felt the desire to move a inch.

Maggie startles me a bit when she changes the channel. She sets up an' gives a stretch, then leans back on my chest so her head's right under my chin. The TV is on a soap opera now.

"How'd that thing with your uncle go?" she mumbles.

"That was tomorrow, but the doc had to reschedule. So it ain't till next week." Ray's been fightin' the cancer for a few years now. His Medicare only pays for so much, an' not for transportation to an' from the chemo treatments, so I help him all I can. It's let up on him lately, but we still gotta keep a eye on it.

"Oh. I thought it was yesterday. What day is it today?"

"Tuesday."

"Don't lemme forget, we're meetin' my brother at the restaurant tonight."

"When? An' what one?"

"Sevenish. And at that nice one."

I don't wanna go nowheres. I'd lay here all day long if'n I could. Ever since she took the cuss off, I don't never wanna get outta any bed she's in. Even if all she's doin' is layin' 'cross me, smellin' her hair an' skin, feelin' her weight on my legs, that's the nicest damn thing I know.

"Jesus, Margaret," her brother John says, "your eyes are still bloodshot."

We set down at his table in the nice restaurant. I been in here before, but I still don't feel comfortable in a tie.

"Sorry, I fell asleep. Jerry woke me up," she says. John looks at me an' remembers. I reach out to shake his hand, pretendin', for now, that we haven't met.

John Kavanagh, 45, 6'1", 210 lbs, brown hair an' same God-damn olive-green eyes as Maggie got. Psychiatrist. Works two days a week at Huntsville Memorial Hospital. I known him since I was fifteen. That's when I got into that last fight that got me kicked off the high school baseball team.

Kavanagh. I never asked Maggie's maiden name. Nor've I met any other of her siblin's. Gordon is her married name. She said her brother's name was John. I'd been thinkin' John Gordon. If I'd known her brother was John Kavanagh, I'da called off the dinner.

"Jerry. Jeremiah, is it? You know, Jerry's a pretty common name in Madison County," he says, takin' my hand in his an' shakin' it real slow an' careful. He's a tremblin' a bit.

"Maggie," I say, "we've actually met before." She looks at me, surprised. "If'n I 'member right, that'd be thirteen year ago." I gotta say somethin', so I tell her, "This gentleman here was workin' when I walked into the ER. He ran some tests for my head injury."

"You never told me about that," Maggie says.

"I got my head mallyhacked with a baseball bat. I'm lucky I can remember your brother's face, forget about his name."

John's got nothin' showin' on his face at all cep'n a little sweat. Like he's a waitin' for me to leave the table so's he can tell Maggie a secret. He's thinkin' right now, I can tell, 'bout writin' "Conduct Disorder" on my chart when I's fifteen. He's also thinkin', I reckon, 'bout the time I just mentioned, a walkin' into the ER when I's nineteen. Probably he 'members I had dirt shoved way up under my fingernails.

He starts right in on a chewin' out his little sister for gettin' high. Asks if she's heard back from any of the positions she applied to in St. Louis, Chicago, or Memphis. He tells her she's just a wastin' her time here. She needs the experience of a larger city. He looks right at her the whole time, just pretendin' I hain't there. He's a pretty big man, lots bigger'n me. She don't get intimidated by him. Just orders herself a Jack an' Coke.

John gets in this habit of lookin' over at me when he takes a sip of his drink. Think it's Scotch, but I hain't sure. Tom drinks that nasty business, but I prefer what Grandma makes back in the woods. For now, I'm stickin' with beer, an' pacin' it slow, so's I don't say nothin' worth regrettin'. John tips his glass up an' peeks at me over the rim while Maggie's askin' him about his wife, Charlene. Looks back at her like it didn't register.

"I asked how Charlene's doin'," Maggie says.

John shakes his head. "She's fine. Forget about her. Look, you're not doing yourself any favors by staying in this place. There's plenty of opportunity elsewhere, Margaret."

"I think I'm doin' fine as is, John. And I already applied to those places, I don't know what else there is you want me to do."

He waves over to the waitress an' drains his glass. Glares at me as he slaps it empty down on the tabletop. Maggie's rubbin' her temples. She's got a little too much makeup on, an' I don't like how it covers up her freckles.

"Mom's pissed over you not calling her," John says. Maggie bumps my knee under the table. John sneaks another glance at me when her drink arrives. He got them bad eyes, that look that says I-know-you-boy-an'-you-ain't-shit.

Right then I'm nineteen again. I's fuckin' 'round with some folks I'd graduated with the year before. I don't 'member how come it happened, but sure enough, I pissed off Billy Thompson good. Think I said somethin' 'bout seein' his sister's panties stickin' outta the Mexican school janitor's back pocket. He was already fuck drunk, so he just went an' got his slugger out the back of his truck. I didn't hear him come up 'hind me. I did notice them boys in fronta me got wide-eyed right then. Afore anybody could say anythin', Billy dropped me with his aluminum practice bat.

"We been through all that, John," she says. "Mom needs to butt out."

"She worries about you, Margaret. You're the baby. You know she worries about you the most. And it doesn't do her health any good."

All I 'member then was feelin' gravel on the side of my face an' hearin' boys a yellin' an' girls givin' a shriek or two.

There was gravel crunchin' 'round my head an' trucks startin' up, then peelin' out. Billy yellin' that they's all a buncha pussies, Jerry ain't dead, he's just fakin', an' who gives a fuck anyhow if he is. Then I got back up on my feet.

"You can tell Mom," Maggie says, "that she oughtta mind her own business. What's that you always say, Jerry?" she asks. "Kill your own snakes. Tell Mom she oughtta kill her own snakes."

I 'member wobblin' a little as I walked up on Billy. He was diggin' through the back of his truck, lookin' for somethin' to wrap me in, probably. His bat was against the tire. I reached for it an' missed the handle the first two times, grabbin' air. Then I got that rubber grip in my hand. Heard Billy yell oh-shit.

He jumped outta the bed of the truck an' ran out into the road, a yellin' for folks to come back. But everybody was gone. When he figured it was just me an' him, an' I had the bat, he ran off the road an' up the hill into the trees. I took off after him, trippin' up a time or two when my legs didn't wanna work right at first. Watchin' Billy trip too, 'cause he was so damn 'fraid of me.

I 'member thinkin' I could smell him better'n I could see him. I 'member feelin' like my feet landed right into his tracks without even tryin'. His breathin' was so damn loud, they musta heard him in town. Then I found the back of his head with a good clank.

"Thanks, dear," John says to the waitress as she brings him a fresh drink. She asks Maggie if'n she wants another'n, an' she nods yes. John just looks away for a bit, like he's thinkin' on somethin' else. She sets her hand on my thigh an' rubs it a little. Not tryin' to get me excited, just wantin' to know I'm there. I drop my hand down into my lap an' squeeze hers.

I'm walkin' Maggie up the back steps of her house. She's drunk an' probably a little high, still. She trips an' falls halfway into the bushes to the side.

"Fuck, Jerry, don't lemme fall, huh?" she says. I have holda her by the waist.

"Don't you worry there, darlin', I won't let the Wowzer get you."

I take her inside, make her drink a glass of water, help her undress an' get into bed. I pull the covers over her, then go an' run a bath for myself. Smoke a cigarette an' think for a bit.

Stoppin' with one good solid hit never was a option. I took that bat to Billy until I couldn't stand up straight no more. Then I started diggin' a hole in the ground with my bare hands. Don't know how far I'd chased him. Don't know how long I dug. I knew enough, after I filled the dirt in on top of him, to find some leaves an' loose branches to cover the spot.

I 'member walkin' down the other side of the hill an' gettin' in the creek. Billy was all in my hair an' on my face. On my shirt an' jeans an' in my socks. I warshed up an' stripped everythin' off but my underwear an' walked back up the hill to Billy's truck. Wrapped myself in the tarp he'd been tryin' to get free. That's how I sat in the truck as I drove it out to Miss Suzie's place. Cars left out there unattended disappear pretty quick. From there I walked down to the highway an' toward town till somebody drivin' past seen me an' give me a ride to the hospital. That fingernail dirt was the only thing didn't come all the way off.

After a while, Maggie wanders in to use the toilet. Then she comes over an' sets on the edge of the tub. She takes my cigarette an' drags on it.

"What's a Wowzer?" she asks.

"Grandma used to tell me 'bout it. Just a story for us hill folk."

She lifts her leg an' sets it along the lip of the tub so she can nudge my shoulder with her toe. I rest my arm along her shin, an' my palm on her kneecap.

"But what is it?"

I drum my fingers on the edge of her thigh for a couple seconds.

"Well. You see. The Wowzer lives up in them woods. He's real big an' like a panther, but it's hard to say for sure, 'cause hardly anyone ever sees him."

"A big panther?" she asks.

"Grandma called 'em *painters*. But he don't never come outta the woods. Not hardly ever. He's real quiet, an' sneaks 'round everywhere so folks cain't hear him. Mostly he keeps to hisself, but he's real picky 'bout who comes on his land. If'n you let your cattle, your hogs, graze back in his part of the woods, he's liable to bite they heads off."

"He'd bite a *cow's* head off?" she laughs.

"Surely. I said he's big, didn't I? Anyhow, if he's in a *real* foul mood, he might just do the same thing to any folk who come a wanderin' on his land. So that's how come you don't never wanna go too far back in them woods by yourself. That Wowzer might get you. That's how the story goes, but my grandma, she said it for everythin'. If you was scared by a movie, or if you thought a bee was gonna sting you, or if you was gonna fall outta the tree, she'd say she wouldn't let the Wowzer get you."

"So you ain't gonna let the Wowzer get me, then?"

"No, ma'am. I hain't."

CHAPTER THREE:

Like a tick in a tar pot.

TOM AIN'T NO strawberry friend, no sir, he's been there for me all year round. Hired me on as a deputy when I's twenty-one. Asked me if I wanted to retire in ten years' time. Said I could do just that if'n I worked for him. Made me study hard to pass the deputy's exam. Made me get my shit together. Looked at me an' seen moldin' clay. If'n I had a dad, I say.

You don't give a shit what I think of Tom, I know. You don't know the whole story, though. He's a good friend to me 'cause he knows I'm good for business. But I know he'd dig a hole for me back in them woods if I ever was to fuck up bad enough. So I keep him informed on everythin' I do an' figure. It's safer for me thataway, so's he don't think I ever wanna hide nothin' from him. Like earlier in the day, 'fore Maggie an' I went out to supper, I called him an' told him 'bout Pam up at Ronnie's place. I said there was just somethin' 'bout it didn't set right with me. I said it looked like she weren't bein' kept right, an' she could get a infection that'd kill her quick. An' Ronnie's so fuckin' high he wouldn't notice till she got cold.

Tom said he thought that was awful decent of me, standin' up for somebody defenseless like that. I didn't figure what he meant right away. Then it come to me. Sure, I guess so, but I was just thinkin' that if she was to die there, an' some panicked kid called it in an' the state patrol took jurisdiction, there'd be a lotta questions raised we don't wanna have to answer. Tom said he thought I was all heart. I reckon he was a jokin'.

That's how come I'm drivin' north on Highway 23 right now. Tom went an' checked on Pamela. Ronnie wasn't there, so Tom took her with him. Said he drove her to a women's shelter in Fayetteville. Guess that's as good a place as any. When Ronnie got back, he threw a shit-fit about it. Them kids was still around when Tom was there, an' they told Ronnie what'd happened.

Tom called up Miles, somebody Tom keeps paid up to buy from Ronnie without Ronnie knowin' he's keepin' tabs on him. Miles went out to Ronnie's house an' popped in for a quick buy. When he come back, Miles said Ronnie was gettin' higher'n all fuck, a snortin' everythin' he could find. Started shoutin' how he was gonna come lookin' for Tom an' me, how this was the last straw an' nothin' else for it.

Tom called up, got me outta bed an' on the road lookin' for Ronnie's car. Probably, I think, he'll just end up givin' a fat lip to one of Miss Suzie's girls, then gettin' his own ass beat, but I always listen to Tom. He's been right enough to warrant it.

I had to borrow Maggie's car to drive down to the station so's I could pick up the patrol car. When I left, Maggie asked me what's happenin'. I told her it was just a damn mess needed cleanin' up.

Sure enough, I find Ronnie, halfway 'tween Huntsville city limits an' his house. His Mustang's parked into a tree offa the shoulder. Them back red lights is glarin' an' he got one headlamp still intact, shinin' on into the trees. I park my patrol car back up the road a ways, on the other shoulder, kill my lights, an' call Tom.

"What you got in the trunk?" he asks.

"You mean 'sides Grandma's farm liquor? Nothin' clean, anyhow."

"Shit," he says. "I suppose I could be there with somethin' in five minutes."

"Don't need nothin', 'cause he always keeps that sawed-off under his seat," I say.

"That'd work, but you gotta be careful how you do it."

While we're talkin', another patrol car drives up. It's that prick, Harold, one of the two deputies workin' the night shift. He pulls up by my car an' steps out in the road. I hang up.

"Thought you were off tonight," he says.

"Coverin' for Junior," I say, "just for a coupl'a hours. You know how he is when Miss Suzie gets a new girl up there." Harold's a bitta Bible-thumper, so he won't ask no more 'bout it.

We look over at Ronnie's car. He's inside, a moanin' an' slumped over. Harold shines his flashlight on Ronnie 'fore I can stop him. I slap it down, on the pavement, but it's too late.

"Fuckin God-damn cunt," Ronnie yells, settin' up straight. "Fuckin' God-damn freeloadin' cunt." He starts a bangin' on the steerin' wheel an' keeps up the yellin'. Anxious as he is, he's squirmin' like a tick in a tar pot.

"What the heck is he on?" Harold asks, lookin' at me.

"You motherfuckin' God-damn whore you don't fuckin' run out on me you piece of trash," Ronnie spits out, still bangin' away at the wheel.

"I gotcha covered, if'n you wanna take him outta there," I say. Harold nods, draws his pistol, an' walks over to the driver's side. I draw mine an' walk back behind the bumper. Ronnie looks over at Harold, then lights hisself a cigarette. Harold looks up at me real quick, then back into the car. He taps on the window, keepin' his weapon trained on Ronnie. So Ronnie rolls down the widow.

"Worthless lazy-ass bitch. Fuckin' worthless," Ronnie says to the tree in fronta the car.

"You gotta get outta the car now," Harold says, his voice crackin'. Ronnie starts laughin' like somebody told a Missouri joke. I watch him real close.

He flicks his cigarette an' catches Harold's neck, an' them little orange sparks fly everywhere. Harold stumbles back, a grabbin' at his neck an' collar. I fire twice.

First shot blows in the back window an' gets Ronnie through the throat, but just passes through meat an' don't catch no bone. Punches a hole out in the front windshield. He starts a turnin' his head to see where it come from.

Second shot goes through the back of the driver's seat an' gets him center mass. Ronnie bounces up an' slams his head into the roof, then flops down on the dashboard over the steerin' wheel. He falls back 'cross the passenger seat an' lays still.

Harold looks over at me, still a brushin' at his collar, confused as all hell, that dumb-as-cow-shit look on his face. I yell for him to get back. I walk 'round to the passenger side an' look in. Thing is, Ronnie's lyin' on top of his shotgun.

Had it out already. I hain't gotta do shit now. Maybe he was gonna reach for it, maybe not, but anyway, it'll look like he was.

You know what Tom said to me when I asked what he got that medal for when he was with the Marines in Vietnam? That's the medal got him elected sheriff here in Madison County back in '86. He's held onto the job for twenty-two years now. He told me he got that medal for killin' folk. That's all. Just killin' a whole lotta folk. Then he said somethin' else I'll never forget. He told me what the general set up as his standin' orders. If'n they was dead, an' they was Vietnamese, then they was VC.

Tom asked me what I thought that meant. I said it sounded like a whole lotta mess is all. Then he said once you been a party to that kinda mess, it don't matter for shit whatever else you do in your life. I reckon I know 'bout that kinda mess, too. But not from no God-damn army, or from no Guards, that's for sure. All I done in the army was drive trucks through the mountains for troop transport in Afghanistan when they activated my unit in '02. That was the last year of my six for the Guards, so I said fuck 'em when I got back to the States an' refused reenlistment. It's not like I wanted to play G.I. Joe anyhow, all that was Tom's idea.

So I'm settin' in Tom's office after hours of paperwork. He comes in, closes the door, takes my coffee mug an' fills it up, then his too. I take out a little bottle from my pocket an' offer it to him. He takes it an' looks at it.

"This your Grandma's?"

"Home-brewed kill-devil since 1920. That was her momma started it, an' she grew up helpin'," I say, pourin' a spot into my mug an' his. He sips at it, coughs, then sips again.

Tom sets behind his desk an' looks at the last form I just finished fillin' out. I always forget how much paperwork it takes to kill folk aboveboard.

"You think them kids up at Ronnie's was the same ones I saw Monday?" I ask.

"You mean them ones I seen yesterday? Sure. Think they're the ones tryin' to start up a gang," he says.

"Thirteen thousand in the whole county, an' they wanna start a gang?"

"What the hell else they gonna do?" Tom laughs. "Some are runaways, some are just high school dropouts who're puttin' off goin' to work at the mine with their daddies for a while yet."

"Hain't that gonna look bad to the Sanhedrin?" I ask. "Seein's how Ronnie was their boy, an' here he was goin' 'hind they backs, sellin' his own shit, usin' kids to do it, an' that whole thing with Pam, too. They ain't gonna be happy."

"That's how come they won't care you clipped him."

"S'pose not."

He sips his coffee again an' looks me over good. "Say, did Maggie hear back from any of them places yet?"

"Not yet."

"You still plannin' on goin' with her?" he asks.

"Surely. But it may be a coupl'a months yet."

He raises his mug. "And your Grandma? Somebody gonna look after her?"

"Her oldest, my aunt Shelly, up in Hindsville. She's seventy-three. Husband died so she just rents out the farm-land. She might move outta hers an' into Grandma's house.

Maybe she'll start rentin' her house out too. Shelly's is just a nice trailer, really. Grandma'll be okay."

"It's gonna be hard to replace you, Jer," he says. "I know you comin' up on ten years, like we said, but still."

"I learnt from you, Tom, keep your head down, keep close to the willows."

Tom nods an' sips some more coffee.

"You seen that tattoo on Ronnie's arm?" I ask.

"No. What 'bout it?"

"Don't know," I say, "but Freddie's got the same one."

"I'll take a look at Freddie's an' see," Tom says. "By the way, that reminds me of somethin' we gotta discuss."

"'Bout what?"

"'Bout Freddie. He cain't go back to Fayetteville."

I sip my coffee.

"I didn't know it was gonna be a problem," I say.

"He weren't caught here last year. If'n he had been, we woulda discussed this back then. Last year it was Big Cal's responsibility, since it was on his stompin' grounds, but Freddie got loose 'fore anybody could do anythin'. Now it's on ours, an' we gotta take care of the problem ourselves."

"That's gonna look bad on us if he takes another walk on our watch. Draw attention from the state patrol, maybe," I say.

"You think I don't know that?"

"So you wanna try an' arrange somethin' to happen in transit? Washington County deputies are comin' out here to pick him up, right?"

"Think so. Hadn't contacted 'em yet. But when I do, that's the protocol," he says.

"So somewhere 'tween here an' Fayetteville, after he's in they custody, Nappy Freddie's gotta get lost."

"Think that can be arranged, Jerry?"

"From what I hear, that boy's slippery as soap."

Half an hour later I'm havin' myself a late breakfast at Bobby's. Maggie come over from the hospital when I called. I told her what happened, an' now she cain't stop touchin' me on my arm, my face, my shoulder, my knee, ever' minute, just to make sure I don't disappear.

"He was gonna shoot you? Jesus, I can't even imagine," she says. She's wide-eyed an' a shakin' her head. "I mean, that's really strange, too. Just Monday you took him to the ER, and then he goes and—"

"Strange, ain't it."

Maggie keeps on lookin' at me like she's waitin' for me to tell her somethin'.

"Well, are you gonna be okay? I mean, I get off at eight tonight, but are you gonna be okay till then? I don't think you oughtta be alone," she says.

"'Bout three me an' my Uncle Ray's goin' fishin' 'cause he got the afternoon off for that appointment got canceled. I'ma hang with Bobby till then," I say.

I can tell Maggie don't wanna leave. She knows somethin's wrong. She's awful damn smart thataway.

"I'ma be fine, baby," I say. "Tom get ya your car back this mornin' all right?"

"Yeah, he did." She checks her watch.

I watch her walk out the door an' from where I'm settin', I can see her go up the block a ways to her car. Both her shoes is tied today.

"You know you a damn fool if'n you don't marry that girl, Jerry," Bobby says, comin' outta the kitchen. "You just 'bout got her wrapped 'round your finger."

"I do believe it's the other way 'round," I say. "An' what 'bout you, hoss? When the hell you gonna get married?"

"When I find me a perfect woman," Bobby says, leanin' on the counter.

"What'd make her perfect, then?"

"She don't care I come home late, stinkin' of stray pussy."

"When's the last time you had any antibiotics, huh?" I ask. Bobby laughs.

"Shit," I say, "you wanna cut out an' go bowlin'?"

"Carlos comes in for his shift in ten minutes. Yeah. Fuck it."

So at the bowlin' alley Bobby wouldn't shut up 'bout Iraq. He was in that first round in the early nineties. Kept tryin' to tell me it'd be okay that I kilt somebody. He done that over there, he said, an' it took him a long time 'fore he could get to talk 'bout it. So I told him it weren't my first time. That made him set back an' look at me different.

Uncle Ray's late again. I'm settin' in my truck out in the church parkin' lot, waitin' on him, thinkin' 'bout what Bobby said. He studied me for a while like I seen Tom do durin' interrogations. Like he's tryin' to figure me out. He asked me if it happened in Afghanistan. If I'd kilt someone there. Fuck no, I said. I just drove them trucks over there, sat in the cab like a bump on a log. No, it was on the job four years ago.

I see Ray comin' out the back entrance of the Church of Christ. He sees my truck an' starts a headin' over. Bobby asked me what happened then. So I told him.

These fuckers down in Dutton, that lived in a house near White River, well, they's makin' meth in they garage. I went there 'cause of some complaint a neighbor give 'bout the noise. They run out the back when I knocked on the front door so I gave 'em chase. Whey they started a shootin', I shot back. Husband an' wife. Dead in the tall grass on the riverbank.

That's what I told Bobby. Mostly, that's what happened.

After me tellin' him, he just looked at me for another minute. "You sure do keep it all shut up tight, don't ya, Jerry," he said. Cain't rightly argue that.

Ray gets to the truck so I open the door to let him in. He puts his rod an' tackle in the back 'fore gettin' inside the cab. Raymond Bowden, white male, 59, 5'10", 190 lbs, white hair, an' blue eyes like mine, starts fiddlin' with my radio, lookin' for his favorite station. His bein' retarded don't show on his face the way it does with them folks that got Down syndrome. With Ray, you notice it when he talks slow an' repeats hisself. How he blinks a lot whenever he speaks, an' makes them groanin' noises when he's walkin' somewheres. If'n you didn't pay attention, you might think Ray was just a normal feller.

"Cast it out further. Try gettin' it out there in the middle. Them channel cats is gonna be in the cooler water with this sun," I say.

Me an' Ray are all set up. We got foldin' chairs, two fishin' poles each anchored in the ground, one cooler for the fish, an' one for the beer. An' we managed to get my favorite spot in the shade all to ourselves.

"I got it," Ray says, reelin' his line back in. He looks at his hook. "Jer, it ain't got no worm no more." He's standin' a ways down the bank. He don't never wanna set still when he's fishin'.

"Well, get another'n," I say. "Here." I toss him the little container of worms, an' he catches it, sets his rod in the anchor, an' starts fiddlin' with the bait.

Ray's worked maintenance for the Huntsville Church of Christ since he was about twenty-five. He's the janitor, the carpenter, the lawn mower an' sidewalk scraper, an' all 'round Mr. Fixit. They let him live rent-free in an old converted garage connected to the buildin', an' pay him a good enough wage to afford health insurance. Also, they made him a deacon.

"You said the middle?" he asks.

"Right plum in the middle if ya can, Ray. That's where they gonna be hidin'."

I been fishin' with Ray since I was old enough to hold a pole. He tries to get me to come to church on Sundays. I give in on occasion. Tom says it's a good idea. Court testimony sounds better to a jury when it comes from a churchgoer.

We've got three fish so far. Ray got two an' I got one. I hain't been payin' too much attention to my lines, though. Mostly I been mindin' the beer. I had to drive home to change afore comin' out to pick up Ray. He won't let me drive him up to the house. Since he moved outta Grandma's place he don't never wanna see it again.

"I think there's a turtle a stealin' the bait," Ray says.

"You seen turtles in there? You 'member what them shells look like?"

"I 'member, Jer. Can you shoot him?"

"If'n I were to shoot at it, them fish'd clear outta here altogether."

"He's stealin' the bait, though."

"That's just the price you gotta pay for a shady spot on the river," I say.

I hear footsteps a comin' up behind me. I got my .22 pistol outta my pocket an' in my palm 'fore I turn to look. Maggie's a walkin' down the path from the road toward us. I don't know why I done that. Who'd it been, anyhow? I pocket it quick 'fore she sees.

"Bobby said this was your spot," she says when she gets close.

"Thought you had to work."

"Mike's gonna cover me for a couple hours," she says. I motion over to Ray's empty chair.

"Ray won't mind?" she asks.

"Hey, Ray," I yell down the bank to him, "you 'member Maggie."

"Hey, Maggie," he yells back, then goes back to lookin' for a rock to chuck at the turtle.

"Guess not," she says an' sets.

"He's good at his maintenance job 'cause it keeps him busy," I say to Maggie, "but he don't really have the *patience* to be that good at fishin'. 'Course that don't stop him from tryin'."

I offer her a beer, but she don't want none 'cause she gotta go back to the hospital in a bit. My lines in the water bob a little bit, but no bites.

"It's nice of you to come out to see me," I say. "I didn't expect to see you till later."

"Somethin' bothered me, Jerry," she says.

"How's that?"

"I'm no shrink, Jer," she says. "But even I can tell when somethin's off."

"What's off?" I ask.

"Your affect. You didn't care that much after shootin' Ronnie. At first I thought you were in shock. That had me worried. So I called Bobby."

I see where this is goin'. Take my cigarettes out an' pluck one from the pack.

"Ray, you care if I smoke?" I yell. I'm not s'posed to now that he's in remission.

"Nope," he says. He's far enough down the bank it don't matter anyhow.

"So you called Bobby," I say, lightin' one.

"An' he told me 'bout your talk today. He told me 'bout that couple four years back. I was thinkin' this was the first person you'd killed, Jerry."

"Sure. Guess I never mentioned it."

"You don't think that's odd? That you never mentioned somethin' like that?"

"No, Maggie, not really. Hain't really somethin' comes up in normal conversation, is it?"

"It's a pretty big secret to hold in for the two years, two an' a half years, we been seein' each other. Pretty God-damn big secret, don't you think?"

"I guess I try not to think 'bout it."

Maggie's quiet a minute. I listen as Ray splashes a large rock in the river.

"I want you to promise you'll go to see someone about it. You'll talk to a counselor about it. Promise that," she says.

"Sheriff's department requires it. I'm off duty until the preliminary investigatin's done. An' I gotta drive into Fayetteville tomorrow an' talk to a shrink."

"Did you before?"

"You mean them other folks?"

"Yes."

"I did. It's required, like I said."

She sets quiet a minute longer.

"I'm still worried. It's too big a secret for me to be okay about it right away."

"Maggie," I say, "you wanna know how come Ray's retarded?"

She sets up straight an' looks over at me. "Okay. Why?"

"Well, you see, it'd be almost sixty years ago. Grampa come home one night. Gone drinkin' after his shift at the mill ended. Plopped down on the couch an' started howlin' good. Callin' out for Grandma to come in an' take care of him. Said she needed to do her job. Well, it's real late, you see, an' Grandma's already taken her Nembutal so she can sleep. She worked hard all day feedin' them kids an' doin' the warsh. So when Grampa don't shut up, the kids go in to wake up Grandma. He's still a callin' for her to come in an' take care of him. But Grandma, she says she's tired. She's awful tired. An' Grampa, he won't shut up. Not for nothin'. So Grandma, she tells her oldest, Shelly, who was then just fourteen, go on in there an' see what her daddy wants. Go'n see to him. Shelly didn't know no better. So nine months later Shelly gives birth to little Ray over there."

"Jesus Christ, Jerry," Maggie says. She looks back down the bank at Ray, who's toyin' with the bait container again.

"I call him my uncle Ray, but I'd do just as well to call him my cousin."

Maggie thinks on this for a moment. "It's probably unlikely that his condition was actually caused by the incest itself, Jer."

"Maybe, maybe not. But there's things most folks know not to do, 'cause of what might happen. An' one way or another somethin' always happens."

"Why'd you tell me this?" she asks.

"'Cause, baby," I say, "there's some secrets y'oughtta not go tryin' so hard to dig up."

CHAPTER FOUR:

Jerry bites the feedin' hand.

"ARE YOU ANGRY about it?" he asks me.

"You mean shootin' him? No. I reckon not. I mean, he got the shit end of *that* stick, didn't he?"

"A lot of times police officers, or sheriff's deputies, like yourself, feel quite a bit of anger after an event like this."

"I hain't. Not yet, anyhow."

We been goin' back an' forth like this for a while, now. The doc sets in his chair, facin' me in mine. He got his yellow legal pad an' blue pen. He wants to know how come I hain't angry. Or how come I hain't broke down an' cried like some little girl yet.

If'n I don't give him somethin', I cain't go back to work.

"I reckon I just tried not to think too much 'bout the whole thing," I say.

"Why's that?" he asks.

"I guess 'cause it makes me feel sad when I think 'bout it."

Tom sent me to see a shrink when I's nineteen. That was part of the deal. Afore I could apply to be a deputy, there's a whole list of things I had to get done. Seein' this other shrink he knew was one thing.

"Why does it make you sad, Jerry?" Doc asks.

"'Cause it's a shitty situation. I knew Ronnie a little bit. I mean, he was pretty fucked up an' all, but he weren't so bad a person inside. His situation got desperate. That's how come it happened."

That other doc, Tom had met him when he worked on the narc squad in Fayetteville. The old fucker had himself a morphine addiction. Tom used him from time to time. Said he felt safer knowin' he had somethin' on the doc. Wouldn't have to withhold. Clean up his story for worry of bein' reported.

"Do you see that kind of desperate situation a lot?" this doc asks.

"Sure. Folks get pushed into things. They don't want 'em to happen, but it happens all the same."

"You're not married, but you said you have a girlfriend. Have you talked with her about this?"

"A little. I talk to her 'bout it sometimes."

By the time I went to see him, that old doc had been retired from practice a coupl'a years. Tom said there was two reasons for goin' to see him. First was in the immediate. If'n I was gonna pass the state psych exam for the job as deputy, I'd need to know what to say. Second was long term. Tom said I had to know myself. Know my triggers. What was gonna set me off. He didn't wanna take the fight outta me. Just control it a little better.

"Do you tell her everything?"

"I cain't do that. She don't need all that burden. All that desperation. All them folks clawin' up at ya, tryin' to get hold an' pull themselves up outta the water."

"Do you have someone you tell everything to?"

"Jesus," I say. "I say my piece to Him."

"Do you feel that's enough?"

"He's the only one I can tell 'bout my momma."

"What do you tell Him about your momma?"

"Like what I said. Desperate situation."

"How was her situation desperate?"

"'Cause she was sellin' her ass when she got pregnant. She was a whorin'."

"Do you know your father, Jerry?"

"I got it narrowed down. Figure it's one of half the men in Madison county, an' a few from Washington County, who liked big-hipped blondes an' visited houses of ill repute 'bout thirty-two years back."

"What happened after you were born?"

"She dropped me off at Grandma's. Then went back to work. Didn't get breast-fed, 'cause there's damn good money to be made from a woman givin' milk. Folks'll pay top dollar."

"How does that make you feel, Jerry, knowing your mother's milk was sold off to Madison County?"

"I don't think about it that much. I guess when I do, it makes me wish I lived some other place," I say. Doc nods, an' marks on his legal pad.

I don't particularly like thinkin' 'bout my momma. But that's what I gotta do in that kinda situation. Give 'em the my-momma-hurt-me story. That's what they wanna hear.

I park the truck in the parkin' lot of Sam's Surplus Store an' stop thinkin' 'bout my whore-momma. Sam's a friend of mine. He was in Guards with me an' Conrad. Left 'fore we got called up, though, on account of that car wreck. I think he resents that. That he never got to be in a war.

Sam sells all kinds of shit. He markets to cops, mostly, but also to some of the homegrown militia types. Guns of ever' kind. Surveillance equipment. Body-armor vests. That sorta thing. Once in a while, Sam'll call me to come down an' I'll go to a gun show with him. I ask him to keep a lookout. Gun shows is a great place to get handguns without havin' to register nothin'.

"What's goin' on, Jerry?" Sam says when I walk into his shop. He wheels out from 'hind the glass display counter. Samuel Dixon, white male, 37, 4'4" in his chair, used to be 5'10", 210 lbs, crew-cut black hair, brown eyes, waves what looks like a Glock with laser sight fixed under the barrel at me. "C'mon an' check this out."

"I'm in a hurry, Sam, I got other places to go today."

"Benny, you know, the stupid one with the ponytail an' the nose ring, well he got conned into buyin' a buncha cases of these fuckin' things offa some guy at the show in Fort Smith last week. I been tryin' to sell 'em to the folks down at the shootin' range. Hey, this is even the same gun you use. Do me a favor an' tell me what you think. Then I can sell more of 'em by sayin' *sheriff's deputies recommend 'em.*"

I take the weapon in my hand. It's a Glock, but a newer model.

"Benny pick up that Winchester you been droolin' over?" I ask.

"The SX-three? Fuck no. I'd never trust him with that. Nossir, I picked that one up myself last month in Little Rock. You know that's the one set the world record."

"You mentioned it."

I look at the little black box mounted under the pistol's barrel. Tiny thing. Depress the trigger a bit an' the little red light clicks on.

"Yessir, I seen the video on that. Watched 'em do it. Twelve rounds in one point four seconds. Fastest semiauto-shotgun in the world. 'Course 'round here I cain't legally put twelve shells in it."

"How much that set you back?" I ask.

"I'd rather keep quiet on that one," he says, then nods to the pistol. "C'mon, what do ya think?"

I point the weapon over at a silhouette target on the wall an' watch where the glowin' red dot falls. Move it 'round the head an' neck an' gut. Like them things kids take into movies.

"I hate these fuckin' things, Sam. For starters, if'n it ain't fixed just right, when you pull it from the holster, it screws up the alignment. An' speakin' of holsters, you gotta buy a special one just to fit it."

"Don't gotta buy it, Jer, I throw it in free with purchase."

"An' 'sides that, Sam, what kinda asshole you gotta be you cain't hit a target without some fuckin' laser guidin' system. Handguns is for close range. I'd understand somethin' like this for a rifle on a SWAT team, but shit, for close quarters it don't mean dick."

"So you don't wanna endorse it, then?"

"You gimme a decent cut an' I'll endorse anythin' you want," I say. Sam laughs an' rolls his chair over to the office door.

"Guess what come for you, Jer."

"I figured. 'Bout time."

We go back into Sam's office. He has me close the door behind me, then he opens the locked door to his private storeroom an' goes in without me. He comes back out with a small backpack.

"You know where you got this from, Jer?"

"Off the back of some truck, I know."

Sam unzips the backpack an' takes out the little black thing kinda like a walkie-talkie with a lotta buttons an' a tiny display screen on the front.

"That the one I asked for? That they discontinued?"

"The BC-296D," he says. "Uniden's Bearcat."

"An' you put that card into it already?"

"Let's just say that it may or may not have been put in," he says.

"Then I may or may not pay ya for it," I say.

"Lemme clarify, Jer. If I, or anyone else, had installed the APCO-twenty-five card, it would be illegal to sell it or be in possession of it. Federal law."

"You done told me this already, Sam."

"Havin' said this, Jer," he says, "an' knowin' what you wanted, lemme just say that it may or may not have been installed, but when you test it out, you'll find the work satisfactory."

"What 'bout the eight-hundreds?" I ask. "I hain't gonna tell nobody where I got from, asshole, I just need to know if'n this'll do that decryptin' on the eight-hundreds range. Them other'ns block that patch right out."

"Just told you. I think you'll find it satisfactory."

"Who the fuck'm I gonna tell, huh?"

"I just wanna emphasize again, Jerry," Sam says. "You know it's both our asses you get caught usin' this. Federal crime."

"I don't know shit, Sam," I say. "An' neither do you."

Maggie ain't called by the time I get over to Marcus's warehouse. I used to work as a security guard when I's nineteen an' twenty after leavin' Huntsville. Tom knew Marcus an' arranged the job. Kept me outta trouble while I's in Fayetteville a waitin' to turn twenty-one so's I could apply for deputy.

The warehouse Marcus runs is one of Big Cal's. Cal's got 'em all over the city, an' some in the suburbs, too. This'n here's the same'n I used to work in when I's nineteen. Just a big metal buildin' in a bad part of town. But since Marcus's office is here, this is the one he uses to watch the business at all the other'ns. Him an' Big Cal keep a close eye on the show.

When they drive them trucks down outta the hills, the warehouses is where they come. Driver'll pull inside the empty buildin' then get out an' walk down the street to have himself a long lunch. Then the crew'll show up an' unload what been shipped. That'll take a coupl'a hours, an' then they leave when they done. The driver comes back to the truck an' drives away, never seein' nor talkin' to nobody. Big Cal always matches one driver to one warehouse. They don't never see no others an' don't never meet another driver. Him an' Tom believe in compartmentalizin'. In fact, I may be the only person that's seen ever' one of they fields in Madison County an' warehouses in Fayetteville.

"What's up, Jerry-boy?" Marcus asks when I walk into his office.

"We gotta talk 'bout this boy up in Huntsville," I say. Walkin' in the office I see Big Cal settin' on the couch to the side, clippin' nails on them thick fingers. He's facin' that wide window that runs the length of Marcus's office, lookin' out over the warehouse floor. I just look down at them nail clippin's. Tom said Cal's thing was young hookers. Like fake-ID young. Said he couldn't never get enough. If'n he's had any today, there's no tellin' what kinda filth got under his nails. Now it's on Marcus's couch an' carpet.

"Jerry, I owe you a drink, boy," Cal says. "You done me a favor."

"No shit? What's that."

"Ronnie," Marcus says from 'hind his desk. "You took Ronnie off our hands."

"Long time comin'," Cal says. He still works with the narc squad that Tom used to be on. He's got up to detective-lieutenant now, an' that lets him pretty near handle everythin' from both sides.

I set in a chair in fronta Marcus's desk an' look at 'em. Both white males in they late fifties. Marcus is 5'9", same as me, but he put on weight since I worked for him, up to 250 now. Hain't got hardly any hair left. Used to comb it over back then, now it's just up an' gone.

"Well, since I'm so popular all the sudden," I say, "how 'bout y'all do a favor for me."

"Name it, hoss," Cal says. He's 6'4" an' 290 lbs of muscle an' gut under his suit. Tom said he boxed. Gray hair an' blue eyes, an' a broad face to match his build, with four little bump scars 'tween his upper lip an' left nostril. Whoever the fuck stepped in a ring with him musta been scared shit-less. Tom told me once how he got them little scars. Tines from a fork. A perp he was arrestin' in a restaurant stuck it right into the bone 'fore runnin'. Cal tackled and cuffed him with it stickin' right outta his face. Still had a piece of sausage patty on it.

"Nappy Freddie MacDonald," I say.

"They found him?" Marcus asks.

"*We* found him. An' he's in a holdin' cell in Huntsville right now. Washington County sheriff's gonna send for him soon I reckon."

"An' with this Ronnie business, y'all'd rather not have him lost on your watch," Cal says.

He puts them nail clippers back in his jacket pocket, brushes his trouser leg clean.

"I s'pose it wouldn't mean too much," Cal says.

On my way back to Huntsville, I stop at a Walmart an' pick up a coupl'a cheap prepaid phones. I get into Fayetteville 'bout once a week, a little more maybe, an' I try to buy all them phones me an' Tom use back there. He makes me swap 'em out ever' week. An' also ever' single time somethin' like this with Ronnie happens.

I think 'bout what Big Cal said when I told him Tom's message. That thing 'bout "where's the fire at?" Cal said it was a coupl'a years after they got to be partners. Probably the late seventies, he said. Tom an' Cal was interrogatin' a perp who was still flyin' on LSD after they brought him into the station. Seein' spots on the walls an' lookin' right through folks. That kinda shit. So Tom wanted to get the name of his dealer.

"Where'd ya buy it from?" he asked. Perp wouldn't do nothin' but laugh in his face.

So Tom started sniffin' 'round the room, askin' Cal if'n he smelled any smoke. Like maybe there was a small fire in the buildin' somewhere. Maybe it was close by. Asked the perp could he smell it? Tom kept lookin' 'round the room for where the fire was at. Got that perp lookin' here'n there for it, too.

Then Tom jumped up an' pointed right at the perp's blue jeans. Yelled out, there's the fire. Cain't you see it? There's that fire right above where your socks is. Right there, cain't you see it creepin' up ya bell-bottoms?

Perp screamed, Cal said, an' grabbed holda his jeans an' ripped 'em open clean up to his knees. He was slappin' at his legs, tryin' to put the fire out. Tom told him he was just spreadin' it 'round, like how that napalm done smeared. Told the perp he knew how to put it out. He'd do it, too, if'n the perp'd be willin' to give up the name of the dealer. The perp give it up right quick an' Tom threw a glass a water on his pants.

Cal said it got to be a joke 'tween them two. They'd say it whenever somethin' strange happened, or if they just needed a chuckle. "Where's the fire at?" "In ya pants, ain't it?"

While I'm standin' in line to pay for the phones, I try an' figure why Tom wanted me to say that. Probably it weren't just for a chuckle. What was it so strange that happened, I wonder, that he'd send me with the message?

Drivin' back from the Walmart in east Fayetteville, I check my phone for messages. Maggie still ain't called yet.

After walkin' with Schnitzel out back in the woods to check on Grandma's still, I set on the porch, smoke cigarettes, an' wait. I can hear them cicadas a screechin' as the afternoon passes by. I wipe my forehead. July in the Ozarks is always wet, even if you ain't got no rain.

Been thinkin' 'bout my momma since I seen the doc. You 'member what I said 'bout bein' a double bush colt? I got maybe three whole memories of my momma. She took me to church when I's five. She was tryin' to clean up an' get religion. Wanted me to learn some more Bible verses. Beatitudes. Twenty-third Psalm. Valley of the shadow of death. I worked real hard on 'em, but I still didn't see her again for a whole year. Then I seen her one last time.

Grandma taught me the Bible says thou-shalt-not-kill. Then how come God's always a killin' everybody He made? When I asked Grandma that, she just shrugged an' told me it weren't no use tryin' to figure. God does just exactly what He wants. Just like that Wowzer.

Close to five o'clock I get in the car an' drive into Huntsville. I hain't heard from Maggie since yesterday, an' that ain't like her. Most days she calls for ever' little thing. Sometimes nothin' at all, cep'n maybe wantin' to share a joke she heard. When I called, her cell phone was off for the first time since I known her. Even when she's in surgery, it still rings four times an' asks for a message.

When I get there, her door's unlocked. I knock an' go on in. She's settin' at the kitchen table, lookin' over a file, smokin' a joint, an' got a glass of Jack Daniels next to her. She looks up at me with no smile at all, an' red eyes. Her face goes all pale under them freckles.

"Are you involved in the drug business, Jerry?" she asks.

I look at the joint in her hand. "Are you involved in the drug business?" I chuckle.

"You think this is funny?" she yells. "I defended you, Jer. I defended you to my brother. Christ, I'm a fucking idiot."

She takes a swallow of her drink an' clacks it down on the wood.

I set down 'cross from her at the table an' ask what John said about me. She slides the file over so's I can look at it.

"This isn't the one in the hospital records. This is the one he wrote before Tom made him *rewrite* it when you applied to be a deputy. He took it out of his locked cabinet and put it on my desk. Look at page four."

I thumb through the pages. It's from when I's nineteen. Trauma to the head. Marks on knuckles from fightin'. I seen all this. Then I see what she got upset over. Either she highlighted it in orange, or John did it for her. Provisional diagnosis: antisocial personality disorder resultin' from severe childhood trauma. Tendency for aggressive psychopathic behavior.

"You ain't gonna base it on just one person's opinion, are you, Maggie?"

She looks up at me an' shakes her head no. "You know how John said Tom got him to rewrite the file? He said that after he refused the first time, Tom took out a photograph of my brother's house in Fayetteville. They'd just had their second baby. He said Tom lit the photograph an' held it over his desk. Just watched it curl up. Then Tom took out a cigar an' lit it off the photo."

"What do you want me to do 'bout what Tom done?" I ask. She just shakes her head again.

"What was it that happened when you were six, Jer? I already looked in the records, but that part was rewritten, too."

"This 'bout what happened yesterday? With Ronnie?"

"Yeah. You could say that, Jer," she says. "The examiner showed me somethin'. John asked him to, or I never woulda known. You couldn't have seen him, Jerry."

"Seen Ronnie? What're you talkin' 'bout?"

"You said you saw his hand reachin' for the gun in the front seat. That's impossible from where you were standin'. He showed me the angles. You'd need to have been up on the back bumper, leanin' over the trunk to have seen that. You were ten feet back when you fired. You killed him before you knew anythin'."

I rub my temples a bit, 'cause my head's startin' to hurt.

"That's a whole lot to assume, Maggie. Them reports don't tell you everythin'."

"Those were just facts, Jerry. An' they weren't in the report, either. That part's been cleaned up, too."

"Did they tell you Ronnie was a pimp, an' he was chargin' for folks, customers, to torture his girlfriend? He had her shot up on junk so she wouldn't give a shit, but he was sellin' her for cheap, an' watchin' folks burn holes in her for fun."

Maggie stubs out the cherry on the joint. Tears start a comin' again. She's still shakin' her head no. She closes her eyes an' asks, "That why you did it?"

"Hain't that a good enough reason?"

I don't make a habit lyin' to Maggie. She's awful smart, an' I know she'd be pissed in findin' out. So I avoid lyin' to her as much as possible. When I have to, it's by omission.

"Are you involved in the drug business, Jerry?" she asks.

She already knows somethin'. If I lie now, it gets harder.

"I don't sell nothin', I don't grow nothin'. All I done was drive the patrol car like a escort for the shipment, from the hills down into Fayetteville. Make sure nobody ever fuck with it."

Maggie doubles over. Makes this gaggin' noise. I think she's gonna have sick up on the table, but she don't. She looks right at me again an' the look says why'd-you-run-my-puppy-over-mister?

"That's all you do?" she asks. I get them little standin' hairs on the back of my neck from the way her voice breaks.

"Once in a while, I do little errands for them folk that grow it. The owners in Fayetteville. Little odd jobs. Nothin' much, really. Just tryin' to keep it all orderly an' peaceful."

"That what happened with Ronnie, then? Peacemakin'?"

"He was already sayin' he was gonna start shootin', Maggie. He was out lookin' for us, me an' Tom, so what I done was self-defense."

"I meant what you did to his arm. That was you, wasn't it? You broke his arm then drove him to the ER," she says. She sets back in her chair, still starin' dead into me.

"Well, shit, Maggie. What do you want? It's called a control apparatus, honey. You want it orderly an' calm, with one dumb-ass kid in the ER ever' year? Or you want no control, an' all them fuckers from the city come out with machine guns an' God-damn chainsaws, a lookin' to take over, an' then you got fifty people in the ER ever' year from it. That sound better to you?"

She reaches for the file, pulls it back, an' closes it. Shakes her head an' says, "I could give a fuck about that Ronnie, but you better explain somethin' else to me. The hospital record said you were brought in, age six, dehydrated, hungry, an' bleedin' from dog bites. That was the *rewrite*. You tell me what I should gather from that."

I set still for a minute. There's a poundin' goin' on in my ear. My hands are a gettin' real warm, my ears, too. My face must be flushed. Then I stand up, grab on to her kitchen table, an' pull the whole thing away, a scrapin' it on the hardwood floor. I look back at her. We're both breathin' heavy.

"Nothin' of that mess concerns you," I say.

"Fuckin' right it does," she says through her teeth, gettin' ready to stand up. "You wanna tell me why you're scared of big dogs, Jerry?"

I rush up to her, grab her throat, an' shove her back in the chair. Squeeze the windpipe good an' feel it shift in my grip. Watch her skin redden a bit more. Them big green eyes is waterin' right up. I expect her to fight me, but she don't even move her arms, just looks up at me. Then I 'member what I'm doin'. I let go of her right away when I realize *whose* windpipe I got my thumb down on.

"I already regret that, Maggie," I say, backin' away. She coughs an' rubs her throat. Shudders. Makes like she's gonna be sick again. She's cryin' now an' looks down at the floor in fronta her.

"Shit," I say. "I'm sorry."

"*You're* sorry?" she says without lookin' up. Coughs. "You're sorry, Jerry? I wanted to have a fucking *child* with you, an' you're *sorry*. Get out," she says, lookin' up at me again.

I pick up the chair I knocked over an' set back down.

"You believe I love you?" I ask her. She shakes her head no, points to the door.

I figure this may be the last time I see her. I get up an' walk to the door.

"Then believe somethin' else," I say. "I enjoyed you."

CHAPTER FIVE:

Kids these days.

THEY FOUND OUT all they needed to, an' I'm back in uniform. Tom calls me into his office an' says we need to take a trip up to Ronnie's place. We both smoke on the way up there. He promised his wife he'd quit, so he needs a excuse. I light the cigarette for him, an' think for a second 'bout how only two days ago I done that for Maggie down by the river.

"So what's at Ronnie's that's so damn important? Didn't the state police already have a go at it?" I ask. Tom rolls down the window an' taps his ash out.

"Your call got me thinkin', an' so when I's up there gettin' little Pam out, I cleaned up some shit that mighta come back on us."

I been listenin' to Tom talk at me ever since I's nineteen. First time he gave me a talkin' to was when I done in Billy back in them woods. He knew I done it. So he had me come into the station an' set down for a polygraph test.

"You know Ronnie kept business records?" he asks me. I shake my head no. Tom drags on his cigarette an' shifts in his seat. Tugs at his seat belt.

Back when I's nineteen, I 'member watchin' Tom from 'cross the room. I's in that chair with them straps on me, a measurin' who the fuck knows what. Now I know they gauge blood pressure, pulse, perspiration, an' breathin', but when I's young an' stupid, they coulda been checkin' sperm count for all I knew. Tom just watched me close while the feller fiddled with the machine.

"I took his notebook, so don't worry 'bout hearin' nothin' from the state police," he says, lookin' out the window as the old telegraph poles with the vines on 'em go past.

I 'member them questions from the polygraph feller. He asked test questions to set a baseline for it. My name an' age. Them little needles didn't move hardly at all. Then he told me to say to him that I'd won the baseball tournament last summer. I told him I did. Them needles moved just the same as afore. The feller looked up at Tom. Tom shook his head no. Feller said for me to say where I lived, an' he watched them needles while I done that. Then asked me to say I lived in Beijing, China. While I said that, them needles stayed just the same. The feller looked up at Tom again, an' I seen Tom's eyes get wider.

"But state boys ain't found his shack. They all over his house, but none of them know 'bout his little shack back up in them woods."

"So you wanna see what he left up there?" I ask. "Like maybe he's got another set of records. Or left some cash. Who knows what, I guess."

"Exactly. Who knows what we gonna find."

That feller givin' me the polygraph said there's no way he could run the test. Said that I didn't respond to the questions in any way that'd register on the machine. Then he said to Tom that he wasn't no doctor, but he knew for a fact that there's only two percent of folks in the country that don't register on them machines. An' he asked Tom if'n he knew exactly which two percent that was. I seen him nod, yup, he knowed it all right. Tom told him he could leave the room for just a minute, but to leave the machine on.

He walked up to the side of the machine an' looked down at me. Said I's gonna answer one more question. I said sure thing. Did I, at the age of fifteen, kill Benny Schafer's terrier an' stuff it into his family's mailbox? Nossir, I didn't. Them needles just keep right on an' didn't budge the slightest. Tom busted out laughin'. Shook his head an' said I was a God-damn natural wonder. Then he let me go. Said I had to walk home.

When I's headed back toward home from the sheriff's station, he pulled up 'side me in his patrol car. Opened the passenger door an' said get in. John's right 'bout you, was the first thing he said. Right as fuckin' rain.

He asked me if'n I wanted to make some good money. Like enough-to-retire-anywhere-I-wanted-to-in-the-world kinda money. I said yeah, sure, why not?

Tom told me I had to prove myself first. He didn't trust me till I done that. First thing was to move outta Huntsville. Just till I could apply for deputy at twenty-one. Get a job in private security. Join the National Guard. When I asked him why I had to do that, he said that was the test. If I fucked up there, if I didn't learn impulse control, I'd end up in a military prison. If I could stay outta trouble in the Guard, an' work my regular job without gettin' fired or arrested, then he'd let me apply.

So I done all that. I think he was surprised I pulled it off. Later on he said it was a win-win situation for him. If I done it, he got himself a new boy just right for the job. If I got into trouble in Fayetteville, or in the Guard, I's outta his hair for good. I could see his point.

Right now, drivin' up Highway 23 to Ronnie's place, I wonder 'bout what he's gonna do when I leave. Even without Maggie in the picture, my time's served. Ten years total, as agreed. Not countin' the one I was in Afghanistan. Had to make that one up.

Tom asks me for another cigarette, an' I fish it outta my front shirt pocket. Probably he's got somebody in mind to take over my job. I hand the cigarette to him an' notice he's still got the other'n in his hand, only halfway smoked. That's when I know he may already have a hole dug for me out 'hind Ronnie's shack.

We park about a quarter mile from the shack, which is maybe two miles down a old overgrown wagon trail that passes behind Ronnie's house. Tom takes the Benelli shotgun outta the trunk. I think that's the one the Marines use now. Tom tries to keep up with 'em. I know Ronnie used to cook up meth there, an' if he still did, I'd understand needin' the shotgun. As is, it just makes me more nervous.

He flips it upside down an' starts fittin' them buckshot shells in the magazine tube. He looks up at me after loadin' in three.

"Seen the other teams yet?" he asks. He means for the bowlin' league.

He fits another shell in. Holds it up an' pumps it to load the chamber.

"I hain't yet," I say. "Different from last year much?"

He turns it over again an' slips in another shell. Four-plus-one. Arkansas state law only lets you load four rounds in a shotgun. You can get 'round it by chamberin' one, then loadin' four. Call it four-plus-one 'stead of five.

"Teams is mostly the same. Shouldn't be too hard. Not with Hollis settin' out this time."

"Then we gonna win the trophy for sure," I say. Tom closes the trunk lid an' clicks it shut soft.

We walk up the wagon trail through the woods the rest of the way. I notice that while my pistol's on my right hip, Tom's walkin' on my left side, an' two steps behind. He's real quiet. But then he's quiet a lot.

I think 'bout my "retirement fund" Tom helped me set up. Right now it's in a bank in Zurich. Long as I was on the force, I's supposed to be patient an' not dip into it. To make it happen thataway, Tom set it up so two sets of numbers was needed to make a withdrawal. He got one an' I got the other. I was gonna use it to buy a house for me an' Maggie. Maybe help her go into private practice if'n she wanted to. I reckon now I'm never gonna see that money.

We walk 'long the trail an' ever' now an' then I look off to the right. That's where the drop is. Down at the bottom of the holler there's a creek me an' some buddies from high school used to fish way back when. Fishin' was just a excuse to go out an' drink, but we had fun. Howlin' like we was wolves or coyotes. One time we got a truck stuck in the mud an' three had to push while the other'n tried to drive it out. 'Member how the back tire spun in that red clay-dirt an' sprayed it all 'cross my clothes an' face.

I 'member walkin' barefoot on them creek stones. Gettin' that moss caught under my toenails. Watchin' them catfish hidin' in the deeper pools. I used to could catch me one with just my hands. Hain't tried noodlin' in years. I'd slip up quiet enough. Wait patient an' still with my arms like a basket under the water. Then one'd come through an' I'd splash him up out on the creek bed. Used to could do that, but I doubt, lookin' down into the holler from up here, that I have the patience for it now.

You know what I'm thinkin' most 'bout, though? Hain't hard to guess. Just Maggie. I swear I got that woman in my blood. Well. Figure that blood's gettin' let out today.

"Go ahead an' kick it," Tom says. The door's flakin' white paint an' looks like it'd splinter in half if'n I just touched it. I watch Tom take the Benelli offa his shoulder an' point it at the door. Kickin' that door puts me in fronta that scattergun.

"Maybe you oughtta shoot the lock off," I say, fishin' through my front pocket.

"What're you lookin' for, Jer?"

I find the plastic package a dishwarshin' gloves. The small roll of tape.

"Lemme get fixed up here," I say, rippin' open the plastic.

"Ain't got time for no nonsense, Jerry," he says. "What the hell?"

I pull them gloves tight over my hands.

"It's called bein' sanitary," I say. "If I'm gonna search through there, I don't wanna slice my finger open on a razor blade Ronnie cut crank with that's still got hepatitis, or fuck knows what all over it."

I wrap the 'lectric tape 'round the open sides of them light-pink gloves.

"Go on then," he says. "Kick the fucker in."

I flex my hands an' stretch out my fingers a coupl'a times.

"Why cain't you just shoot the lock?" I say, poppin' the snap on my holster.

"He used to cook meth in there. Maybe he stopped, maybe he didn't. I don't wanna blow myself up, Jerry. Just kick it in," he says. I take my weapon out an' look down at it. Hain't no safety on a Glock. I know I chambered a round. I can just pull the trigger.

Ronnie's shack is 'bout fifteen by fifteen, outside walls covered in roofin' shingles, windows got tinfoil on the inside. Doorjamb looks rotten. There's a TV antenna on the roof. I don't know what the layout is in there, whether there's furniture or boxes. I figure on some kinda half-ass plan to duck an' roll once the door gives. So I go.

'Steada kickin' it, I shoulder through the door an' commit to a roll once I'm inside, bangin' my shoulders, rather'n my head, on the plank floor. It's plenty dark, an' once I'm back up, crouched on my feet, I crawl back away on the floor outta the light. I can see Tom out there, pointin' the gun inside, raisin' it up to his shoulder. Lookin' for where I'm at.

"What the fuck's wrong with you, boy?" he yells.

He cain't see me now, but I can see him. He starts a backin' away from the door.

I take a careful aim on him.

Somethin' cracks me hard on the shoulder, then twice on the head, real quick. I turn to try to get away from it without gettin' near the light, an' I get hit in the face. Tom shouts somethin' from outside. He can hear it happenin'. I'm on the floor an' I fire up at the ceiling an' my ears go a whinin'. Tom comes in the door an' I see somebody, a small somebody, step in 'hind him an' stick a knife in his back. Tom yells an' fires the shotgun into the floor close enough to dig splinters in my bare arm an' neck. I fire again an' scoot back 'long the floor. Point my weapon to where the beatin' was comin' from an' stand up. Head back to the doorway an' grab Tom on the way out. Catch the light switch, damn near by accident, an' click it up. There's two of 'em. Them little fuckers from Ronnie's house.

The one in the middle of the room been beatin' on me got himself half a pool cue. The one on the left, nearest the door, got a big old huntin' knife, blood on the tip. I shove Tom out the door 'hind me, an' motion with my gun for the one to drop his knife. He does, an' I grab him by the shirt collar an' pull him outside. I stay at the doorway, kick at the back of his legs till he falls, an' put the kid facedown with my knee in his back. I tell the other'n to drop his cue. His pants get wet an' he drops it. I look back at Tom.

"How you doin'?" I ask, forgettin' neither of us can hear from the shootin'. Tom's on his knees, reachin' 'round to feel the wound in his back. The kid picks up the cue to throw it at me when I look away. I shoot him in the chest 'fore he lets it loose.

"Jesus, Jerry," Tom yells loud enough for me to hear. The kid under my knee's squealin' pretty awful, legs a kickin'. I slap him on the back of his head with my gun.

"You gonna live?" I mouth to Tom. I stand up an' back away from the kid on the ground. Then I see the bushes shake over to the right of the shack. Spot two more kids runnin' back into them woods fast as they can. Maybe they was a waitin' to ambush us an' chickened out bad.

"Think he got the rib," Tom shouts. "I ain't gonna die. But what'd you do to that kid?"

I look into the shack. There's a fifteen-year-old body in a ripped-up Guns N' Roses T-shirt facedown on the plank floor 'tween a workbench with tools an' boxes in fronta the TV.

"You was gonna kill my friend," I say to the one on the ground under my knee. I grab him by the belt at the back of his jeans an' drag him on his stomach a few yards out from the shack.

"Hold him, Tom," I say. "I wanna ask him somethin'."

Tom moves over real slow, slings the Benelli on his shoulder, an' stands above the kid. He gets down an' kneels over the kid's legs. Puts his hands on the kid's upper arms, holdin' him in place.

I shoot the kid twice in the back.

Then I point the gun right at Tom's flushed, sweatin' face. Probably he's got a after-glare in his eyes from bein' so close to the muzzle. Hearin' ain't gonna come back no time soon neither now.

"What the fuck you doin', Jerry!" he yells. I have to read his lips, 'cause the ringin's loud as ever. I back up a few more feet.

"Now I got a question for you, boss," I shout. "Keep them hands right there."

Tom loses all that color in his face.

"You got a hole dug for me?" I yell. He don't say nothin'.

There's another loud crack, muffled though my screechin' ears, an' I'm thrown on the ground, covered in stingin' spots. Tom got it too. I see the smoke where it come from the bushes to the right of the shack. I grab Tom an' drag him back to the side of the buildin'.

There's small blood spots a burnin' on my arms an' legs, an' one or two on the side of my head. They's startin' to leak out some. Tom's got 'em on his chest, his arms, one above his right eye. I can feel a dribblin' offa my earlobe.

"Sawed-off," I shout into his ear. "Ronnie loved 'em." He musta give them little fuckers one with some birdshot. Never told 'em what range they gotta be, though. I laugh a little, an' Tom looks up at me, wide-eyed. I peek 'round the corner to the opposite side of the shack them kids is at. There's a half-rusted shovel lyin' on the ground. Maybe Ronnie used it, or somebody 'fore him.

"You see where they are?" I say in Tom's ear, cuppin' to it with my hands 'round my mouth. He wipes the blood outta his eyes, an' leans far enough to see 'round the front edge. I point to where I think they are, right 'hind them trees back there.

He nods an' looks up at me, pullin' out his pistol. I'ma grindin' my teeth from bein' peppered with that shot. Some of them got deep in the muscle, maybe a couple even caught bone.

"Watch the one on the right. When he comes a runnin' out, drop him," I say. I hope to shit he heard me an' them boys didn't. I point to them extra two magazines on his belt, an' then to the shotgun. "Gimme cover for the next coupl'a minutes." I pull back from Tom's ear, grab the shovel, an' run the other way, into the woods, with the shack 'tween me an' them.

You know what'd be the smart thing to do? Oughtta just set back an' wait. Let them little bastards kill him when he runs outta bullets, then clean up whatever mess is left. But I hain't sure. There's more to consider.

Tom got my retirement fund. If'n I live now, an' he die, then it's gone for sure. Gotta figure whether he's worth that much. Hain't just right now, though. Probably he had a hole dug for me back there. Might be he'd dig me another'n. There's that shovel in my hand. 'Member why I took it. If'n I do this right, he'll never think of diggin' one for me again.

I'm in the woods, a runnin' back over the ridge that shack sets near. Headin' back 'hind it thisaway, I know I'm gonna come up over the ridge 'bout a hundred feet 'hind where them kids is a hidin'. My chest is gettin' tight, like I'm bein' tied to one of them trees. I know that ain't happenin' right now; that was what my momma done when I was six.

There's branches slappin' my face, briars snaggin' my slacks an' scrapin' my arms. That light spottin' down through them trees overhead's a blindin' me a little. I cain't hardly hear nothin'. Cep'n my blood a poundin'. There's that. An' them elastic ropes get tighter an' tighter 'cross my chest. They's a burnin' the skin on my neck. Momma pulls 'em real tight an' works on a knot 'round the other side of the trunk.

I trip on a half-rotted root an' nearly spill on down the steep slope, afore I catch my balance. I think one of my shoes come off, but I hain't got time to look. It's gettin' harder to breathe. There ain't no path where I'm at, it's just dry leaves an' loose dirt an' rocks under the trees. Hain't nothin' but what's not been warshed off the side of the hill from them rains. I 'member watchin' some clouds gather overhead when I seen my momma walk on up the path. I 'member thinkin' God was gonna warsh me right away. Watchin' her a stumble on up that path, that's the last time I seen her. Leavin' me in the woods was the last thing she ever done for me. Don't reckon I ever found no reason to find my way out, neither.

When I come up over the ridge, I slow down. I try slowin' my breath down, too, as I walk up on them kids. I said the one on the right for Tom. That leaves the one on the left for me. From my side now, that's on the right. When I get close up enough to see him, I can tell he ain't but about fifteen or sixteen. Hidin' 'hind a tree trunk, peekin' 'round to spot for Tom. He's got a mess of sweaty black hair on his head an' ripped-up jeans with paint spots on 'em. His arms look pink from bein' out in the sun. Fingers spread out, grippin' at the bark. Must be the other'n got the gun.

I cain't hardly hear nothin' right now, but I swear I can feel ever' sound on my skin. I creep up 'hind him quiet as I can. With that gunfire from Tom, an' what they been returnin' with that sawed-off, they can't hear shit neither. I'm five feet away when his head turns a little to the right an' I recognize him for the one watched me put the fur on Ronnie.

I tighten my grip on the shovel an' feel the rubber of them gloves a bendin'. Lift it up shoulder high. One more step to him. I count six pimples on his right cheek. Shift my weight onto my back leg. I drive the point of the shovel into the boy's neck an' feel that metal bite the tree trunk.

Shears maybe a third through the side of his neck an' scrapes a little on the spine. Kid's shoulders throw back an' his head jerks over to the right, where the wound is. Blood's spittin' a little out on the bark, some in a pulse, some's mist from a windpipe been nicked good. I give the handle a hard yank back to pop the point outta the trunk. Kid's knees is givin' out an' he turns to look at me as he's sinkin' down onto the moss an' leaves an' roots. Them wide eyes blink 'hind sweaty hair as his face goes pale.

I drive the shovel into his neck again. This'n goes further 'cause he's turned around now, but it slips off to his left side, diggin' another respectable gash 'fore stoppin' in the trunk. Blood spreads down his shirt more regular now. Not just specks'n drips, but a flow. I jerk the shovel outta the bark again an' step a little to the side. Give a wide backswing. Good'n fast, an' hard as I can, I bring it 'round an' connect the side edge of that shovel with what's left to go through the boy's neck. Them blinkin' eyes shut tight as the handle snaps in my grip.

My pants an' shirt get wet from what's sprayed up on me, but that only lasts a second. That bark's good'n moist from the wet weather this summer, an' the shovel's bit right in with the head settin' on top. I reach up an' grab by the ears. Gotta work it back an' forth, 'cause a flap of the skin's pinched good into the bark. I get it free an' grip in his hair good. That rubber's surely squeakin' 'gainst his wet hair. Don't matter. Everybody's deaf today.

I come a walkin' outta the brush toward where the other kid's at. I know Tom sees me a carryin' that head at my side, like a bowlin' ball on league night.

"Hey, buddy-boy," I yell. "I got your friend here. Wants a word with you."

I chuck the boy's head at the ground to the left of the tree so's it'll roll into view. Other boy stumbles out from 'hind his tree, an' I can tell from how his face looks, he's a shriekin'. He gets ten feet or so from the trunk when Tom opens up a hole in the kid's lower gut. His legs give out an' he goes down. Tom limps out from 'hind the shack an' walks over to the boy. He don't waste no time. Just puts another'n in the head.

Me an' Tom's down by the creek a warshin' up. I got my clothes soakin' in a little pool, held down by my feet. My gun's out in my hand, but I don't reckon I need it. Tom ain't looked at me since right after we got shot at. I just set, jaybird-naked on a rock, smokin' a cigarette, watchin' him clean up on the other side of the creek. My hearin's startin' to come back.

"Hey, Tom," I say.

"What?" He don't look up from scrubbin' his hands.

"Did you see any tattoos on them kids 'fore we covered 'em up?"

"I didn't think to look, Jerry."

"I's a bit preoccupied myself. Cain't 'member if I seen any."

"Fuck's that matter anyhow?"

"Just tryin' to figure somethin'," I say.

It took a lot to get Tom down the side of the hill after everythin'. He's started gettin' kinda white. Don't know if that's all shock, but it sure ain't from blood loss. Them peppered spots clot up pretty quick. Problem is, eventually they gonna have to go back in to get out the birdshot.

I had to shoulder him on the way down. Couldn't hardly walk, much less climb. I'm watchin' him tryin' to get at the dirt under his nails now. His head's shakin' like he wants to say no. Like he wants to wake hisself up from a dream.

He looks up at me real slow.

"Jesus," Tom says.

"Uh-huh," I say. "Kids these days, right?"

"I ain't seen shit like that since—"

"Yup," I say. "Listen, we gotta figure—"

"I mean, you come outta them woods, with that fuckin' head, man, and it was just like that Wowzer they used to talk about. 'Member? Them old-timers used to talk about it?"

"Sure I 'member," I say. "But right now we gotta figure what we gonna say when we get back."

"Shit," he says.

"The hole we dug was deep enough, an' far enough back in them woods, we don't gotta worry 'bout nobody findin' nothin'. But maybe we oughtta burn the shack an' the area 'fore we head back," I say. "Less evidence 'round means our story'll go further."

"God-damn, Jerry," Tom says, lookin' back down at the river. "Just like that Wowzer."

Tom got it real bad. A lot worse'n me. He's been in the hospital ten days now since that day back in the woods. I was wrong 'bout that blood loss. His was internal. Got himself a infection, too. They let me out after a overnight stay. I went to see him a few days back. Said I wanted his numbers for my retirement account. He said he'd see. I reckon he figured tables been turned. Like them numbers is the only thing keepin' him from gettin' his own hole dug. Cain't deny but I thought of that, too.

I'm by myself in the office right now. Schnitzel's sleepin' under my desk an' on top of my feet. I bring him when I've got the night shift 'cause nobody's here to tell me different. Them sores from that shot are itchin' pretty bad. I cain't stop pickin' at 'em.

Got a letter from Maggie today. It's folded up in my pocket. Said she accepted the position in Chicago. She don't never wanna hear from me again, she says. But Christ, I got that woman in my blood. I checked the postmark, an' it was Chicago. Then, after me an' Ray got back from fishin', I dropped him off an' then went by the car dealership that rents the U-Haul trucks. They let me look through the records. She drove the truck to Memphis.

I'm lookin' at my computer right now. At a map site on the Internet. Huntsville, Arkansas, to Memphis, Tennessee, is exactly three hundred miles. Five hours an' twenty-four minutes by car.

Schnitzel moves his legs in his sleep, lets out a grunt that ain't quite a bark.

Dreamin' of chasin' rabbits, I reckon.

CHAPTER SIX

Jerry's up-an'-gone Miss-woman.

SO HERE'S WHAT I do with my vacation. First I call Aunt Shelly up in Hindsville an' see if she'd be willin' to watch Grandma for a week, startin' on Sunday. Then I call Sam in Fayetteville Saturday night an' tell him to have a box of things ready for me, an' I'll be in to pick 'em up early Sunday mornin'. By the time I get back from Fayetteville, church's gettin' out an' Shelly's already come over. I run through Grandma's meds with her, an' show her where I hid the grocery money. Then I get my bag I packed up last night an' toss it in the trunk of the car I rented. Put a blanket in the backseat for Schnitzel an' let him check it out. I say good-bye to Grandma an' Aunt Shelly, an' then start the drive to Memphis.

I get there in the early evenin' an' head over to where I think the place is. I 'member the place she applied to was the Regional Medical Center. The big one downtown, not far from the Mississippi River. I have to drive 'round the area a few times 'fore I find the restricted lot where the docs all park. Like I expected, it ain't in that big leveled garage connected to the buildin', it's a isolated one on the other side. Docs an' administration only, gated in with a security guard. 'Cross the street, there's a buncha places to eat. Fast food an' a diner or two. A ice cream shop. I park outside the diner, facin' 'cross the street, 'hind some low hedges.

There's a patch of grass an' bushes back on the other side of the restaurant strip, an' I open the door for Schnitzel an' let him out. I get a plastic bag from inside the car an' then wrestle to get his leash on. He don't like that one bit.

"You in the city now, boy," I say. "They got laws for it."

After he done his business, I take him back to the car an' set in the front seat with the binoculars I got outta the trunk. Hain't them big ones I got for bird-watchin', these is the ones Sam sold me, an' they's a lot smaller. I'm lookin' over the lot for Maggie's gray '99 Saab. Some cars I can see what plates they got an' some I cain't. She works a lotta evenin's an' nights, I know, so she'll probably be here in a minute. Less'n she has the day off.

I get out an' head into the diner to get somethin' to eat. A steak sandwich from the feller at the counter, with some onion rings an' coffee, all to go, 'cause I don't wanna take my eyes offa the lot for too long. When I get back in the car, I set out Schnitzel's food dish an' some water. He keeps sniffin' at my sandwich, so I give him a little strip of beef. After we're done eatin', I let him up in the front seat with me so's I can scratch 'hind his ears. He lays his head in my lap an' I sip my coffee.

"Where she at, buddy-boy?" I say. Schnitzel looks up at me, then sets his head back down. I cain't see all them cars from the way they parked in rows. I recognize some of what could be Saabs. There's only a few gray ones. That's what I gotta watch. An' I can see the door to the buildin'. I can see who comes in an' out. It's gettin' on to dark now.

After my second trip with Schnitzel over to the bushes, I'm gettin' his leash unhooked from his collar an' I look up an' see her car pullin' into the lot. I grab my binoculars quick an' just catch Arkansas plates as she pulls in through the gate. It's near ten p.m. Usually that means a twelve-hour shift. But I don't know how they work the schedule here. I got no idea. It could be just eight hours.

She parks in the corner to the right an' by the fence. Gets out an' reaches back in for her purse. She's got on her gray slacks an' a sleeveless blouse. Tryin' to make a good impression her first week on the job.

When I first seen her 'round the Huntsville ER, if she wasn't in scrubs, she was in jeans or sweats. Don't think she never thought that mucha me 'fore that night I pulled her outta her car. Always thought she was awful pretty, right from the beginnin', seein' her leanin' over the counter at the nurse's station, readin' some chart, chewin' on the end of her pen. I know a time or two I leapt at the opportunity to take some statement in the ER on the chance she was workin'. Just so's I could get a look.

Cain't stay parked in the same spot for eight hours or more. Gotta move it 'round the block an' switch sides of the parkin' lot, less'n I wanna draw the Memphis cops. So I set the alarm on my phone to go off in a hour an' curl up in the backseat with Schnitzel.

She comes out at ten fifteen a.m. If I coulda got into that lot last night, I coulda put a tagger on her car, so's I wouldn't lose her in traffic. Still, even if I do, there's tomorrow. I been watchin' since eight this mornin' an' my eyes is already tired.

Seein' her walk 'cross the lot wakes me up good. I get the tinglin' in my fingers an' my stomach jumps a little.

Maggie takes Interstate 240 south to the airport. She's real easy to follow, even though I hain't used to the city traffic. She gets off at 23A, Airways Blvd. Then a right on Democrat an' pulls into the drive for Holiday Inn. I pull in after her an' drive 'round to the hotel 'cross the lot from it, the Econo-Lodge. I park in the lot an' watch her go inside.

So this Mexican kid who works in the kitchen, Juan, works me up to two hundred for the room number. *Doscientos y no mas, hombre.* Surprises the hell outta him I know a little Spanish. He calls the front desk an' says he needs to take up Maggie's order but lost her room number. Two twenty-four. Juan's smilin' wide, a countin' the twenties in his hand, when I walk to the back door of the kitchen.

I turn an' ask, "Cuál lado del edificio?"

"Qué?" Juan asks. Maybe I got that one wrong.

"Cuál fachada? Norte? Oeste?"

He nods an' I see he gets it. "Oeste," he says.

West face of the buildin'.

Maggie was awful surprised I knew a little Spanish, too. I didn't tell her till we got to Puerto Vallarta last year. Then I ordered dinner our first night out an' she stared at me while I's speakin' like I had two heads. Told her my high school teacher wore these tight skirts. An' when she erased the chalkboard, she done it from side to side 'stead of up an' down. That ass shakin' was enough to get me through four years. Plus, it helps on the job. Fair amount a Spanish spoken down in the mine. A lot more out on the farms.

Didn't tell her 'bout my buddy Jose, though. The Sanhedrin brought him up from Mexico to run the growin' side of the operation. Jose, he been teachin' me quite a bit. Then when me an' Maggie was walkin' 'round Puerto Vallarta, I got to show off a little more. Readin' street signs for her. Pickin' out some song lyrics when they's spoken slow enough. Asked her if'n she knew what *mi cielo* meant. She knew *cielo* was sky. Heaven, I said. It means my heaven.

I pick the room that's cheaper. Not 'cause I cain't afford it, I took one of Tom's credit cards from the top drawer in his desk that he reserves for emergencies only. Of the two rooms available on the east side three floors up, one was the honeymoon suite. That'd be just too much, so I take the other. Had to leave a deposit on Tom's card for them to let Schnitzel in the room. I take my bag an' box from the trunk an' head on up.

The 1000 mm color spot telescope is ten pounds, eighteen inches long, an' black all over. I set up the tripod at the window an' hook the adapter up to the scope so I can plug it into a outlet. Open up the laptop that I'm rentin', like everythin' else, from Sam, an' dig through the box for the connector cord. I turn on the telescope an' plug it into the laptop. I don't know which room's 224 yet, but after she leaves for work tonight, I'll check the floor layout.

Schnitzel's gettin' antsy, so I set up his food an' water in the bathroom. Just a couple more things to do 'fore I can walk him. There's the Bearcat scanner. I take it outta the box an' set it next to the laptop on the bed. There's another cord for that, too. I turn on the TV an' put the earpiece in from the scanner.

I start scannin' through the 800 mhz range. It don't take long 'fore I find out what the Bearcat 296d can do when you fit it with the APCO 25 card. You get to listen in on folks' cell phone calls. That's how come it was discontinued. I reckon I'm 'bout half a mile, at most, from her room, which should be plenty close. I set it to run through the 800s slowly an' just listen for Maggie's voice while I play with adjustin' the image from the scope on the wide laptop screen. There's six room windows along the second floor. Two got they curtains open. Cain't see Maggie in any of them, though.

I walk Schnitzel out in fronta the hotel an' clean up after him. I got the scanner on my belt, inside my shirt, an' the piece in my ear. Still searchin' through the channels. Schnitzel barks at a basset hound that wants to get near his ass. I take him back up to the room.

Outta the six west-facin' rooms, now three got they curtains open. Cain't see Maggie in any of them. I get up offa the bed an' swivel the scope down to where her car's parked. It's still there, so I move the scope back to the hotel. Lay on my back an' stare up at the ceilin' fan. There's all kinds of voices talkin' in my ear.

Deep tenor male voice says, "I love you too," followed by alto female with probably a German accent sayin' good-bye. Then fuzz 'tween signals. Slight soprano female chattin' with scratchy alto female about somethin' or other. "Such an asshole," alto says, followed by soprano agreein'. Fuzz 'tween signals. Alto male laughin' with a tenor male. Fuzz 'tween. Alto female askin' tenor male how the trip was. Fuzz 'tween. Soprano juvenile female askin' tenor female, probably in old age, what she's gonna get for her birthday.

I look over at the six rooms on the laptop screen again. This is stupid. I swivel the scope back on the car an' leave it. Find the animal channel on the TV. Switch my eyes back an' forth from the screen on the bed next to me to a scene where there's a crocodile a waitin' just under the surface of the river for the gazelle to stretch out its neck an' lean in a little more. Just needs to be a little closer.

Eight twenty-five p.m. the lights on her car come on. I focus the picture on her as she's gettin' in. Shoulda recorded it. Her car backs outta the space an' leaves the lot. Move over to the edge of the bed an' slip my shoes on. Schnitzel looks at me like he's expectin' his walk.

"Not yet, buddy. First things first."

The inside of her hotel looked just like mine, cep'n for nicer carpets. I walked right in the front entrance an' headed over to the west corridor where the rooms was. Room 124 was the second from the north end. So now, back in my room, I fix the scope on the second from the north on the second floor. Curtains drawn. They been drawn all day for this one. Again, I'm bein' stupid. Gotta watch the parkin' lot 'fore I switch to the room. An' I gotta figure how long she'll be gone. Probably she's clockin' in at nine. But maybe she's late for the eight p.m. shift. No way to know. Shortest shift she'd work is a eight-hour. That'd mean four a.m. Probably it's a ten or a twelve. No way to be sure, though. I set my alarm for three forty-five.

Cain't really sleep, though. With her days off, an' when she don't work the night shift, I got used to sleepin' at her place four nights outta the week. Gets me thinkin' how warm she was by me. How much I liked all that. Layin' my arm 'long the curve of her hip. Smellin' her from just havin' had sex. Maybe it was the first night we done it without a rubber, I 'member, an' that took a long while to get there, but anyhow, I got up to piss. An' so when I lifted back the toilet seat an' pulled out my pecker to aim it, I felt a little somethin' stuck on the end. Pulled it off an' it was a little curly hair. Flipped the switch on an' held it up to the light above the medicine cabinet. That tiny curled hair glowed orange. Had it belonged to any other'n, I mighta retched, but hers didn't bother me none at all. Damn, I 'member thinkin', guess what's mine is yours, an' yours is mine.

She's on her cell phone when she gets outta the car at ten forty a.m. I grab the scanner off the bed an' turn it on. Plug in the earpiece an' set it to scan quickly. Set the laptop to record the image from the scope an' audio from the scanner. I follow her by watchin' the screen an' movin' the scope, which is hard to coordinate. She stops by the side door an' fishes out a cigarette from her purse. Lights it an' waves her hand like she's pissed 'bout somethin', an' tellin' whoever's on the other end of the line.

I light me a cigarette, too, an' watch her on the screen. She turns north, still movin' her hand around, an' I can see the curve of her ass in the skirt. I touch the screen with a coupl'a fingers, an' a flake of ash sticks to it. She turns back east, lettin' me look her full in the face. I still got my finger on the screen. I pull it back so's I can see everythin'.

Then it hits.

"No, God-damn it, Mom, I am not tryin' to cut you out."

My stomach jumps when I hear Maggie's low alto. Hain't heard her voice in a coupl'a weeks. It's a little more raspy today than usual. That makes sense if she's started smokin' again regular-like. I hit the lock button quick on the scanner an' make sure I'm still recordin' on the laptop.

"Nothing's going on right now, okay? I don't care what John said," she says.

Mom says, "He was awful worried about you, hon."

My fingers are a tinglin'. I zoom the image in on her face till I can make out her freckles.

"He overreacts. You know he does. There's nothing you need to worry over. I promise. Understand?" she says.

Mom says, "Maybe I would if you'd come and see me. You haven't been home in years, hon. Not since before that accident."

Her eyes close an' her face gets a whole lot redder. She's gonna yell, now.

"Jesus Christ, Mom! I just need you and Dad and the whole crew to leave me the fuck alone! That's what I fucking need right now, okay?"

"Margaret, don't swear at me," Mom says. "And certainly don't you dare take the Lord's name in vain!"

"Shit. I'm sorry, Momma. I'm sorry, okay?"

Mom says, "Well, I can understand losing your temper, but some things, Margaret, some things are never acceptable."

She closes her eyes on the screen. There's them tears a startin'.

"I'm sorry, Mom. I can't come and see you now. I will soon. I promise."

Mom says good-bye, an' I drop ash on the keyboard when Maggie hangs up an' the line goes to that fuzz. She stands out on the sidewalk for a few more seconds, then uses her key-card to walk in the side entrance. I try blowin' away the ash, an' Schnitzel comes over to see what the big deal is. Maybe he recognized her voice, too.

I move the scope to get the second room from the north side. Set back in the bed an' wait. I cain't yet figure what I'm gonna do. Waitin' here's like havin' a limp dick. I gotta see her. But I know what'll happen if'n I do. I know she'll get scared of me. Call the police, or try at least. She ain't gonna set still an' let me talk. Don't really wanna talk anyhow. It's itchin' me somethin' awful not to be seein' her.

With the earpiece still in, I walk downstairs. Cross the street an' walk on down the block. There's a liquor store I seen. I pick up a bottle of tequila an' head back. There's these little paper cups in the bathroom I use for doin' shots. I try not to do too many.

We drank a awful lotta tequila in Mexico last year. Margaritas an' straight up. Stayed at this little shack near the beach. Seen me a iguana as big around as Schnitzel, an' twice as long tail to snout, just a sunnin' himself on a rock above where the tide come in. Maggie started gettin' a little sunburnt, so I had her come back with me to the hotel room. She asked me why it was such a big deal. 'Cause, baby, I said, you're no good to me if I cain't put my hands on you.

I 'member she laughed at that.

When she opens up the curtains, I 'bout shit. It's three p.m. an' I reckon she cain't sleep, or she's got a early shift, or maybe the day off. I watch her on the screen a minute 'fore I start recordin'. She got a desk by the window an' she sets at it in a chair. She's watchin' TV with her legs crossed an' propped up on the bed. Got her joggin' shorts on an' them little white socks. Hair's back in a ponytail. There's a sweat stain on the back of her T-shirt. Reckon she went excercisin'. Her feet's movin'. Wigglin' her toes the way she does when she don't think of it.

Bobby calls on my cell phone.

"Where you been, hoss?" he asks.

"I'm on vacation," I say.

"Where you at, then?" He has to repeat the question 'cause I'm watchin' Maggie stretch her neck from side to side.

"Mexico."

"Bullshit. You probably just holed up in your grandma's house layin' on the couch."

"Uh-huh. You got it."

"Listen, what you doin' right now, Jer? Anythin' important?"

"Just watchin' some porn," I say, as Maggie starts clippin' her toenails on the screen.

"'Cause there's these fine-ass girls down here playin' pool at Willie's place that come in from Fayetteville, Christ knows why, but they cruisin', man. Drop your pecker an' get down here in time, an' we might just be able to pick us up some strange, Jer."

"Rather just watch what I got here," I say. Maggie's leanin' in with the toenail clipper to get a better angle. I can make out her sports bra under her T-shirt.

"No shit? What you watchin', then?"

"This short redhead. Cute as a button," I say.

"I see," Bobby says. "So she let you do that, huh?"

"I'm on vacation, Bobby. I'll stop by when I get back," I say an' hang up.

Schnitzel gets walked again, an' when I come back in, the curtain's still open. She's still in the chair at the table by the bed. An' her right arm's up. An' her hand's open. An' her head's turned to look right at her palm. She's lookin' at somethin' there. There's a tiny little glint of light from her hand as she closes her fist. I reckon I know what she got in there.

Brought it with her.

She don't leave for work at ten. Curtains is closed, but her car's still there. Schnitzel's done with his supper an's just settin' on the bed a lookin' at me. I drunk maybe half that tequila in the last day. Don't know how much I slept. Nor when I et last.

Fuck it.

She's there an' I'm goin' to see her. She brought it with her. I grab my bag an' empty my clothes out. Throw on my light jacket. Then I dig the last toy outta the box. What I got from that hardware store 'bout a block an' a half down from the liquor store. A 22 oz. rip-claw hammer. Shiny metal head an' neck, black rubber grip. I stick it in my bag an' swing the bag over my shoulder. Take a half a mouthful of that tequila 'fore headin' out the door.

I stumble in the hallway an' catch myself quick by grabbin' the wall. I walk a little slower down to the elevator. I got my hands inside my bag, movin' things 'round. I cain't stop fidgetin', hands in the bag one minute, then in my jacket pockets, then makin' fists at my sides. They won't set still.

I walk out 'cross the parkin' lot an' head 'tween all them cars. Cain't go in the front door right now, 'cause they got folks up at the desk that ask your business this time of night. So I head 'round for the back entrance of the kitchen, where I run into Juan a piece back. I wait outside by the dumpster till some kids come out for a smoke.

I know Maggie ain't gonna wanna let me in. I know that. An' I cain't shoulder this kinda door in too easy. These hotels got pretty thick'ns. Kickin' it'd be hard, too. So if she don't open up, that hammer in my bag's gonna pop that latch right back through the frame. Pickin' the lock'd be a hell of a lot quieter, but they got that keyless entry in this hotel. Them damn little plastic cards.

Gotta figure how long it'd take her to get from the door to the phone. Or her purse on the dresser where she'd keep her cell. Four seconds, maybe. She could get to the phone. Pick it up. One an' a half seconds. Punch in nine-one-one. Another second. Figure it don't ring too long. Prime time for calls right now, but think on the safe side. Four more seconds. She can do all that. She just cain't speak to the operator. Got ten an' a half seconds to get the phone hung up.

The kids from the kitchen head back inside, an' I creep on up to the door after they's already in. Slip my arm in the gap as it's closin' an' go right into the maintenance hallway. I think I 'member where the stairs is. Couldn't use the elevator the other day when I checked the floor layout. Find the stairs an' head on up to the second floor.

Hain't nobody in the hallway when I peek my head out. Then a door opens down to my right an' a man an' woman walk out, talkin'. I duck back in the doorway for the stairs an' wait a minute till they pass. Then I check again an' walk into the hallway. Move on down to 224. Still ain't decided whether or not to knock first. If'n I knock, she'll come to the door. Once she hears my voice, she gonna head for the phone. But if I just start in a pryin' with the hammer, she'll call with the first noise, an' she could be right next to the phone. Which means I'd lose a few seconds.

I settle on knockin' first to draw her to the door an' away from the phone, then settin' right in with the hammer. That'll give me the most time. Get the hammer outta the bag an' set it to slide 'tween the door an' frame. I raise up my fist to knock on the door an' see I got a light-blue pair of dishwarshin' gloves on, an' taped off too.

Shit.

Didn't mean to do that. I just look at them gloves on my hands for a second. Don't know when I put 'em on. If I done it in my hotel room, that means I walked all the way 'cross the parkin' lot with 'em on. Through the lobby of my own hotel, even. Cain't remember it.

I didn't mean to put 'em on.

I put the hammer back in the bag. Shove my hands in my pockets. Head for the stairs.

Some days left on my vacation, so I spend 'em down at the bowlin' alley. Not really workin' on my game, 'cause I'm so drunk I cain't hardly stand up straight. So I settle on just tryin' to keep the ball on my own lane. An' smokin' at the same time, that's quite a accomplishment.

"What ya doin', Jer?" Fat Bobby calls out from 'hind me. I miss my last step an' let the ball go wrong, so it jumps the gutter an' lands in the other feller's lane, an' goes in his gutter. I wave sorry to him, an' he just shakes his head at me.

"What's up there, homeboy?" I yell to Bobby.

"Where you get off callin' me homeboy, cracker?" Bobby says, teasin' me.

"Would ya rather I said tar-baby?" I say, steadyin' myself on the ball return.

"Don't gotta be a asshole, Jer," Bobby says. "Just come over to say hi."

"Shit. I didn't mean nothin' by it," I say. "I'm just fuck-drunk, tryin' to bowl an' not piss myself all at the same time."

Bobby grabs my arm an' starts walkin' me toward the bathroom. We walk in, an' he has me splash some cold water on my face.

"Hollis said you been out here the last two days. Open to close, far as he knew. Drunk the whole time."

"Well, I hain't bowled no three hundreds, that's for sure."

"Or two hundreds, or one hundreds neither, I bet."

"Damn, Bobby, that's just mean."

"You call me a tar-baby an' I can knock your rollin' abilities as I please. Fair's fair."

He gets a handful of paper towels an' has me dry my face. Then he opens up the end stall an' walks me in.

"Gotta piss now?" he asks.

"Don't think so."

"Then just sit."

It's the handicap stall, so I use the handrails to guide myself on down. Bobby leaves an' closes the stall door. Then

I hear him open the one next to mine. The toilet seat creaks under his three hundred pounds. We done this plenty of times.

I fish my cigarette packet outta my pants. Pick through 'em till I find the one with the twisted end. Pull it out an' puff on it while I light it. I pass it under the stall to Bobby.

"So," he says 'tween hits, "better 'fess up, cuz."

I lean 'gainst the wall an' prop my elbow up on the handrail. Shake my head. Bobby passes it back to me under the wall. I take the hit. Cough.

"She up an' gone, Bobby. For good."

"Sure enough, Jer."

Pass it back to him. Kinda hard to stay straight up 'cause of how dizzy I'm gettin'. Cain't help but fall over a little bit. Head's slidin' along the metal dividin' wall.

Bobby says, "What're you gonna do 'bout it, though. That's the question. You gonna be a pussy? Gonna sit 'round an' bitch an' moan over spilt milk, or you gonna get back on the horse? Don't be a bitch, Jerry. Grow up an' be a man. You smoked some fuckin' guy two weeks back without flinchin', an' then this is what happens you get dumped? Where's that badass motherfucker I seen who didn't give a shit? Gotta get back on the horse, Jerry."

"Hain't no horse to get back on. Hain't there. Fuckin' gone."

Bobby passes it back to me, an' I hit it a coupl'a more times.

"Just seems thataway now, Jer. That Maggie, she's one that's gonna hurt a bit gettin' over. But you cain't let her take it from you. You can get it back. Folks always do."

Shake my head again an' pass it back to him. He don't know nothin'. He don't know 'bout me standin' out in the hallway with the rip-claw hammer an' gloves taped over my hands.

"She was somethin' else, though. Smart as all hell," I say. I slide offa the toilet an' set with my back to the wall an' rest my arm up on the toilet seat. The floor feels wet through my jeans. Don't know if it's mine or someone else's 'cause right now I cain't tell the difference 'tween hot an' cold. "Pretty like them little lambs the Lowrys used to raise up an' bring to let the school kids pet durin' show-an'-tell. An' I got in trouble for pullin' this little'ns tail tryin' to make him go baa-baa. They made me set on the other side of the room an' watch while all the other kids got to pet them little lambs. An' they was just the prettiest little things I'd ever seen. Maggie's like that. Pretty like how you feel it when you just a kid."

What was I gonna do with that hammer? You already know the answer to that. Wouldn'ta needed no gloves otherwise. She's my favorite thing in the whole wide world, an' I was gonna put her down just like that.

"Still there, Jerry?" Bobby asks, passin' it under the wall to me. I take another quick hit an' pass it back.

"I mean she was educated, you know? A regular Miss-woman."

An' I's gonna put the claw end of that hammer directly into her brain.

CHAPTER SEVEN:

Jerry's off-cast ruckus.

TOM CALLS ME at seven. I reckon he tried to reach me Saturday, but I slept all day yesterday. Heard my cell phone ringin' an' just said fuck it. When I finally pick up he asks me if I'm back yet. Hain't s'posed to be on duty till Monday, but sure, I'm back.

"Need you to do somethin' off duty," Tom says.

I'm wary of anythin' Tom asks right now. Considerin'. But what the hell am I gonna do, say no? All he's gotta do is call them fuckers down in Fayetteville an' we got round two comin' up. Less'n this here's round two.

"What's the doin's, boss?" I say.

Charles Spiedell, white male, 46, 5'7", 205 lbs, recedin' black an' gray hair, blue eyes, stands in the middle of his kitchen in his green bathrobe offerin' me coffee.

"No, I don't want no cream, Chuck," I say. "Fact, I don't want no coffee at all."

Chuck's one of two locksmiths that live in Huntsville. The other one's in church right now, along with most the rest of town. Chuck's family goes to the Free Baptist service, but he says if'n God wants to speak with him, then He can knock on his door.

"What ya need, Jer?" he asks.

"For starters, close up your bathrobe. Them boxers don't hold the fly all the way shut."

He closes his robe up an' sips from his coffee mug. I can see he's hung over, like me still, so I let him have his coffee a minute more an' light a cigarette.

"So tell me what you need. I assume this ain't about the bowlin' league?"

"Them metal briefcases. Can you get 'em open?" I ask him.

"Maybe. Sure," he says, noddin' his head an' draggin' his cigarette. "If it's a keyed lock, then no problem. But if you got a combination lock, that's a whole other animal."

"I reckon it's a key," I say. "How's a grand for half a hour's work sound?"

"You cain't get it open yourself?"

"I can get it open, sure, but not without breakin' it. I need you to pop it open, look the other way while I check what's inside, then shut it back the way it was so's nobody'll know it been messed with. Then after, you keep your mouth closed on the matter," I say.

"I'd need to stop by the shop, pick up my fine-picks. Half an hour, you say? You got the cash with you, Jer?"

"In my back pocket. Don't worry, you'll be back under the covers, dreamin' 'bout the babysitter's legs 'fore your family even gets done with the service."

Chuck rocks back on his heels a moment. Looks over at me an' smiles.

Stevie's house is on the edge of town. He ain't home, 'cause he an' his family go to the same Church of Christ as my Uncle Ray. An' after the shit that went down with Ronnie, he's been tryin' to get in all the religion he can. I park the patrol car in the back driveway. Right away his big black lab comes a runnin' up to the fence an' starts barkin' at me.

"You on dog duty, too," I say to Chuck.

"What I gotta do?"

I take some of them dried pig ears outta the glove box. Conrad makes those when he hunts razorback, an' Schnitzel loves 'em. I hand two of them dried ears to Chuck.

"I hain't gettin' outta this car till you got that fucker's full attention."

Chuck gets out an' heads to the fence. Shushes the dog. Leans over the chain link fence an' lets him sniff his hand a minute. Gives him a ear an' pets his head while the dog starts a gnawin' at it. After a few more minutes, he got that tail a waggin'. I get out an' head 'round to the front a the house. I know Stevie's spare key's hid under the ceramic frog in the flower bed.

Stevie worked for Ronnie. Runnin' errands, far as on the record goes, but under the table he was settin' up some of Ronnie's cook-spots without nobody's say-so. Since Ronnie had to maintain the appearance of respectability for Tom an' the Sanhedrin, he needed somebody else to do the leg-work in settin' up his own operation. Stevie was off-limits to me an' Tom 'cause he worked for Ronnie. Now Ronnie's in the ground, it's open season.

I walk on into the livin' room an' head down the hallway by the bedrooms. Smells like lemonade in the house. Walls got little crayon marks here'n there. As it goes, it's a nice house. Stevie's a accountant by trade. Started workin' for Ronnie just to pick up some extra cash to help his family through the recession. The air conditioner clicks on right when I find what I'm lookin' for. The door to the attic's in the middle of the hallway ceiling, an' I tug the little rope to open it. Unfold the ladder an' climb on up, duckin' my head down. Tom said back in the southeast corner by the big stack of boxes. He found out about this little stash from Ronnie's books he left 'hind in his house. Records of who he'd given money to an' who kept it safe for him. Tried codin' it by usin' nicknames, but if you already know all the folks, it ain't hard to figure.

I can smell bird shit as I pull out my flashlight. Feathers, mice, cardboard, an' bird shit. I walk back to the south end of the attic an' check the corner to my left. Start pullin' down the boxes from the pile. Dust gets in my eyes an' on my uniform. There's a open box of kids' toys that tips an' spills when I grab it. Little plastic gardenin' things—a hoe, a rake, a waterin' can. A buncha matchbox cars. Coupl'a naked dolls. I try an' imagine Maggie at five years old, combin' her dolly's hair with a little brush. Talkin' to it. Dressin' it up an' puttin' it to bed.

I kick the rest of the toys outta the way an' pull aside the last few boxes. Sure enough, there it is, right in the back behind the last box. A shiny metal case. Time for Chuck to earn his pay. I take the empty toy-box, put the metal case in, an' close the flaps over it. Gotta 'member to set everythin' back the way it was when I put the case back. Head back to the patrol car.

"Now when it clicks open, buddy," I say, "do yourself a favor an' look out the window."

"Sure. Okay," he says. He unfolds a rolled leather flap that has his picks inside. Starts to work on the case's lock with a coupl'a thingamajiggers. I light a cigarette, look at my watch, then roll down the car window. Chuck fumbles a little.

"Lemme try another'n here," he says, reachin' back to his picks.

I don't get that cigarette but halfway smoked afore I hear the double click. Chuck looks up at me, an' I nod. He turns his head to look out the passenger window, an' I open the case.

It's a lotta money, just like Tom said it'd be. Stacks of hundreds an' fifties. Could be half a million. I take the package he gave me from outta my lap an' pull the tiny little gray box from the paper sack. Hain't no bigger'n half a my cell phone, an' Tom said the only reason it was that big's 'cause of the battery. Gotta make sure the switch is clicked on for the signal. I pull out the razor blade an' cut a hole in along the edge of the black fabric linin'. Pull it back. Slip the little thing inside the linin', an' then there's the click of the magnet attachin' to the steel shell. I put the loose flap back where it was an' pull out the little bottle from my pocket. Maggie's clear nail polish. She left it in my bathroom at the house on one of the two or three nights she stayed over. I take the little brush an' pat it along the two-inch cut. Next to me, Chuck sniffs 'cause of the fumes, then rolls down the window, but just keeps right on lookin' out the whole time. After coatin' where the slit is in the fabric, I blow on it to dry. A few more minutes an' I close the case shut.

I drop off Chuck an' give him his money. On the way back to Stevie's place, I'm thinkin' 'bout her toenails. Watchin' her paint 'em. I swing by Conrad's place to ask if I can borrow his shovel. He ain't there, so I go ahead an' take it from his tool shed an' throw it in the floor of the backseat. I know he won't mind. Gotta secure it with some nylon rope from the trunk. I tie it by the head an' also by the far end of the wood handle, slippin' the rope under the metal partition, to the mounts under both front seats. I take one of them cheap blankets outta the trunk an' cover the shovel up. Get back in the front seat an' feel that bottle of polish in my front shirt pocket.

Maggie couldn't have painted fingernails for a regular shift in the ER, so she almost never did 'em, 'cause she'd have to undo 'em the next day. But her toenails, she was serious 'bout those. She coulda paid for them pedicures in the beauty shop, but she liked the ritual of paintin' them herself.

Red, usually.

Stevie's family minivan shows up 'bout one thirty. Guess they had a potluck. I'm parked up the street a bit, so he won't notice right away. Give him a few minutes. Then I get out my cell phone an' punch in his number. He answers on the fourth ring.

"C'mon outside, Stevie-boy."

"Who is this?"

"It's your friend Jerry. C'mon out, we gotta talk."

"What's it about, Jer? I'm kinda busy right now."

"C'mon out an' I'll tell you. I'm parked just up the block."

"Why don't you just come inside? We can talk in the basement, in my shop."

"You want me to do that, Stevie? You want me to come into your house?"

He's quiet a minute.

"What's this about, anyhow, Jerry?"

"One a Jose's new kids. I need you to clear somethin' up. He's been spreadin' rumors, an' I'd rather hear the truth from you, buddy."

"I'll be right out," he says, an' hangs up.

When he gets out his front door, I pull up along his sidewalk an' get out. I open the door to the backseat. Point for him to get in.

"Why the back?" he asks.

"'Cause we gonna pick up that little punk-ass kid, too. I want you to set next to him an' coach him on what to say. Tell him not to lie, 'cause of what gonna happen if he does. Whisper it to him. Scare the kid good. Get him to 'fess up."

"What do you want me to say?" he asks, settin' down in the backseat.

"Just put the fear of God into him," I say, shuttin' the door.

"What you got down here on the floor?" Stevie asks.

"Go on an' see. Pull up the blanket there."

"Holy Christ, Jer," Stevie says. "You gonna use this to scare him? Show the kid what's in here an' make him shit himself?"

"Kid?" I say. "We ain't meetin' no kids today."

Takes him a second.

Stephen Jeffries, white male, 35, 5'11", 160 lbs, brown hair, brown eyes, bouncin' in the backseat, bangin' on the mesh metal barrier with his fists, eyes streamin' tears, face flushed red, screamin' bloody murder.

First I make Stevie take off his clothes, cep'n his boxers, socks, an' shoes. I fold up his shirt an' pants an' put 'em on the ground next to me. I throw the shovel on the ground near two large oak trees. Not too close, 'cause I don't wanna waste time with him cuttin' through roots.

"You gotta dig it yourself, Stevie-boy," I say, pointin' to the ground with my pistol.

"Uh-huh," he says, wipin' tears from his face as he picks up the shovel, "but how come I gotta be naked?" 'Cause I had to check your arm for tattoos, I don't say to him. He looks 'round the area. Maybe thinkin' where he could run to. We're plenty off the main roads. Gravel path got us most the way up here, then had to park 'hind some bushes a bit up the hill from the road. Followed the dried warsh-bed, where the water runs down the mountain when it rains hard. Found this clearin' a ways back.

"'Cause after you're done, I'ma donate your clothes to the Salvation Army, an' I don't wanna soil 'em," I say. "I believe in bein' charitable for the community."

I tell him to get to work diggin' or I'll make him do it with one arm broken. He starts makin' a hole in the ground, an' I riffle through the pile of clothes. Look through his wallet. Take out his family pictures. Look real close at the one of him an' his wife. They look awful happy together. I wonder how they done that.

"I didn't know Ronnie was doin' it without no one's say-so," he yells, sobbin' again. "I thought it was just another branch comin' up. Like they was expandin', you know, diversifyin' like businesses do. Didn't know it was goin' against nobody."

I know that. Ronnie had everybody under his wing conned good.

"Listen here, peckerwood, just keep diggin' an' shut up an' we'll get along fine."

"Jerry, I got a family, you know?" he blubbers.

"How'd you like to lose that tongue, Stevie? Got pliers an' a razor in the trunk back there. Maybe I'll put it in a little box for 'em. You can write the note."

He goes back to diggin'. Don't shut up, though. Keeps right at the bawlin'.

After forty minutes, he's made some real progress. I check the time on my cell phone. Tell him he's done. Have him crawl out an' kneel over the pit. Put the muzzle of the gun against the back of his scalp. Lean into him a little.

My cell phone rings, an' I step back to answer it.

"What is it?" I say.

"Okay, well, you said to call you right at three, so that's what I done," Tom says on the other end.

"Huh? What're you sayin'?" I shout into the phone. "You said I had the green light on this'n. Hain't no goin' back, I got the hole already dug."

"All right, Jerry, I'm gonna go now. Stop over at Miss Suzie's later tonight an' we'll talk." Then Tom hangs up.

"I don't understand. You said this was for certain," I say into the dead phone. "No, he says he didn't know Ronnie didn't have no say-so, but so fuckin' what, he done it, an' ain't that enough?"

Stevie's a shakin' his head an' groanin'.

"No, but how can you believe him?" I say. "I mean, if it's a toss-up, I'd say put him in the ground. Don't mean nothin' to me but fillin' in the dirt."

Stevie, naked an' covered in mud an' sweat, pisses on the ground under him.

"Fine," I say into the phone, clack it shut, then put it in my pocket.

I walk back over an' grab his clothes. Drop 'em on the ground next to him. He starts up bawlin' again. I kick him over on his side.

"Somebody just gave you a pass since you didn't know nothin'. Don't need two missin' bodies to account for when you could just have the one, I reckon. But that don't mean you're welcome in Madison County. You got twenty-four hours for you an' yours to clear out. Otherwise, I'm gonna need a bigger hole. Stevie, you're a off-cast fucker now, you get me?"

I stop at the station an' check to see if I got any messages on my desk. That picture's still there. Me an' Maggie in Puerto Vallarta. I changed outta my uniform after droppin' Stevie off, an' while I'm at my desk, Rhianna comes up 'hind me.

"Can I ask what you're doin', sir?" she says with that bite in her voice.

I turn 'round, an' she laughs. "Didn't recognize you outta uniform, Jer."

"I hain't back on duty till tomorrow. Just checkin' in, though," I say. "Hey, has Tom been back to the station yet? I mean since he got outta the hospital?"

"He just got out yesterday," she says. "An' no, he ain't been in yet."

"Sure. Okay. You got the key to his office in your desk, still?" I ask.

"Yeah. But you're not on duty, Jerry. What is it you need?"

"Nothin'. It can wait till I see him next."

She nods, turns to leave, then stops in her tracks. Rhianna Beaulieu, white female, 28, 5'8", 145 lbs, blonde hair, blue eyes, rubs her temples an' looks back at me with trouble wrinklin' up her forehead. "Got a question for you, Jer," she says. I've always enjoyed the soft Avoyelles-Cajun in her voice she tries to cover up. Not like Bobby. He's proud of his accent. Two years ago when she come up here, I told her I had another friend from Louisiana. She asked which part, an' I said that Fat Bobby was from Nawlins. She corrected me. That ain't Louisiana, she said.

"What do you need?" I ask. She shakes her head, lookin' down at the carpet.

"Nappy Freddie MacDonald."

"What of him? When did they finally pick him up?"

"They didn't," she says. "He's still in the same cell."

She opens the office door for me, an' right off I start diggin' through the papers on Tom's desk. Pull open the drawers in it.

"Where's he keep the key for the file cabinet?"

"It's here," she says, holdin' up the same key-ring.

Rhianna's the only one Tom trusts with the spare keys to his office. He tends to trust the women he fucks. I take the key ring from her an' unlock the file cabinet. Thumb through prisoner transfer records. Tom's real meticulous 'bout record keepin'. Everythin' goes in the file room, an' duplicates of important papers go in his office. I don't have the password to his computer, so if'n it ain't in hard copy, I won't find it.

"I already looked, Jer. It ain't here. In Records neither."

"How come they didn't pick him up?"

She scratches the back of her scalp an' just keeps lookin' at me.

"Rhianna?" I say her name louder, startin' to yell. "How the fuck come they didn't—"

"I don't know what happened, Jer," she says. "I called Washington County Sherriff's Department, an' they never got a request for prisoner transfer."

I look up at her from the file cabinet. Shut the drawer. I move over an' set in Tom's chair. He wanted *me* to do it. He wanted me to arrange Freddie's escape from custody, an' to have a hole dug for him, too. What does that mean? I cain't figure it.

"Jerry?" she says, settin' in the chair 'cross the desk from me. "What's goin' on?"

Needed to get rid of me. An' Freddie. Fucked up mine. But if he could still get me to take Freddie, he could have somebody waitin' for us. Two birds with one stone.

No. That cain't be right.

"Jerry? You gotta lemme know what you're thinkin'. You know somethin' I don't? 'Cause folks 'round the station are wantin' to know how come Freddie's still in that cell after near three weeks with no paperwork."

"I'm workin' on it. Gimme a minute."

Tom planned to do it that way first. Has to be. They find Freddie by sheer luck, an' Tom sees his chance to have the Sanhedrin take care of the whole thing. They get a dead little Freddie, an' all they gotta do is clip me along with.

Tom don't gotta do nothin'. Let the professionals handle it. Then that shit with Ronnie happened, an' he couldn't wait on it. Had to act fast.

No. That ain't right. He'da done somethin' afore now, even in the hospital. Just has to make a phone call. Shit. What am I missin'?

"Just tell me he forgot," Rhianna says. "Okay?" She looks shaky. Mostly she's cool as a cucumber. But she's gettin' anxious, I can tell.

"What's that?" I say.

"Freddie MacDonald's been in a cell with no paperwork of any kind filed. An' he don't know the difference, really, just reads comic books an' magazines an' talks to himself. Brain fried like that egg in the skillet on TV, you know? Hasn't even asked for a lawyer." She rubs her temples again. There's this birthmark under her left ear. I get why Tom's dippin' his pen.

"I can understand if he forgot. 'Cause of the shootin' back in the woods. But I don't wanna entertain other possibilities, Jerry. Just tell me Tom forgot. He was going to have him transferred, and 'cause of that business that put him in the hospital, he just plain forgot."

"Probably right," I say, still lookin' at the papers on Tom's desk. No idea what I'm s'posed to be lookin' for. Maybe a Post-it that says *use Freddie to get Jerry*.

She nods her head again, gettin' up to leave. I get up, too, since she's gotta lock up.

"Yeah, you're probably right. He just forgot, what with that infection an' all. Them damn antibiotics can really throw you through a loop."

I'm itchin' at the scabs on my arms from that birdshot a couple weeks back. They don't wanna just heal up an' leave me be. I'm settin' on the back pew at the emptied-out Church of Christ, waitin' for my Uncle Ray to finish wipin' down the communion table. Promised I'd take him up to Miss Suzie's this weekend. He's in love with a coupl'a them girls up there.

Ray wipes 'round the edge of the offerin' table with his rag, coverin' the same spot four or five times now. He gets like this afore goin' out there. Then when he comes back, he's just as bad. I seen him work at it for more'n a hour. Gettin' in each of the corners 'round ever' letter of This-Do-In-Remembrance-Of-Me. Tom asked me one time if'n I oughtta be takin' somebody retarded like Ray up to a place like Miss Suzie's. I asked him, who'd he think took me for the first time when I's fifteen? Sure weren't Santy Claus.

"Let's go, Ray," I say. "Hain't got dirty since ya cleaned it a minute ago."

"I gotta clean it good, Jerry," he says, lookin' up at me.

"You done that, now let's go."

He shakes his head an' goes back to wipin' at the table. He'll do this other times, too. Church of Christ is a no-drinkin' religion, so whenever I bring over a coupl'a six-packs for us to watch a late movie on his TV, he's got to go an' wipe it again 'fore he goes to bed. One time I made the mistake of askin' him how come he had to clean it like that ever' time, when he already does it as part of his custodial job. He said it's so's the devil don't get in. Then he had to start a cleanin' it all over again.

I check the time on my cell phone. Tom wanted to meet up 'round six. It's five fifteen now, an' it's a twenty-minute drive through the hills to get there. I cain't do nothin' wrong by Tom right now. I just cain't. Need to play along. Seein' Maggie made me wanna not fuck it up again. Maybe she'd even wanna see *me* if I didn't fuck up for a while. I know that ain't likely, but I don't wanna consider the other option. Don't even wanna think it.

I get up from the pew an' head out through the lobby to the front doors. Cain't smoke in the buildin'. I set myself down on the top step an' fish out my cigarettes. Light one an' lean against the red brick. The mortar's a crumblin', an' some falls on my shoulder. I don't know what Tom done back in them woods. He may've dug a hole for me, an' he may not. Only way I'ma get my retirement fund is by playin' along a bit more.

You know I cain't even begin to describe how bad it reeks of Lysol in here. Swear to God, ever' time I walk in it liketa chokes me an' I gotta step outside for fresh air. I tell Ray I'll catch up with him later an' stand out on the front porch a minute, tryin' to keep my throat from closin' shut. I watch a few cars drivin' down the road on the other side of the holler.

Miss Suzie's place is right near the bottom of the old Huntsville Road loop. But you cain't get to it from the bottom, you gotta take a county dirt road in from 295 on the west side of the loop. Then you gotta take four or five switch-backs down into a holler, cross the creek on that rusted bridge, an' follow it back the way you came. Then you park in a lot an' walk 'bout a hundred yards or so up the path to the buildin'. When some of them older folks from the city council come in, Suzie'll have a golf cart sent down to bring 'em on up.

There's two buildin's all covered in metal sidin', right next to each other, stickin' out the side of the hill, an' connected by a covered walk. When Suzie took over for the colonel forty years ago, there was only the one buildin', an' that was just a old barn. The house that the barn went with fell down a long ways back. I look down at my feet on the white rock path. Used to be plain old gravel when I come here regular as a dumb kid. I watch a coupl'a fellers walk on up the path an' head in. When I got my breathin' under control, I head for the bar.

This is how Tom keeps everythin' goin' his way in Madison County. He got a arrangement with Miss Suzie. Any elected official in the county gets whatever he wants at her place, an' it goes on Tom's tab. Mayor. County attorney. Council. Assessor. Hell, even the Huntsville chief of police. Tom don't even look at his tab. He just bills the Sanhedrin for it an' calls it business expenses. For twenty-two years, he's been the most popular sheriff the county's ever had.

"I don't recognize you," I say. Bartender looks me over. Big fucker, like he works as a bouncer, too. Got a barbwire tattoo 'round his neck.

"Second week here," he says. I nod an' look up at the small camera lookin' over the bar. Suzie's watchin', but nobody's seen her come outta her private room in a decade. Not since that feller come up an' stuck her with a knife. She was right friendly with folks up till then.

"Since I don't know you, I got some special instructions."

"What's that?" bartender asks. He's fillin' up the well bottles with the cheap stock.

"Got bleach under there?" I point to the rack under the dishwarshin' machine tucked away in the corner. They got another'n in the small kitchen, but the little'n they keep out here.

"Sure," he nods.

"Take that bucket where you got the dishtowel, dump it out, run the rag under hot water."

"What for?"

"'Cause I'm the customer, shithead," I say. So he does it, an' I watch him real close.

"Now pour two capfuls of bleach in the bucket. No, three. Then fill it with that hot water from the tap. An' make sure you got that rag wrung out real good. You sure you ain't got a clean one?"

"Just this one. Unless you want me to get one from the back?" he says. I don't know where it'd be from. Somebody's come-towel, maybe.

"No, that'll be just fine. Now drop it in that hot water an' let it set for a minute. An' don't bunch it up like that. Let it spread out. It's gotta soak through."

"Okay. Now what you want done?" he asks, pickin' it outta the bucket.

"Take that glass outta the dish rack there an' wipe it down. No, not that glass, the one on the back side. Yeah, that one."

Bartender shakes his head like he cain't believe it, but he does just what I ask. Picks up the Collins glass an' starts wipin' it 'round the outside. Hain't doin' it right.

"Give it here," I say, reachin' my hand out. He gives me the glass an' the rag. Laughin' at me now. Like I'm some kinda headcase. So I'm scrubbin' the rim an' shovin' the rag all the way down on the inside.

"That really necessary?" bartender asks. I just nod an' set down the glass an' the rag.

"Some guy's lips was just on here a minute ago. 'Fore that, them lips was probably on some diseased snatch. Or it was a hooker's lips on it, fresh from suckin' dick, an' probably got herself oral herpes anyhow. So yeah. I'd say it's necessary."

"Then what do you want?"

"Tomato juice."

I hain't seen Tom yet. There's Christmas lights up 'round the bar. Folks walkin' 'round I try not to look at. Some got they clothes on. Others not as much. There's a small lounge room out in fronta the bar, with a coupl'a tables an' several couches that got red slipcovers on 'em. Mosta the private rooms is down the hallway to my left, through that walkway, in the connected buildin'. Suzie's office is upstairs in this'n. Hain't too crowded tonight. Some nights it's standin' room only. I don't like the smell of that Lysol. There's all kinda other scents, like some cinnamon, some vanilla, an' some kinda orange spice, but that Lysol's underneath it all. It's that lemon kind that don't smell nothin' like lemons. I sip my tomato juice. Maggie gave me a taste for that. Somebody comes up behind me from the right side.

"You're up here all alone, honey," a woman's voice says. "You want some company?" Then she slips her hand through my arm an' my throat wants to close up right quick.

"GODDAMNIT YOU NASTY FUCKIN' CUNT GET THEM HANDS AWAY!" I yell, an' spill my juice all over the bar. She steps back quick. I reach over the bar for the rag, but it ain't there no more. I gotta clean my arm with somethin' quick. I stand up from the barstool an' reach for my wallet. Leave the bartender a twenty 'cause I was rude. I'm gettin' ready to head for the bathroom when I notice who it is.

Pamela Hillman, white female, 33, 5'5", 125 lbs, blonde hair, hazel eyes. Hain't seen her since back at Ronnie's place. Guess she didn't like the shelter too much. She got her hair done up, lotta lipstick an' eye shadow, an' she's in some lacy pink teddy-type number that covers her burns. Probably she's just givin' folks head till they heal up a little better an' some makeup'll cause them scars to disappear. She just looks at me like I got a dick growin' outta my forehead.

"Nice to see you, Pam," I say. I turn away to head for the bathroom, but then reconsider. If'n I go into the bathroom, I'll have to touch the handle. Don't wanna do that. I look back at the bartender. "Just hand me that bleach bottle, huh? An' the rag, too."

While I'm wipin' at my bicep an' elbow, Tom walks up right when it's gettin' to sting a little. I toss the rag back over on the bar.

"How do you find Jerry in a whorehouse? Just gotta listen for the feller screamin' don't-touch-me. How was your vacation, Jer?"

He's in uniform, but got his shirt open an' hairy beer gut hangin' out. All sweaty. There's them same birdshot scabs on him, too. Got a drink in his hand. I can smell that cheap Scotch over the bleach an' Lysol.

"What'd you need, boss?"

He leans in to whisper. "Seen Stevie packin' up his shit. You gave him twenty-four hours like I said?"

"Sure did. But I could see him wantin' to take off soon as possible."

"You gotta get on it, then."

"Thought you were gonna handle that end of things, boss."

"*Was* gonna. Somethin' came up. An' somethin' else, too. You gonna have somebody ride along with you. I was gonna show him what we do. Since you're leavin', I gotta find a replacement. I'd do it, but I'm still too weak for that kinda duty."

"What parts he from?"

"Fayetteville. He's got a security job now like you had. If he works out, I'll hire him on as a deputy. So you gonna do some evaluatin' tonight, in addition to this thing with Stevie," he says, then nods to my elbow. "That arm's turnin' red, Jerry. What you put on there?"

I walk back behind the bar an' turn on the faucet over the little metal sink. Let my arm run under cool water for a minute. I don't know why, but it occurs to me as the water's coolin' my burn that I need to return Conrad's shovel to him. Bartender just stares at me. I peek my head over the bar at Tom. He's wrinklin' up his forehead. Reckon he thinks I'm fit for the nuthouse.

Ray's quiet in the cab of my truck. Guess he had botha his girls tonight, 'cause he took twice as long. Tom's offered to let me put anythin' I want from Suzie's on his tab, but I don't have no use for it. So I charge what Ray does to his tab. Works out for all parties involved. I wanna light the cigarette I got stuck 'hind my ear, but with Ray in the cab, it wouldn't be kind to him. After I drop him off, there's this kid I gotta meet up with. Tom's new guy.

Park outside of Ray's little house 'hind the church. He gets outta the cab, an' I say good night. He shuts the door an' asks me if it's gettin' on to froggin' season yet.

"Reckon so, Ray. We'll have to dig out them spears. Sharpen up them tines."

CHAPTER EIGHT:

Jerry licks the flint.

"JUST SHUT UP, Jimmy," I say. "Don't wanna hear nothin' from you for the next hour. At least the next hour."

James Howell, white male, 22, 5'10", 150 lbs, curly black hair, blue eyes, has been talkin' nonstop since we left Huntsville half a hour ago. Tellin' me 'bout all the pussy he got in the army. 'Bout what a badass he is in his MMA club. Tellin' me how many seconds he knocked the last feller out in. When he asked me if I done any of that, I asked him what the hell MMA was. Mixed Martial Arts, he says. Okay, I said. Sure, I heard of that. Then to shut him up, I said all that was for faggots. Miscalculated, though, 'cause he ain't shut up since.

Stevie left his house at 'bout two thirty a.m. Like Tom said, he took the briefcase with him. Got Tom's laptop open while Jimmy drives. There's this trackin' system. Signal gets sent from the case up to satellites, or over to towers, or God knows what, an' then the company that makes the little tracker puts the data on a private webpage, so's only we can see it. Tom showed me how to use the little Aircard that plugs into the laptop like them jump drives an' connects it to the Internet with the same reception as a cell phone.

So long as Stevie stays on the highway an' don't go too far into the hills, we can follow him by the little dot on the map-screen.

I told Jimmy to keep at least a mile back from Stevie. Better if it's two. How's come I think MMA's for faggots, he asked. Told him to shut up. Not that he listened.

"Keep back, I said. Nobody on the road right now. If you can see his taillights, he can damn sure see your headlamps."

There's nothin' outside the window now. Middle of the night. Passin' through the hills. A light ever' mile or so when there's a house. Some chicken barns. In between it's black.

"Tell me how's come you said that, huh? I can beat the shit outta folks on the mat."

"An' I said to shut up for at least a hour. You don't listen so good. An' slow the fuck down, kid. I don't care there's curves in the road now, it goes straight nearin' Fayetteville."

"Just tell me how's come you said that, an' I'll shut up," he says.

I shake my head an' just watch the screen. Stevie's on Highway 45, 'bout where it turns into Mission Street, which means he's almost in city limits. Neither me or Jimmy's in uniform, an' I don't like that. Done it plenty of times, but it just ain't my favorite. I like the way folks read you in uniform.

"Well, I take it back, okay? You wanna go'n bruise up your brain, play footsie with fellers in tight shorts, you go right ahead."

"What do you mean?" he asks. Keeps lookin' over at me while he's drivin'.

"Pay attention to the road. He's gettin' close now. I hain't got nothin' against the mat, kid," I say. "It just don't mean nothin' to me's all. I learnt different."

Red dot starts movin' north offa 45.

"Okay, looks like he took a right on North Oakland Zion. You know what's up in that area?" I ask.

Shakes his head, lookin' out in the black. "Fuck, I don't know. Mostly residential. So tell me what you learnt different."

"Later. Focus on the road. We gonna turn in a minute so keep your eye peeled. Shit. Took a left on Skillern. Jimmy, here's the turn for Zion."

"Got it," he says. "You said left on Skillern?"

Everythin's been dark for the last forty minutes. Now on the edge of the suburbs, my eyes gotta adjust to the street lamps.

"He's on two sixty-five north. Map says it's by the country club," I say.

"He's goin' to the mall," Jimmy says, noddin' his head.

Little red dot gets on Shiloh. Then East Shepherd Lane. Then stops. As we're headin' up East Shepherd, Stevie drives past us in his little yellow Toyota in the opposite lane, an' botha us 'bout shit.

"Fuck. Was that the guy? What's the screen say?" he asks.

"Just stopped. He dropped it off. Looks like the mall's east parkin' lot," I say. Jimmy looks back'n forth from me to the road, panicked.

"Think he saw us?" he asks, jittery-like.

It's in the east lot, all right. Little red Honda, late eighties model. Only car in the lot. The case is in there. Jimmy parks the car on the tiered level above, overlookin' the Honda maybe a quarter mile west. Turns off the engine. Lights a cigarette an' rolls down the window.

"Hain't fightin', kid, that's all I'm sayin'."

"What do you mean? I even heard of guys gettin' killed on the mat."

"I mean, it's got rules. You can get disqualified. Fightin' in a competition's like puttin' on a show. Hain't fightin'. It's like startin' a bar brawl. Just workin' up a sweat. When you aim to *kill* a feller, then that's a fight. What I learnt was from a guy in my Guard unit. He was a cab driver but also taught classes part time, too. Karate. Judo. Jiu-jitsu even. Probably some of the same shit you learnt. Only he didn't teach us no forms. Just some principles to work from. Like *economy of motion*. That's what he called it. Economy of motion. Least amount of effort producin' the most amount of damage."

"Like what?" he asks.

"Go ask him yourself, he still teaches here in Fayetteville. Two classes on Thursdays an' one on Saturday. Name's Alan."

"But gimme a example."

"If it'll shut you up," I say. "You drove, so I'll take first watch. For two hours?"

"Sure thing."

"Okay. Like this. Usin' someone's momentum when they come at you to twist they arm back 'round an' pop it right out the socket. Or like puttin' your thumb through somebody's eyeball till it goes right into they brain. Practice it by tapin' a ripe orange to a feller's face, directly over his eye. You learn there ain't no rules. You get in a fight, there ain't no lines to cross. An' first rule in real life is, if'n you got down to just your bare hands, you already lost. Now shut up'n get some sleep, kid. Wake you up in two hours."

Jimmy's leaned back in the driver's seat, eyes closed. I shut the laptop an' stuff my hands in my pockets. I got my .22 in my right palm. I don't know this kid from nobody. An' even if I did, I wouldn't put it past Tom to use him.

Maggie's in the dark with me. My arm's still burnin' from that bleach, an' that makes me 'member her drippin' candle wax on me that one time. Watchin' her eyes get wide as she done it. Right now I feel like she's settin' right there in the backseat. I could just look back an' see her. 'Course I don't wanna do that. That Wowzer's back there, too.

"You know what's in the case? How come it's so damn important?" Jimmy asks, eyes closed. Like he don't know. Good actin'.

"Hain't the case we want," I say. "That's just a little bribe money somebody gave Ronnie to smooth things over for the operation. Ronnie give it to Stevie to hold on to. So now Stevie's off-cast, he gotta return it, less'n he wants some feller to come a chasin' after. What we want is to know who give it out in the first place. 'Cause that's who's tryin' to move in on us."

"What're we gonna do when we find out who done it?"

"Tell Tom, I reckon. He can rain down a lot more fire'n just the two of us."

I'm tired, but thinkin' of Maggie got me antsy, tappin' my fingers on the steerin' wheel. I wanna go back to Memphis. I gotta see her again. But it's gonna be hard to stay in a hotel room an' just watch her 'cross the way. Or see her walkin' from her car into the hospital. If'n I don't stay put in that room, I liketa hurt her. Not that I'd mean to, but she'd start screamin' on seein' me. Tryin' to get away. Makin' her set still would probably hurt some. So I'd have to just set in a room an' pull my hair from stayin' put. Still. That's better'n doin' this bullshit.

Hain't quite light yet when I see another car come into the lot. Looks like a silver Ford, late nineties model. Circles 'round twice in the parkin' lot below an' stops a few feet away from the red Honda. Two fellers get outta the back an' go over to it. One opens the door an' pops the trunk. The other looks in the trunk an' nods to the driver of the Ford, an' it takes off. I open up the laptop again as they start up the Honda.

While I'm gettin' it to the map-screen, I see Jimmy textin' on his cell phone.

"What're you doin'?"

"Tom said to let him know when the others showed up."

Thought he didn't know what was goin' on. Maybe he didn't say that, exactly. I don't 'member his words. I reach back into my right pocket an' feel for the .22. The red Honda pulls outta the parkin' lot an' heads back down East Shepherd Lane. I reach over with my left hand an' start the car while I cock the pistol with my right hand. When I pull my hand out, I bring my cigarettes. Jimmy looks over at me after he closes his cell phone. Puts the car in reverse an' pulls out.

Half a hour now. Monday mornin' an' folks is gettin' on the road to go to work. Followed these fuckers through Fayetteville, from Highway 180 to 156, then all the way south to the old 71 scenic route that winds through the mountains on its way down to Fort Smith. I call up Tom. Don't know if that'll help or not.

"Think they saw you?" he asks.

"No. Hain't been in line of sight. We're at least three miles back."

"So you think it ain't no goose-chase?"

"How would I know? I'm just doin' what I been told."

The further south of Fayetteville I go, the less comfortable I get. The further I am from home. I don't know the country here. Hain't been down old 71 but maybe twice in my life. Any second it could happen. All Tom has to do is call them in the car up ahead, tell 'em to pull over. Maybe at a gas station. Jimmy'd know the doin's, of course. So when we walk up on them fuckers in that little red Honda, Jimmy sets his sights on me an' puts me down. Or if he don't get the first draw, while I'm puttin' holes in him, them folks from that Honda put some in me. I cain't get 'em from both sides.

"Follow 'em as far as Fort Smith. If they don't pull over 'fore then, pull alongside an' shoot 'em while they on the road. Then grab the case an' head back. Bodies, too, if you can. We wanna know who these guys are," Tom says. "Call me right back when it's done."

An' grabbin' that case'll mean Tom knows right where I am.

They pull over a ways 'fore Mountainburg, maybe a hour yet from Fort Smith. This little tourist spot, a buildin' right on the highway made outta white cut rocks that been mortared together, that looks out over the Ozarks. Got a wooden deck built on the other side over a hundred-foot drop, with them pay telescopes. There's this fat white rooster with a bright red face a scratchin' in the flower bed next to the shop's front door. There's nobody in the Honda when Jimmy parks. But there's a café next door. Maybe they went in there. Don't matter. We'll see 'em when they come back. We're four spaces from that Honda, an' not another car in between.

I take out the clear plastic egg. Break it open in my hand.

"What's that?" Jimmy asks.

"Hain't you never had a girlfriend, Jimbo?" I say. "It's panty hose. Thought ya legs might be gettin' cold."

"Funny. You want me to put that on my head?"

"Our heads," I say, cuttin' the hose in half with my pocket knife. One leg for him, one for me. "Jimmy, it's broad daylight, get it?"

"Sure, okay."

"But not till we see 'em come out. Then real quick. Have it rolled up in ya hands already so it goes on fast. We do it like this, one-two-three."

"How's that?"

"When we see 'em come out. One, we put the stockin's on. Two, when they get to they car, we step outta ours. Three, as they gettin' in, we walk up fast. Walk, not run. An' shoot ever' bullet you got in your gun. You take the driver, an' I'll get the other'n."

"Then what?"

"Then we'll see. May be we gonna do some heavy liftin'."

Afore the stockin' can go on, I gotta get my gloves ready. Jimmy's got his leather'ns. I gotta get mine out. Jimmy's hands is a shakin', an' the smoke comin' offa his cigarette is makin' this little wavy pattern from it. Gettin' ash on his knee. When I got my gloves on tight, these ones is pale green, I start in on the tape.

"Why you gotta do that?" he asks.

"Shut up'n mind the door. They probably comin' out soon."

I reach in the brown paper bag an' take out the .38 an' the .357 Tom give us. Check the cylinders to see they loaded. Give Jimmy the .38, since I know he carries one of them for his security job. Check the hammer by clickin' one turn an' lettin' it down soft. Smooth action. This is gonna make a whole lotta fuckin' noise. One last thing 'fore I get my stockin' on. I pull some foam earplugs outta my pocket.

Jimmy don't wait, he just bolts outta the door. Hadn't expected that. I get outta my side an' stay there while he strides quick 'round the car. He ain't lookin' over at me, just at his target. The two men gettin' in the open doors of the Honda, one of them slappin' a new pack of cigarettes, look up as Jimmy raises his .38. I stay right where I am an' aim mine. Jimmy's now right 'tween me an' them. If'n he wants to shoot me, I got the drop on him. Jimmy fires the first shot.

It misses the feller an' blows in the back driver's-side window. That rooster next to the door starts flappin' an jumpin' up an' down. Both them is reachin' for they own guns. I still don't know who to aim for yet, but I lift up the .357 an' point. Jimmy fires a second shot an' hits the feller on the driver's side of the car right in the shoulder. The feller on the passenger side got his pistol out now, an' I squeeze my own trigger. The shot gets him through the collarbone.

That'll put him down for now, least till I get over there. If'n he gets Jimmy afore that, boo-fuckin'-hoo.

Jimmy steps in closer to the driver an' shoots him in the chest. I jump back in our car an' scoot over on the driver's side. We left it runnin', so's all I gotta do is back out an' head over there. I stop just on the other side of the Honda's back bumper an' pull the trunk release.

Jimmy shoots his last three shots into the driver's body on the ground. As I get 'round the back side of the Honda, I see that the passenger feller's on his butt backin' away from the car, an' he turns white when he notices our car pulled up right next to him. His face ain't but ten feet from mine. I point the .357 as he's liftin' his pistol from the ground. Got his lips pulled back from the pain, I reckon. Shoot him through the teeth.

I rush up to the Honda. Lean in the shattered window an' click *that* trunk release. When I head back for the trunk, I notice there's folks startin' to gather 'round the entrance to the café an' the tourist shop. Fire two more shots, one at each place to get they heads down, an' hope to God nobody in there got a concealed handgun permit. Pick the case outta the trunk an' throw it into ours. Grab the passenger feller an' drag him over quick as I can. Jimmy starts draggin' his over, an' gets there just after I have mine lifted up. Drop him inside. Help Jimmy lift up his. They's pretty awkward to lift when they ain't bound or wrapped up an' arms an' legs can just flop all 'round. Shut the trunk lid an' hop back in our car.

As we screech outta the gravel parkin' strip, I see a feller comin' outta the tourist shop with a marker an' a notepad. He's got the plate number for sure.

"Well, sure, there's a APB out for the car," Tom says on my cell. "Goin' north on Seventy-One, right? Are you north or south of the turnoff for Devil's Den?"

"South yet," I say. Jimmy's in the passenger seat, havin' another cigarette, tryin' to get his hands to stop shakin'.

"You're comin' up on Winslow, then. Take the right onto Koyle, I think. That'll take you to Old Ridge, then to County Thirty-Eight, an' you know how to get to Two Ninety-Five from there. Just stick to the back roads an' you'll be fine. Call me when you get there."

"Hain't goin' to your spot. Got my own picked out. Hole's already dug."

I park the car back behind the bushes like I done yesterday with the patrol car. 'Fore we get outta the car, I have another cigarette. Notice I still got my gloves on.

"What time is it?" Jimmy asks. I shake my head.

"Calm your nerves now, 'cause it's real important you don't fuck up durin' this part," I say. "We're almost done." I pull the trunk release. Unwrap the tape an' pull them gloves off. My hands is awful sweaty now.

I get outta the car an' head back to the trunk. Left my .357 in the backseat. Seen Jimmy reload his .38 on the way in an' stuff it down the fronta his pants. He takes off his shirt 'cause he's gettin' so hot. When I see what's on his arm, I look away, but not too quick. We wrangle the bodies outta the trunk an' start draggin' em up the hill to where the hole is. I'm awful glad I forgot an' left Conrad's shovel up there when I's with Stevie yesterday. There's a small fold-up one in the trunk, but that's just for diggin' outta snow drifts an' such. Take forever to fill in with that one. When we got the bodies up to the top of the hill, we leave 'em right near the hole.

"That gonna be big enough?" Jimmy asks.

"Just shut up an' set a minute."

I call up Tom.

"You got a inkpad an' roller up there? How 'bout them fingerprint cards?" He sounds kinda pissed. "We need to know who they were, Jerry. That's the only direction we got left to look in. You got that shit where you are? 'Cause I was all set up here."

I bet he's all set up. I just bet.

"I'll take care of everythin', boss. Just you leave it to me." I hang up.

"Grab that shovel, Jimmy," I say. "We gotta do somethin' afore we cover 'em up."

"What's that?" he asks. I kneel down by the body Jimmy shot. Take the arm an' pull it out to the side. Lay it palm up.

"Put the point of that shovel on the wrist, right here, where the joint is. Then jump hard down on it with both feet, like you would startin' to dig. Should pop right off."

"Jesus, Jerry, what the fuck for?"

"Tom needs fingerprints. There's a APB out on the car, so I cain't exactly drive it up to the station to get what I need. We gonna put 'em in one of them trash bags in the car, an' then get what we need from the station so I can do it at my house. An' I hain't drivin' this car to my house, neither. Just leave it down the road a few miles an' let Tom come an' get it while we walk to my car. So get over here an' steady this shovel."

Jimmy walks up an' stands behind it. Grabs the new ash-wood handle an' adjusts the point over the wrist. I nod for him that it's right. Look one more time at what's on Jimmy's arm.

When he bends his knees to jump, I take my .22 outta my jacket pocket an' shoot him three times through the chest. Jimmy falls back, right hand grabbin' at the holes, left still holdin' onto the shovel. I get up an' move in over him. Take the .38 outta his pants. Glance over at that thumbprint tiger on his upper left arm.

He's coughin' blood up now. Red bubble comin' from his left nostril. Looks up at me all confused-like. Eyes don't wanna stay on one place. The sky. Oak tree. Gun in my hand. If he knew somethin', maybe I'd ask him a question or two. But he's like me. He don't know nothin'. Compartmentalized.

I put the .22 on his forehead. His arms come up to try an' stop me. Movin' his eyes to my face, down to the gun, an' back up. Grabs my hand an' tries to get himself a grip with his slick fingers. I pull the trigger twice.

"You burn out that car like you said?" I ask.

"Yeah, I did. How'd James do?" Tom asks.

I shut off the water in the bath. Schnitzel's whinin', beggin for a treat. I been givin' him them chicken-an'-liver-flavored ones from the store he just loves. His nails clickin' on the tile as he moves from beggin' on one side of my feet over to the other.

"Hold your horses," I say to my dog. He sets still, tail waggin', lookin' up at me with them sad droopin' eyes. "Jimmy done just fine," I say to Tom.

"Sure. Good. How'd them fingerprints turn out?" he asks.

I look up at the cards on the edge of the sink. Schnitzel whines again, so I give him another treat. I can hear Grandma's TV in her room down the hall. It's just after nine, an' the comedy show she watches is on now. I can hear her rockin' chair squeakin' the floorboards.

"Have 'em to ya in the mornin', boss."

I look back over into the tub at the six hands layin' in four inches of water. They's bound together in pairs at the thumbs with my 'lectric tape, so's I'd know which one went with which. Right now, the water's got a tint of red, 'cause of what's left on the open part of the wrists an' the blood that smeared on the skin while they was in the trash bag. That's how come I gotta soak 'em now. Clean 'em good 'fore I take them prints.

"It's good to have you back, Jerry," Tom says.

"Great to be back," I say. He hangs up, an' I close my cell phone.

I hain't gonna do this no more. Waitin' for the other shoe to drop. It's stupid. Cain't make no plans this way. He's gonna do it now, whether he was afore or not. I give him three sets of prints, an' when he runs 'em, Jimmy's gonna pop up on his screen. I've half a mind to stop by his house tonight an' finish him off 'fore he knows anythin'.

Them pairs in the tub look like little pink birds with they wings spread out. My dog whines again, an' I shush him. I pick up the first pair. Take the fingernail brush an' start scrubbin' away dirt an' what clotted. Dip it in the water a few times. Scrub it again. Set it on the towel spread out in the sink to dry. I reach in for the next pair.

Only reason I hain't gone into Tom's house tonight an' shot him in his bed with his wife, or whoever else is there, is 'cause I don't know for sure. There may've been another'n.

Scrub over the skin good. Get the specks an' clots. Get under them nails. Doin' palm prints, too, so gotta clean that good. Schnitzel's still whinin'. Shake my head no.

If'n I was to move on Tom now, an' there's other parties to consider, then I'm fucked good. Wait an' see what he does when he gets Jimmy's prints on his screen. Grandma's rocker's creakin' louder now. I doubt he'd try an' use her. That'd be funny. Interrogatin' a woman cain't talk. Don't even know what year it is.

Set the pair down on the towel to dry. Pick up the last pair an' start scrubbin'. By the time he figures it out, I'll be gone. No reason for me to be here. Cain't learn nothin' by stickin' 'round. He'll dump his cell phone right away. Probably won't even use one for a while. Set the last pair on the towel to dry.

I get up from the side of the tub, dry my hands on the face towel, an' walk outta the bathroom, through my room, an' down the hall to Grandma's room. She's settin' in her old rockin' chair with a quilt over her legs. Sewin' a date on some pattern, probably for a weddin' happened forty years back that she thinks is comin' up soon. I check the pill box on her nightstand. Kiss the top of her head an' tell her good night. She squeezes my hand.

Them pairs in the sink is dried by now, so I head back down the hall to my room. I like this bathroom. Everythin's fairly new. Put it in four years ago when Conrad first moved out here. He'd worked construction for God knows how long an' said he'd give me a deal. I wanted a bathroom that weren't all the way downstairs, an' he needed a little extra money. I helped him out on the whole mess of groutin' an' wirin' an' plumbin'.

Reckon I hain't gonna do nothin' with Tom right yet. Just head for Memphis, soon's I'm done here. If he's gonna kill me, well, then there's no reason not to go an' see Maggie. Say what's on my mind. Or don't say nothin' at all. I done licked the flint good with this business. I'll be ready for whatever comes.

Gather up them three cards with the rows of spaces that say R. Thumb – R. Index – R. Middle – R. Ring – R. Little. An' the row under it has the Ls, too. Open up the inkpad. Get the roller out.

Maybe she'll see me now that I'm a dead man.

I give Schnitzel a treat.

CHAPTER NINE:

Somethin' dead up the branch.

I spot 'em right away. Me an' Schnitzel settin' in the front seat of the car I rented from the airport counter back in Fayetteville. Northeast corner of the lot, opposite side of where her gray Saab is parked. I'm drinkin' from a water bottle. He's lappin' from the bowl I put on the floor. It's a quarter to noon, an' hotter'n fuck today. Don't help that the parkin' lot's black asphalt. Got my binoculars on Maggie's hotel room window. Listenin' to static on the Bearcat. Then her voice comes through the earpiece, just sayin' hi to answer a call. I set up straight, an' some water dribbles on down my chin. I bend down to grab a tissue, an' that's when I see 'em. Southeast corner. Mid-nineties silver Chevy Lumina. Two in the front seat. One got binoculars, too.

"Listen, John," she says in my earpiece, "this shit you been tellin' Momma. I don't appreciate it. You don't need to panic her, given her nerves."

John says, "I'm sorry for startling Momma. But I do think you should come and see her. Fayetteville would do you some good."

I find the tissue an' wipe at my chin. Move my binoculars over toward the Lumina. As I lean over him, Schnitzel starts lickin' my face. Pat his head an' tell him to stay down.

"And this crap about being traumatized. Thank you very fucking much for your diagnosis-sans-consultation mister shrink-asshole. And thanks for sharing that with Momma, too. That was the icing on the cake, you prick."

"You are traumatized," he says. "And if it doesn't come out in treatment, Sis, it'll come out someplace else. I don't need to consult with you to know that."

The one in the driver's seat with the binoculars got himself a crew cut. Got a marked-up face, like from gettin' beat down on. Scars on his nose an' chin. Skin stretched tight on his cheekbones. Stubble an' sweat on his face. White short-sleeved collared shirt. He's got a slight build. Looks like a cop. Don't see no earpieces, though. That'd be regular on a stakeout.

"Butt out, John," she says. "I'm on my way to work right now. Just on my way out the door. Don't have time to talk about this fuckin' thing right now. And who the fuck said I was traumatized, anyhow? I'm pissed, John. And it's nothing kickin' the bag in the gym for a few weeks won't fix. That and some Jack Daniels."

"A psychopath brutalizes you, Sis, and you're going to be traumatized," he says. "You find out your life has been in danger, and that'll happen anyway. Forget about him putting his hands on you. The stress from that experience is going to...Maggie, I shouldn't have to even say this."

The other'n in the passenger seat is asleep. Got his head leaned back, mouth open. Cain't see mucha him, cep'n his shirt. Looks like blue silk. Maybe he's taller.

"Fuck this, John. I'm leaving now. You wanna talk later, then call. Maybe I'll answer or maybe not. I know you're just concerned for me is all, but you're bein' such a dick."

"Listen here," he says, "you're not gonna screw this up like in Fayetteville. You fuck up here, missy, and I can't get you another job. You don't take care of yourself here, and there's nowhere to go and no one to cover for you. It'll all be on your head this time, you get me?"

Hain't nothin' but quiet on the line for a minute. I lay down 'cross the front seats. Scratch Schnitzel 'hind his ears. Look up at the ceilin'. The burnt-out dome light. Car shakes a little as a delivery truck passes.

"You talk to Momma again 'bout me, and I'ma tell her 'bout that woman you keep in Huntsville. But I'll tell your *wife* first, John. You want Charlene and the kids to know what Daddy does when he's out in the hills? Better choose your words careful, big brother."

Line goes dead.

They follow her to the hospital. License plate says Arkansas, so they ain't locals. She talks to her oldest sister on the way in. Cries a little 'bout how she doesn't know what she's doin' with herself. Sis tells her it's gonna be okay. Promise. Maggie says she misses folks back home. Even Momma. Says she's gonna visit real soon.

The Lumina stays two or three cars behind her. I stay three or four cars behind it. When we hit a traffic jam on the 240, I just set, real patient-like, an' smoke a cigarette. Three cars in fronta me I see 'em. Try not to guess at why they followin' her.

They park at one end of the restaurant strip on the other side of the hospital. I park at the other, six businesses down. Gotta think. I don't know nothin' yet. Probably, they's from Fayetteville. Since they was here already, watchin' her, when I showed up, then they musta followed me from the last time. Followed me down from Huntsville. Why'd they wanna stay on Maggie, though? If they followed me down here, then I gotta stay outta view the whole time.

I call the sherriff's station in Huntsville. Ask for Rhianna. 'Bout now's when she'd be gettin' ready for shift change, so maybe I can catch her 'fore she heads out on patrol.

"Thought you were on today, Jerry," she says. "Yesterday, too."

"Call it a leave of absence," I say. "But I need a favor from you. I need you to run some plates for me."

"Sure, I guess. Long as that's all you need. An' long as you don't mind I tell Tom."

"Go ahead an' tell him," I say. "But wait till after they been run."

I give her the number, an' she reads it back to me.

"Oh, hey," she says, pullin' the receiver away, "speak of the devil."

"Don't waste none of my time, Rhi, just run 'em quick for me."

"Run what, Jerry?" Tom says.

Fuck. Take a deep breath. Scratch 'hind Schnitzel's ears. Let him lick my wrist a bit.

"Hey, boss. I's just gonna ask if'n you got my message," I say.

"Uh-huh. Sure enough. You know what I been thinkin' the whole time in my office this mornin'? After I run them prints?"

"What's that? How to build a better mousetrap?"

"That I oughtta," Tom says, "I oughtta trust your instincts, boy."

"How'd you mean, boss?"

"Name wasn't James. That was a alias. Anthony White. Done a four-year bit on manslaughter two. Some weapons charges later on. Several warrants still out on him even. Kid's muscle, Jerry. But I don't figure for who yet."

Exhale. Grab me a cigarette an' light it up. Fingers feel light. So's my head.

"I figured somethin' was up. So I done you a big favor, then. Pickin' him off 'fore he could get close to you."

"Reckon so," Tom says. "How's come you ain't at work today?"

I glance down the strip at the Lumina. "Leave a absence. I'll come on back when I'm good an' rested. Mexico suits me."

"You ain't in Mexico, Jerry," Tom says. "You really think I don't know where you are? It's called a credit card bill, dumbass. Checked it when I seen it went missin'. An' speakin' of it, you owe me for that room, kid." He's quiet a moment. "I'll just assume you went right back to Memphis, then."

"Okay, sure," I say. "You gonna take these two fuckers offa tailin' Maggie, then?"

"Maggie? Thought you said she was in Chicago," he says.

"Did. But she ain't. Found her in Memphis," I say.

"Fuck, Jerry. You're trottin' on thin fuckin' ice, buddy. You ain't a native there. Plum off the reservation. Do best by gettin' your crazy ass back into the hills, kid." He waits a second, an' I hear him suckin' on one of his hard candies he always has 'round when he's tryin' to give up cigarettes. "Okay, I'll bite. Who's tailin' Maggie?"

"You think I know? Shit. I thought you sent 'em."

"What'd they look like?"

"Cops," I say. "They look like fuckin' *cops*, boss."

"That ain't good, kid. What you gonna do?"

"Got me maybe half a idea. Them files you got from runnin' them prints. Check known associates. Then look up *them* fuckers' files an' send 'em to me. Make sure they got profile pictures."

"Call me 'fore you do anythin', Jer," he says. "Oh yeah. Almost forgot. You gave me a empty case. What'd you do with what was inside?"

"I'ma use it to have me another pecker attached, right above my left kneecap. An' I'ma buy Fat Bobby a seat on the city council so's he can have all he wants at Miss Suzie's for free. An' then I'ma get Conrad one of them Russian mail-order brides that cain't speak English an' looks like a ice skater. That'd be perfect for him, don't you think? Help the man outta his shell a little. Be good for the bowlin' team, too."

"I'm serious, Jer. I gotta know."

"Wait, you ain't even heard what I'ma do for you, boss. With what's left over I'ma pay me some Mexican to lock you in a closet, tape you down, an' spread honey all over you with one of your wife's paintbrushes. Then he's gonna cover you in about a hundred thousand ants. The kind that got a sweet tooth, an' sharp'ns at that. Then, when you gimme my retirement fund back, maybe he'll hose you off. I'd do it myself, but you know how I hate that kinda noise."

"Jesus Christ, Jerry," he says, chucklin'. "What the fuck am I gonna do with your money, huh? Cep'n maybe dangle it a little to make you behave. Takes two sets of numbers to withdraw, 'member? I only got the one."

I look down at Schnitzel. I cain't think of any reason to believe anythin' he's said.

"All right, so what'd *you* need the cash for?" I ask. With all Tom's got stashed away, this'd be like a drop in the bucket. I look back over at the Lumina. They switched drivers an' now the other feller's asleep.

"State police been investigatin' that shootin' that put us in the hospital. Hain't lookin' good, Jerry. They found your shoe back in the woods. Don't know what that means, but they think it fucks with our story somehow. Half a million'd go a long way toward fixin' it."

"Well, shit. Guess Conrad ain't gettin' his mail-order bride."

Rhianna called back with the license plate records. The car was stolen outta Little Rock two days ago. So it don't mean shit. Just that they're switchin' out the vehicles they use. I'm gettin' anxious, now. Fidgety, too. I drive outta the strip. Cain't remember the last time I had more'n two hours' sleep.

Put the car in a shaded space next to Forrest Park, just a block southeast of the hospital. Crack all the windows. I know you ain't s'posed to leave dogs in cars like this, but I hain't got no choice. Pat his head an' tell him I'll be right back. I'll tell Maggie hi for him.

I start walkin' north up Manassas Street, which runs the west side of the park. When I get two blocks up, past the block where them fellers in the Lumina is parked, I cut over to Jefferson an' head a block down to the front entrance of the hospital.

Her office is on the second floor on the opposite side of the main entrance, above the ER. All office doors down the hallway. Small waitin' area at the end of the hallway with tinted windows overlookin' the park. Lights off inside now. I walk down to the end of the hall an' check out the few couches an' chairs. The tint-film on the windows gives a decent reflection of the hallway. I set on the couch hidden behind the corner an' watch the hall. She's on the floor as much as she can be, but I know she's always runnin' up to her office to take private phone calls. Least she used to. I look at the magazines out on the table. One on Memphis life. Four-month-old *People*. Eight-month-old *Cosmo*. *Newsweek*. Kids stuff. Today's paper. I pick up the paper an' hold it up so's anybody comes into the area'll think I'm not just starin' out the window. After thirty-five minutes, I see her comin' down the hall. Heels clickin' on the tile 'steada tennis shoes. Still wantin' to make a good impression.

Wait till she gets the door open. She steps inside. I get up an' sprint down the hallway. She musta heard my soles squeakin' on the floor as she started closin' the door, 'cause she opens it again to peek out her head right as I stop. She looks up at me.

Turns red.

'Fore she can shut the door, I push it open an' walk inside.

"Jesus fuckin' Christ, Jerry!" she yells as I shut it 'hind me. She backs up to her desk an' reaches for her phone. I move in an' slap the receiver away when she picks it up. She raises up her arms to shove me away when I get close to her, takes a deep breath to scream. I wrap my left arm 'round her body an' pin her arms to me, an' plant my right hand over her mouth.

Check to see her nostrils is uncovered. Noise comes outta them. She starts kickin' at my shins, wigglin' like a calf caught in a rope. Screamin' an' moanin' through her nose. Tears wellin' up in her eyes. Catches me in the shin with her heel, makes me wince an' grit my teeth.

"Fuck, baby," I whisper in her ear. "You can beat on me all you want, but I didn't come to hurt you. Promise."

She tries to break free, a movin' her weight back an' forth, but only allows me to get my arm a better hold. Kicks at me again till I hear her shoe plop on the carpet. So she switches feet an' kicks at me with that'n. I move my leg outside hers, an' real quick she tries to knee me right in the balls, but only gets my thigh. Does gimme a charley horse, though. I push her over my leg to trip her up, so's I can carry her, slidin' her heels 'long the carpet, over to her little leather couch. I lay my legs on top of her legs. It's weird how much this is like one of her games.

"There's some men wantin' to hurt you waitin' in a car outside," I say. "I'ma take my hand away, an' I need you to be quiet an' just listen for a second. I mean it. There's some crazy fuckers followin' you 'round right now."

I pull my hand away.

"You mean 'sides you!" she yells, an' tries to bite my face. "Get off me, Jerry, right now. Swear to Christ I'm gonna scream if you don't."

I shift her so I can move my arm, an' I move offa her. She just lays still, lookin' up at me as I back away. Wipes at her eyes.

She sets up an' straightens her skirt. It come up to her midthigh when I's on top of her. Button come offa her blouse. She squares that up, too. Wipes her eyes again an' sniffs.

"You can't be here, Jerry. I'm serious about that."

"Just walk down the hall with me. Down the next wing over. There's a window that looks out over that restaurant strip. Then you'll see what I'm talkin' 'bout."

She's lookin' out the window, like I said. There's other folks in this area, so she feels a little safer. Got them little binoculars from my pocket up to her face. She looks over at me with them green eyes real quick, then back out the window.

"Sure. I see the car. But that doesn't mean what you said."

"How come that other'ns asleep, then?"

"I don't know, Jerry. But that doesn't prove anything. And you have to leave now."

She hands me back the binoculars. Starts walkin' back to her office. I wait just a second to watch her ass walk away, then hurry to catch up.

"I mean it, Jerry. When I get back there, I'm callin' security," she says when I get alongside of her.

"I can show you. Just lemme check my e-mail in your office. Probably he's sent 'em by now. I can show you. I promise. I'll print 'em off an' we can go check at the window again."

"What're you talkin' about?" she says, lookin' sideways at me. "No. Forget it. I'm callin' them right now." She reaches into her pocket an' takes out her cell phone.

I grab it outta her hands quick an' head for the stairs. She yells after me. On my way down the stairwell, I call my cell phone with hers. When mine rings, I answer an' hang up both. On my way outta the hospital, I leave the phone with the receptionist an' ask her to have it returned to Dr. Margaret Gordon.

I give Schnitzel plenty of water an' treats after I get back. Wasn't gone more'n an hour, but he's a little pissed for it. Take him on a walk in the park. Move the car back to the strip. It's another six hours 'fore she comes out. I wouldn'ta had to steal her phone if she hadn'ta changed her number. I call her when she gets on the 240. Prayin' they don't got the same kinda scanner I got.

"You clever dog," she says. "You know this is just gonna add to the restrainin' order?"

"You got a smart mouth, woman, but that's how come I love you so damn much. Just shut up a minute an' listen. Look in your rearview mirror."

"It's dark, Jerry, what the fuck am I lookin' for?"

"Watch me flash my brights real quick." I flip it up an' down fast.

"Okay. Now I know where to tell the cops to look," she says.

"Look four cars up from there. Should be two behind you."

"I'm hangin' up, Jerry. Then I'm changin' my number again."

"Just look, for fuck sake."

"Fine. Okay, two back. In my lane?"

"Yup, now change lanes. Like you gonna get off at the next exit. Then get back on."

I watch her car blinker come on. She moves her Saab one lane over toward the exit. Then the Lumina changes lanes without a blinker. She moves back on. So does the Lumina.

"Fuck," Maggie says. "Oh my god oh fuck. Okay. Now I'm scared, Jerry."

"That's okay. I'm here, an' you're gonna be just fine. Gotta figure out somethin' real quick. Hold on."

I put the phone on speaker an' pull over in the breakdown lane. Reach in the back an' grab the laptop. Open it up an' plug in Tom's Aircard.

"Jer, what's goin' on, huh?" she asks.

"I fucked up, Maggie. I'm sorry." I type *Memphis motels* into a search engine.

"What do you mean, you fucked up?" Her voice is gettin' shaky.

"Sometimes I cain't see the forest for the trees. I led 'em right to you."

"Who? Led who, Jerry?"

I click on the map an' focus on the motels near the airport. Somethin' cheap. Somethin' with hourly rates. That takes cash with no ID. I'll have to call the places.

"They don't want you, Maggie. Rather, they only want you to get to me. I'm awful sorry, I led 'em right to you."

"*When* did you do that?"

"'Bout a week ago. Tried to find you so's I could say my piece. Couldn't do it an' went back home. I didn't know they was followin' me then. Don't know who put 'em on me, neither. But they only want you to get to me. I'm awful sorry. I didn't know nothin'."

"You tried to find me? Jerry, I don't like where this is goin'."

"Me neither. So here's the plan for now. Just listen an' do what I say."

"Okay."

"Shed the tail. One-two-three. One: you go back to your hotel room. Get dressed up like you're goin' out on a date. Did you bring any of them titty-shirts with you? An' them high heels, too."

"Like I'm goin' on a date? What's that gonna matter, Jer?"

"So's they don't get suspicious of where you gonna drive to. An' I want you to bring your big purse. I mean that giant one I made fun of now'n then. Pack what you can in it. Your pills. Toothbrush. A change of clothes. 'Cause you ain't gonna go back to that room for a few days."

"What're you talkin' about? I can't go back at all?"

"Not for a few days anyhow. Hain't safe till we're sure. Two: you'll get the address texted to your phone. Head for the motel, an' get a room facin' the street."

"Okay, an' then what? Once I'm there, then what?"

"Three: I'll text you again to open your curtains. They'll be distracted by that. Then I come up behind the car while they're lookin' at you. Shed the tail."

"What do you mean by that? What are you gonna do?"

"What's that gonna matter? Them that lives by the sword, Maggie. You know the rest."

Hain't yet nine when I get to Walmart. I'm lookin' for them throwaway phones when Tom calls me on mine. I got no idea what to say to him.

"ID'd 'em yet?" he asks.

"Figure I recognize one from the pictures you sent. The other'n I hain't sure."

"Tell me which one you recognize, an' I'll run *his* known associates. Try it again."

"Sure. Okay. Look, Tom. You know what's gonna happen, right?"

"You mean you're gonna clip 'em right off once you know who they are. That what you mean? Think I didn't know that?"

"I mean, is there anythin' you wanna tell me 'fore the doin's?"

He don't say nothin' for a few seconds. "Jerry, do you think I'd be helpin' you set these fuckers up like this if they was workin' for me this whole time?"

"Reckon not."

"Now lemme ask you somethin' a little more personal. What're you gonna use?"

"I brought a couple with me in the trunk. There's the Browning thirty-two an' that Beretta M-nine. Reckoned I'd use that Beretta 'cause it holds more."

"An' these ain't been used, right?"

"I hain't stupid. Least not when it comes to this."

"What're you gonna do 'bout Maggie? Have you figured it yet?"

"Been a workin' on it."

I find the motel on the east side of the airport, 'bout two miles from 240 down Lamar Avenue. I wait parked out on the street, 'cross from the exposed room entrances. Send the address to Maggie. Set in the car an' pull on my gloves. Tape 'em good while Schnitzel watches. I decide to move the car a block over, behind the motel. Get out with the M9 in my jacket an' walk over to the alley 'cross the street from the room entrances. This is where they gonna park, since it's the only spot with a view of the rooms. The alley's blind to 'em.

I set behind a dumpster, smokin' a cigarette. Watch them white curls move up 'tween lavender rubber fingers. They just gonna pull up on the street, an' that'll be that. Keep an' eye on the motel entrances 'cross the street. Check the gun again. Fifteen in the clip. One chambered. Fifteen-plus-one. Check that the safety's off. Cock back the hammer. Leave it set in my pocket. Crush the cigarette out an' put the filter in my pocket. Breathe deep a few times. I just done this shit.

My cell phone flashes in my hand. Maggie sent a message that she's checkin' into room twelve. I look out from 'hind the dumpster. See her headin' outta the front office, down the walk to the line of rooms. She's in her tight black skirt that comes just above her knee. Low-cut pink sleeve-less blouse I'd always go crazy over. Still do. Looks like she might fall over in them heels. They pink, too, an' look like snakeskin. Called 'em her fuck-me shoes. An' God-damn that hair. Done up somethin' fierce.

That Lumina pulls up on the street. Parks with the back end in fronta the alley, cuttin' off the view of room twelve.

That's good, though. I'll be comin' from behind. I get the earplugs an' put 'em in. Then the last thing I got from the Walmart. Outta season, but I found one on clearance. Looks just like the one Maggie got me. I fit the black ski mask over my head.

Over top of the Lumina, I can see Maggie's door open an' shut. Light comes on through them curtains. I told her not to set anythin' down. Use tissues to handle the doorknob an' the fabric. Not that it'd matter in a hourly room with all of them different sets of prints, but then I don't want her pickin' up nothin' nasty on her hands neither. Wanted to tell her to wear gloves, but that'd look weird in the summer. 'Cause of *my* gloves, I gotta use the end of a pen to send her the message to open the curtains.

The light appears over the roof of the Lumina. I get up an' walk along the wall. Pull the Beretta outta my jacket pocket. Come 'round behind the Lumina. I can see botha them inside, a lookin' over to they left, right at the window. I'm five feet back from the corner of the car bumper. 'Member where Maggie's window is. Gotta keep the line of fire outta her window an' a ways over so's she don't catch none. Left hand under right to steady the grip. Raise the M9 to aim. Start squeezin' the magazine empty.

First four or five shots I go back an' forth 'tween driver an' passenger heads. Blood spits out on the dash. Puffs of glass blow outta the windshield an' into the street. Then I move down the back of the seats an' put eight or nine through the center mass of both. For a second I gotta guess at it 'cause not enough of the window's been punched out an' them shards block the view. They bounce around a bit inside, but the seat belts keep 'em put. Last coupl'a shots I try for the heads again an' get one more in the driver's, which goes in under his jaw right through to the top, 'cause by then he's leanin' half out the window on his side. Takes less'n five seconds altogether.

When the slide locks back, I look up an' see Maggie watchin' me from the window. Her mouth's open an' eyes're wide. Real quick I lean in the window on the passenger side an' check the arms under they short sleeves. Nothin' I can see on either. I shove the M9 into my pocket an' take off a runnin' down the street back to my car. She closes the curtains 'fore I'm outta view. Take off the mask as I get back to the car. Pull out the earplugs. Yank off the gloves. Take off my jacket an' wrap everythin' up in it. She's on her way out the door an' headed back to her car. After she drops it off I'll pick her up at her hotel on the other side of the airport.

Take the 240 back up to the city. The Greyhound station's downtown on Union Street. Two blocks from the Mississippi. She don't say a word to me on the way there. Schnitzel's waggin' his tail an' tryin' to get up in her lap. She holds him for a bit, but don't look down at him. Just stares out the window.

"You smell somethin'?" she asks, lookin' 'round the front seat an' into the back.

"Gun was hot. Barrel probably melted into my jacket a little."

"Oh," she says, starin' out the window again. "What were you lookin' for on those men? You were lookin' for somethin' after it happened."

"There's this tattoo. This tiger I seen. Reckon maybe it's got somethin' to do with this business, but I cain't figure it yet."

There's a line at the concession counter in the bus station. Maggie's settin' on a bench under a advertisement for women's perfume. She's got this long stare Tom always talks 'bout soldiers havin'. Focused on nothin'. Not blinkin'. I pay for the Coke an' the Diet Coke an' head back over to her. Set down beside an' hand her the Diet. She takes it without changin' the way she's lookin' out into the crowd of folks. Mosta them's black an' Hispanic.

"So now what?" she asks, sippin' her drink. Looks over at me for the first time since back at the motel. An' it reminds me of somethin'. I cain't place it.

"When you done with that drink, I'ma follow you into the ladies' room."

"What for?" she asks. Eyes ain't blinkin'.

"Gotta show you somethin' afore I go."

When I lock the stall behind us, I take the .32 outta my back pocket. Hand it to her. She takes it an' looks it over.

"Put that in your purse, hon. Just remember that it's there."

"Is it loaded?" she asks. I nod.

"Hain't chambered, though. You gotta pull the slide back to do that. That'll chamber the first round an' cock it, too. Then you just point an' pull. You 'member how I showed you to do that last year? How to chamber it? An' how to shoot it?"

"Was it this same one?" she asks, lookin' up at me from the black an' silver pistol.

"No, but it was a thirty-two, like this'n. Just point an' pull, like at them bottles. This'n here has a ten-round magazine. Keep it in your purse just in case."

She nods, lookin' back down at the gun. Opens her purse an' puts it in. Closes it an' looks back up at me. She's goin' pale now. I open the stall door an' help her walk over to the sink. This black lady looks us up'n down. I set her purse on the counter. She leans on me with her full weight, an' I see she's gonna fall if'n I don't steady her. I get her under her arms an' lean her against the wall. Her eyes is real wide.

"Your face is awful red, Jerry. You know you're sweatin'?"

"Sure. Might be gettin' sick. Hain't slept in three days."

"Shouldn't drive like that, Jer," she says. "Bad for everybody." Then just that quick, her eyes roll back in her head, knees give out, an' she falls to the side. I catch her an' help her to set on the floor with her back to the wall. Holdin' her upright. I look over to see if that black woman's still watchin', but she's gone.

Maggie's eyes pop open again, an' she just looks right at me a minute, not a bitta understandin' on her face. Then her forehead wrinkles, an' she starts cryin' just like that. Snifflin' an' sobbin' hard. Gaspin' an' moanin' a little. Shakin' her head side to side. Color flushes back to her cheeks. She ain't moved her arms up from her lap yet.

"Oh my God oh my God. Are you gonna kill me, Jerry?" she sobs. Winces.

"No, honey," I say. "No way. Never."

She shakes her head again an' finally moves her hands up to wipe her eyes an' nose. I reach up for them brown paper towels an' grab a few for her.

"How do I know, though?" she says through a coupl'a gasps, an' still snifflin'.

"'Cause, baby," I say. "You're my favorite thing."

She looks up from blowin' her nose. Moves her hand to my face an' touches it. Moves it up to my forehead.

"An' don't you 'member, hon? I said I'd never let the Wowzer get you."

She blows her nose a little more with her other hand still on my face. Takes the paper towel away from her nose.

"You're really warm, Jer. Maybe you shouldn't drive like this."

"I'll be fine. Just gotta get back to some familiar country's all."

We're back on the bench in the middle of the station. She's got her head down 'tween her knees, hands folded on the back a her neck. She's groanin' now. Says her head aches.

"What are you gonna do now, Jerry?" she asks, a little muffled from 'tween her knees.

"I'ma go home, Maggie. You're gonna get a ticket for anywhere you want as soon as I leave. Call your work an' tell 'em *family emergency*. Stay gone a week."

"What's in a week?" she asks.

"One of two things. I'ma sort it out one way or the other. Either way, it'll be safe for you to go back to your hotel room an' back to work."

"How's that?" she asks, settin' up, lookin' at me with her face all flushed.

"Like I said. I'ma sort this shit out. An' if I do get it taken care of, then nobody'll need to mess with you." I look down at the openin' of her blouse.

"Look *here*, Jerry," she says, pointin' to her face. "And tell me what you mean by *either way*, huh?"

"Like I said. I get it sorted out, an' there'll be nobody left to mess with you. Or I get done in for the doin's, in which case nobody'll need to mess with you."

"So you mean either you kill *them* or they kill *you*, and either way, they won't need *me*. Is that what you're sayin', Jer?"

"I reckon so."

"Then why'd you give me that gun? I shouldn't need it."

"It may take a week for it to get all sorted, hon. You're in danger durin' that time. I wanted you to have it just in case. Help both us feel better."

She's quiet for a minute an' puts her head back 'tween her knees. I watch folks walkin' all 'round with backpacks an' luggage an' baby strollers.

"How'd they find me in the first place?" she asks, settin' up again.

"I led 'em to you. I'm sorry 'bout that."

"When? Did you tell me this already? At the hospital today?"

"I did. I came to see you maybe a week or more back. I's gonna come an' meet you, but it didn't work out. So I just left an' went home. But I didn't know they followed me here. So I led 'em to you without knowin'. I'm sorry. I fucked up."

"Who's *they*, Jer? You haven't said."

"If'n I knew, I'd say. Hain't figured it yet. I thought I knew, but probably I's wrong. So I got some more askin' 'round to do yet. All I know's this whole situation smells bad, like there's somethin' dead up the branch."

She elbows my side an' motions for me to look at this twelve-year-old Hispanic kid a starin' right at her cleavage from a seat twenty feet away.

"He's almost as bad as you," she says. I laugh. "Why didn't you try to see me before when you were here? What didn't work out?"

"I's still mighty angry. I liketa hurt you if I'd come to see you. An' I didn't wanna do that again. So I left. Best thing to do."

I move to get up from the bench. She looks up at me with them wide eyes again. Puts her hand up on my arm.

"Where you goin'?" she asks.

"Fayetteville, to drop off my rental. Then home. To sleep for the next twenty-four hours. Wait till I'm gone to buy a ticket. Got that?"

"Why's that important?" she asks. I get down on my knees in fronta her. Take her hands in mine.

"'Cause I know myself. If I know where you're goin', I'ma get halfway to Fayetteville 'fore I start headin' back to wherever you're at."

"Okay. Sure," she says.

"I'll call you in a few days an' let you know it's over. An' if I don't call in a week, you'll *know* it's over." I squeeze her hands. Wish I had somethin' special to say. "I'ma kiss you 'fore I go, Maggie. One time, okay? Just in case I don't never get to do it again."

Afore she can say anythin', I lean in an' put my lips on hers, kiss her hard an' quick. Then I get offa my knees an' head for the exit.

My head's startin' to ache some. Feels like I'm comin' down with a fever maybe. That's what you get for stayin' up for three days straight. Stop at a twenty-four-hour gas station in West Memphis, just across the Arkansas border. Fill up. Walk Schnitzel a bit on the grass. Buy some cheap coffee inside. Bottle of Tylenol for my fever. Flip through the country CDs they got on the sales rack by the register. No bluegrass. Further down the road, I find a trash barrel where I can throw in my jacket with all the other shit inside. Squeeze a little lighter fluid I got from the gas station on top of everythin'. Burn it good.

Gettin' harder to keep my eyes open. Startin' to figure I oughtta pull over an' sleep a bit 'fore I get any further down the road. Gonna be in hill country soon, an' it don't suffer no fools. Get over on the shoulder an' park in the ditch. Lean my seat back. Roll down the windows a bit. Shut off the car an' light my last cigarette for the night. Listen to the semis blow past an' rock the car. Schnitzel yawns in the backseat. Ash drops on my chin. Chuck the cigarette out the window so's I don't torch myself. The orange cherry catches a tailwind from a truck an' goes swirlin' off, scatterin' little sparks.

That look she give me tonight. Now I can 'member where it's from. First night she came on to me. Not the first time I went home with her, but the very first time she let me know she wanted me to.

"I thought a lot about what you did," she'd said, sippin' on her Jack an' Coke through a straw. Lookin' up at me, totally serious.

I asked her what she'd been thinkin' 'bout it.

"Well. Yeah, you saved my life," she said. "An' that's somethin'. But I do that for folks every day. An' they don't owe me nothin'. So it don't mean all that much."

I 'member I just nodded.

"Havin' said that, Jerry," she said, grinnin', "I'd like to buy you a drink."

I'm thinkin' of her lips on me when my phone rings. I cain't 'member where it is now. Don't particularly wanna answer it, neither. Probably Tom wantin' to know what happened. So I let it go to the voice mail. Then it starts ringin' again a coupl'a seconds later. I shift in my seat an' dig it outta my pocket.

"What's up," I say.

"I'm in the bathroom stall right now, Jerry, an' fuck me am I scared."

Maggie don't sound good. Shaky, teeth a chatterin'.

"What is it? What's goin' on?"

"I seen it, Jerry. I seen what you were lookin' for."

"What'd you mean?"

"This guy. Came in an' sat a few seats down from me. Waitin' on the same bus. I was gonna head for Little Rock. An' he sat not ten feet from me. Big guy. Ponytail an' sunglasses on top a his head. Then I saw the tattoo on his arm. It's that tiger you were lookin' for."

"You sure?" I set up in my seat an' start up the car.

"How big was the one you were lookin' for?"

"Um. I reckon it's the size a my thumb. Real little. You sure that's it? 'Cause it could be some guy who likes cats. Maybe he's got a bobcat on the other'n."

"No. I'm sure of it. It was real small. Almost didn't see it. So I got scared an' went into the bathroom. I've been tryin' to get a hold of you, Jerry. How far away are you?"

"Maybe a hour. Stay in the stall. It's a public place, an' he knows he cain't go in the women's room without gettin' noticed. Get your thirty-two out an' chamber the first round. Don't open the door till I get there."

I peel outta the ditch, cross Interstate 40, bounce through the median, an' pull onto the eastbound side. Slap myself on the face a few times. Wish I'd brought another gun with me.

It's near midnight when I get back to the station. I go in a different entrance from where I come in last time. Take a minute an' look 'round the place. Folks thinned out. Look for the guy she described. That was a hour ago. He'da split if'n he thought she'd made him. Least that's what I'da done. Don't see him anywheres. So I walk over to the ladies' bathroom. Knock into the garbage can on the way by accident an' damn near tip it.

"Maggie?" I call out when I walk in. "It's me. It's Jerry. C'mon out."

She does. Door swings open an' she steps out real slow. Gone white all over an' shakin' again. Got the .32 in her hand. Purse on her shoulder. I go on over to her an' take the gun. Hammer's cocked back, so I release it down soft. Stick it in the back of my pants. She's shiverin' now. I put my arms 'round her for a little warmth, an' she jerks away some. Then she rests against me.

"Is he still out there?" she asks, teeth still chatterin'.

"Nope. Let's go quick 'fore he come back," I say.

"You want me to take you somewhere else? Another bus station, like maybe the one in Little Rock? You could go anywhere from there."

We're drivin' through West Memphis again. I spot the
gas station I stopped at earlier. There's another'n up ahead,
so I'll go there instead.

"I thought about that," she says "the whole time you
were gone."

"Hold on a second, I gotta pull in here," I say, an' get off
the interstate.

Pull into the gas station. Park next to the store an' head
inside. On my advice, she uses the bathroom 'cause we're
headin' into hill country. Not that there ain't plenty a places
to go there, but only if you don't mind squattin' by a tree
an' usin' leaves for toilet paper. Prayin' you ain't grabbed no
poison oak.

First I grab a cheap gettin'-stuck-in-snow blanket off the
shelf. Then a coupl'a coffees. Some tater chips to snack on.
Some water bottles. A Arkansas road map, 'cause I don't
know the area 'round Little Rock all that well. Pay for it an'
take everythin' to the car. She's still in the bathroom, so I
get Schnitzel an' walk him on the grass a bit until she comes
out. When she gets to the car, I turn to walk back an' trip on
the curb. Fall flat on my face. Schnitzel starts yappin'.

Maggie comes quick an' looks me over. Puts her hand to
my forehead again.

"Damn, Jerry, you're still burnin' up. You can't drive like
this."

I try to set up, an' my arm just wobbles an' gives out an' I fall back on my stomach again. Think my nose may be bleedin'. Lip, too. Legs feel dead.

"Help me get back to the car," I say.

Put my arm 'round her shoulder. She helps me stagger over an' get into the backseat.

"Here, get this blanket over you," she says, spreadin' it out.

"That was for you," I say. "You were shiverin' earlier."

"I'm better now. An' that coffee'll warm me up."

She shuts the door to the backseat an' gets in the front. Takes some Tylenol outta my little bottle. I swallow 'em right from her hand. She starts up the car. Grabs the map off the front seat an' unfolds it. Traces her finger on it. Folds it up again. Backs the car outta the parkin' spot an' heads to the on-ramp.

"You can just leave it in the parkin' lot," I say from under the blanket.

"Doc says you need rest, Jerry, so hush."

"I'll sleep all day, but just so you know, you can leave the car at the bus station an' I'll drive back when I feel up to it."

"I was gonna tell you, Jerry," she says. "I'm not gettin' on any bus."

"How come?"

"After tonight, believe it or not, I feel safer *with* you."

"They know right where I live, Maggie. You'd be in harm's way."

"And you'll guarantee these fuckers couldn't find me? Could you promise that?"

"No. You know I cain't."

"Then hush up. I decided. If you're gonna clear things up for me, I wanna be there to make sure you do it right," she says. "I'm not sittin' in some motel room God knows where waitin' for some double-Y-chromosome to kick in the door. I'd rather deal with you than that."

Last thing I hear is her sippin' at the coffee.

"You look pretty shitty, kid," Tom says. I set up in bed when I realize it's him. Slept all the way back. Things is kinda fuzzy after she started drivin'. Maggie's standin', arms crossed, in the doorway to my bedroom. It's light outside. Probably eleven in the mornin'. Tom's settin' in the chair beside.

"Where's Grandma?" I ask. He puts his hand on me an' eases me back layin' down.

"She's diggin' up weeds in the garden. Or maybe she gone to check on her still. She's fine, Jer. Just lay still. I got some more work for you tomorrow, so you gonna need to rest."

"It's gotta be tomorrow?" Maggie asks. "Can't wait another day?"

"'Fraid so. No choice on that."

"Then you better leave so he can rest," she says.

"On my way out," he says. Gets up from the bed, an' I notice he's got a cane. He walks to the door an' winks at me as he passes Maggie. I hear him goin' down the stairs.

I move my legs over the side of the bed to get up, an' find I'm still pretty dizzy.

"How'd I get up the stairs?" I ask Maggie. She comes in to help me set up.

"You don't remember?"

"I don't 'member nothin'," I say. She helps me stand up an' stays there till I can steady myself. She walks 'hind me when I head for the bathroom. I'm still in the clothes from last night. I start undoin' my belt buckle.

"If you gotta piss, Jer, you better sit to do it. I don't want you tryin' to steady yourself an' aim it all at the same time."

"I'm not that brave," I say, settin' down easy.

"When you're done, I got a question for you," she says.

"What's that?" I ask.

"How come you got a bag full of money in the trunk of that car?"

I sleep a little durin' the day, but mostly I'm just tired. Don't hardly move at all. Set up in bed an' watch TV. She sets in the chair by the bed an' watches with me, quiet. Or works on the crossword in the Fayetteville paper. She gets me some crackers to eat when I feel hungry. I cain't bear nothin' but soda crackers, the way I'm feelin'. All the while she's in that chair she's got that .32 in her lap an' is facin' the doorway.

Told her the money was a little bitta leverage. Gonna help with a problem she probably don't wanna know 'bout. Business that didn't concern her.

After a while, she stretches out her legs on the bed. Rests her feet next to mine.

"You think we're safe here?" she asks. I look over at her.

"Reckon so. I'd thought Tom was tryin' to kill me, but I figure different now."

"Tom that was just here? That Tom?" she asks, lookin' worried.

"That Tom, sure. But it ain't him that put them fellers after you. But, anyhow, this is Tom's turf, an' I doubt anybody'd try hittin' a sherriff's deputy at his own home," I say. I don't know if this last is true or not, but it don't make sense gettin' her worked up when nothin' cain't be done 'bout it anyhow.

When night comes, she sleeps next to me. Puts the .32 on the stand next to the bed. Crawls under the covers with me an' curls up to my back. Lays her arm 'cross my waist. I don't reckon she wants to do nothin' else, an' even if she did, I'm still too weak for it.

"You smell bad," she says.

"Hain't showered in a few days. Sorry."

She pulls herself closer. Her breath tickles on the back of my neck.

"There weren't no tiger you seen back there. Was there?" I ask.

"Are you mad?" She don't move. Just lays still an' breathes.

"No, I hain't mad. An' it was a good lie, too. You turned yourself white an' everythin'. Thought I's lookin' at a ghost. But how come you lied?"

"Guess I didn't think you'd come back if I just asked you."

"Then, honey, you don't know me very well at all."

"Maybe I wanted to make you worry some about me, too," she says.

"You sure done that."

There's them cicadas out the window. A screech owl out in them woods. Schnitzel's nails on the wood floor out in the hall.

She says, "That's why you came back to see me the second time. Said you were worried 'bout hurtin' me the first time, so you couldn't approach me then. But you were willin' to risk that the second time."

"I thought I was a dead man," I say. "An' if'n I was gonna die, then nothin'd stop me from seein' you again. I didn't care who'd get hurt. Not even you, an' that's the plain truth. I needed it, an' that's what mattered."

"Then why'd you wanna put me on a bus?"

"'Cause by then I knew it wasn't for certain. Had more of a chance. An' it didn't make no difference where you went to, I knew you'd be comin' back. I'da found you when the mess was all over."

"What do you think your chances are now?"

"Fifty-fifty," I say. "Maybe better."

CHAPTER TEN:

The carrot or the stick.

ME AN' MAGGIE'S settin' at the breakfast table while Grandma stands at the stove, fryin' up the bacon. I don't know if she 'members Maggie or not. But she set a place for her an' poured her coffee. When Maggie tried to get up an' help, I just told her not to. Better to let Grandma do it. Probably she thinks I'm Uncle Ray an' Maggie's my Aunt Shelly. Ray always has orange marmalade with his toast, which is what she give me when I set down. An' she gave Maggie black coffee. I never seen Shelly put a drop of cream in hers.

"She gonna sit down with us?" Maggie asks.

"It's already seven. She has hers 'round five," I say. I pour a little cream in Maggie's coffee while she's butterin' her toast. I 'member she hates it black.

"You know where we're goin' first today?" she asks me.

"Tom called while you was in the shower. We're gonna go'n see us a Mexican."

"Qué pasa, rinche?" Jose asks as me an' Maggie get outta the patrol car. His house is 'bout ten miles southeast of Huntsville an' near the bottom of the holler. No neighbors 'round for a mile or so. Knew I'd find him here since he don't never go in to work till after lunchtime anyhow. Rinche's what they called the Rangers in Texas. An' comin' from him, that ain't a compliment, but it's his sense of humor. He cain't get over the badge.

"Solo un viaje de negocios, hombre," I say.

"What kinda business, Jerry?" he asks, lookin' a little worried. Jose Pepe Martín-Rodriguez, Hispanic male, 45, 5'7", 150 lbs, black hair, brown eyes, stands in his front door-way, lookin' back an' forth at me'n Maggie, inchin' his hand 'hind his back where I know his .45 is.

"Cool it, Jose," I say. "Para tus campesinos. It's about your employees, buddy."

"Bueno," he says, scratchin' his goatee. Turns his attention to Maggie, gives her a wide grin. "Who's the lady? Tu novia?"

"A veces," I say. Only sometimes. "Maggie, this here's Jose, the hardest workin' Mexican I know."

"Nice to meet you," she says, extendin' a hand.

"Me gusta, Señorita," he says, kissin' the back of her hand. Then looks up at me. "Por qué traes tu novia aquí?" I chuckle at that. If'n I'd had a choice, I wouldn'ta brought her.

"Para precaución, hombre. Bad folks 'round these days. Cain't be too careful."

Jose calls up his employees. It works like this. For each of twenty or so growin' sites, there's a dozen or so workers, an' one team foreman. Each of them takes his orders from Jose. When he's got problems with his boys, Jose turns to me for a disciplinary action. *Una acción disciplinaria.* Rarely do I ever gotta do more'n slap somebody 'round for laziness. Knock out a tooth once'n awhile for pocketin' some product, or for drawin' too much attention at the bar. Tom said not to waste time with the regular field hands, for now anyway, an' just check out the foremen. Jose calls 'em up one by one as me'n Maggie sip iced tea on his front porch swing. I got one arm 'round her shoulder. Her free hand's feelin' along the trumpet vine growin' up the latticework.

"They'll be here in half an hour," Jose says, closin' his phone.

"You'll wanna go inside pretty soon. Have a seat at the kitchen table. Away from the windows," I say. She looks at me. Don't say nothin'. Gets up from the porch swing an' heads to the door. I walk in with her. Motion for Jose to follow me.

While Maggie walks into the kitchen, I walk with Jose downstairs to his basement. Under the old wooden stairs there's a cupboard. Have him unlock it. Open the doors up. I reach inside an' take out his Chinese AK-47. An' two of the thirty-round banana clips settin' next to it. I take out my 'lectric tape an' bind them clips together, staggered a coupl'a inches, loadin' ends at top'n bottom.

"All you gotta do is pop it out, flip it over'n pop it right back in," I say. "An' don't forget to pull back the bolt."

"You think there'll be a problem, Jerry? I mean this bad a problem?" he asks. I unclip the strap on both sides an' set it back on the cupboard shelf. Then unfold the wood'n metal stock. Move the safety lever to automatic. Hand the rifle to him.

"Like I said, amigo, with bad folks 'round, cain't be too careful."

I wait inside the front door where them kids cain't see me when they show up. Jose keeps 'em on his front lawn. He's on the porch, talkin' to 'em. Hain't showed 'em the rifle yet.

"I need you all to sit on the grass. There is a thing we must check out. Don't worry," he says. "It's just a business matter."

The foremen—'bout twenty college-age boys, mostly white, one black, a few Hispanic, in holed jeans an' ratty T-shirts, with bandannas or ball caps on they heads—look at each other a minute then start settin' down on the grass. When they all settin' down I walk outta the front door. That's when Jose picks up the rifle from behind the little wall along the porch. Some of the foremen turn white, an' I can hear some breath sucked through teeth, some murmurs, some shiftin' on the lawn. But don't nobody stand up, or even speak out loud.

I start on the left side of the group an' walk through 'em. My yellow dishwarshin' gloves is taped on, an' I got the holster unsnapped for my Glock. I check the arms, the upper biceps, one by one. Lotsa tattoos. Barbwire. Death's head. Yin-yang. Chinese characters for God knows what. Bugs Bunny. Superman. No tigers, though. I have 'em all take off they shirts just to be sure. Still nothin'.

I leave 'em an' walk back up into the house. Jose sets his rifle down. Then I decide to walk back outside on the porch. Stand next to Jose as he's dismissin' them.

"Which ones worked with Stevie?" I ask. He looks over at me. "Don't play dumb, now. You heard what he an' Ronnie was doin'. Settin' up cook-sites. Tell me which ones he was usin'. Which of the foremen?"

"Paul," Jose calls out. "Stephan. Both of you can stay behind for a moment."

I walk down into the yard where the two young men are waitin'. The others gettin' in they cars parked along the dirt road an' peelin' out. When there's only the two of them left, I size 'em up. Two white males, 19 to 22, 5'8" an' 6'1", small one's 135 lbs with black hair an' green eyes, big'ns 200 lbs with blond hair an' gray eyes. I don't say nothin'. Just take out my expandin' steel rod, clack it out hard, an' bust the tall one's right kneecap.

He falls on the grass an' starts screamin'. Jose's picked up the rifle again. Big'ns just holdin' his knee, tears a pourin'. Small one's got his eyes switchin' from me to the big'n to Jose's rifle, but he don't dare move. I keep my eyes on the small feller while I slap the big'n on the ground a few more times. Once 'cross the ribs. On the chin. Collarbone. Little feller's shakin' now, an' I stop hittin' the big'n.

"I's just warmin' up on him. You gonna get worse'n that in a minute. Less'n you tell me somethin' right the fuck now."

"What is it? What do you need?" he says with a hoarse voice. Through all of them screams from the big feller on the ground, I can barely hear the kid.

"Where'd Stevie go?"

Maggie's quiet in the patrol car. Schnitzel's in her lap, paws propped up an' lookin' out the window. She's just starin' straight ahead. She wants to ask, I reckon, but she won't ask.

We stop at Shawnee's motel where Highway 412 meets 127 an' have lunch at the café. I'm eatin' a ham-an'-cheese sandwich. Got a basket of them curly fries. Maggie's stealin' glances at me now an' then, but don't wanna look straight on. She's not nervous, I can tell. Unsure, maybe, but not nervous. She starts in on her chicken sandwich.

"Is it easy for you?" she asks, lookin' up at me finally.

"What's that?" I say, swallowin' a bite then warshin' it down with ice water.

"I heard, Jerry. That guy screamin'," she says. "I know, I'd already seen what happened in Memphis. But, I don't know, somehow that seems different. That was more personal. I don't even wanna think about it now, but I know they were gonna—maybe kill me. And you prevented that from happenin'."

"How's this different?" I ask her. "Roughed up some kid 'cause of what he was into, 'cause of what he knows. The only chance we got, an' more for mine than yours, is to follow the trail an' find out where this mess is comin' from. Roughin' up that kid was just another step in makin' sure we don't end up in a hole in the ground. You ask me if it's easy. Don't reckon I know what you mean."

She don't say nothin'. Finishes her sandwich an' sips her Diet Coke through a straw. I watch her lips pucker up to suck on it an' cain't help but shift in my seat.

"So what's next? Did you get the information you needed?" she asks.

"Sure. But I cain't get done what I need to today. It's too far a drive, an' I got other business to 'tend to."

"What other business?" she asks. Curious now.

"Gonna get ridda some of that money. Take care of another matter. Unrelated to this."

"Can you tell me what it's about?"

"Sure. I's gonna do that anyway. You gonna be there."

"Do I need to be there?" she asks, settin' up straight.

"Hain't got no place to put you. Not anywhere I'm sure you'd be safe. So you're gonna stay in the back of the patrol car. They ain't gonna see you anyhow. Just stay down an' under a blanket. Shouldn't be no trouble."

I take the key Tom left for me at the front desk an' head down to room fifteen. Maggie's in the front seat of the patrol car, parked a few spaces down from the brown van that ain't got no windows. I fit the key into the lock an' turn it. Open the door. Fuckin' reeks of cigarettes an' weed an' empty beer cans even 'fore I walk inside.

Shut the door 'hind me. Nappy Freddie MacDonald, settin' over on the bed watchin' TV, looks over at me. Stubs out his cigarette in the crowded ashtray on his lap. Opens the blue cooler beside him.

"Hey, Jer," he says. Scratches his scalp under his blond dreadlocks. "Did Tom say you'd be by? Can't remember. Wanna beer?"

"Sure, Freddie," I say. He throws me one. I set at the table by the bed an' crack it open. Let it foam all over the carpet.

"You smoke any shit this mornin'?" I ask.

"Not too much," he says. What *too much* is for him, I won't venture no guesses. Tom stuffed him in this room a few days back. Give him a brick a weed, ten cartons of cigarettes, maybe six cases of Coors—Freddie's favorite—an' told him not to leave the room till somebody come'n got him. Promised him cash, like six figures, if'n he'd set tight an' do what he's told.

"C'mon, then," I say. "Time for a cold shower."

"Can't I just have some coffee?" he asks.

"Nope. Shower first. Then coffee."

I make him scrub all over hisself while the water's cold as it can get. Warsh his dreads out. Scrub his armpits an' privates. While he's warshin', I look at the tattoo on his arm. He's nothin' really but a burnt-out shell of what he used to be. Can barely 'member his name some days. Don't seem to 'member his wife at all. Nor killin' her. He can follow orders, though. Stayed put this whole time. I wonder if he 'members where that tattoo come from. Wonder if Tom even thought to ask.

"Freddie," I say through the shower curtain, "where'd you get that tiger on your arm?"

"Ain't a tiger," he says.

"Why not?" I say. "It sure does look like one. Where'd you get it?"

"Ain't no tiger. It's the mark of the beast."

"What, like from the Revelation?" I ask.

"Then flew one of them Seraphims unto me," Freddie says, "havin' a live coal in his hand he'd taken with tongs offa the altar."

I step back from the shower curtain. Freddie ain't scrubbin' himself no more.

"An' he laid it upon my mouth. An' said lo this is touched thy lips. An' thine iniquity is taken away. Thy sin is purged."

That ain't the Revelation. I 'member that much. Isaiah, maybe.

"That got somethin' to do with your mark, there?" I ask.

"Ain't no mark at all," Freddie says, goin' back to scrubbin'.

I decide not to push the issue any further. Make him brush his teeth when he gets out. I brought him a little hair dryer for his dreads. It's a cheap'n Maggie left in my bathroom last year. I knew Freddie'd need it. Cain't imagine how long it'd take for them awful things to dry on they own.

After he's done gettin' ready, I give him a good stingin' slap 'cross his face.

"Fuck me, Jer, what's that for?"

"You sober enough to drive? 'Cause you're no good to me if'n you cain't drive."

I make him walk in a straight line. Count backwards. Touch his fingertips to his nose. Mostly, it's just to scare him into stayin' sober till he gets back to the room. He knows me, an' he knows I don't fuck around. He'll stay sober.

Put him in the van with the map an' the laptop. Camera's already plugged in. Tell him all he's gotta do is open it up an' press a button when I text him. Point the camera where I said. Then he's just gotta close it up an' drive back. He can get higher'n all fuck after that. Just cain't screw it up 'fore then. I grab his nose ring an' twist a little. Not hard. Just enough to make his eyes water.

"I won't screw it up, okay?" he says, an' I let go. Shut the door. Watch him drive off.

I walk back down to the patrol car an' get in. Maggie looks over at me.

"You didn't need me in the backseat after all?" she asks.

"That's later. We got about four hours till then. What you wanna do in the meantime?" I ask her. I give a grin, an' I can see she ain't happy with what I'm thinkin'.

"I got a better idea," she says.

"Don't worry 'bout your feet so much. Just find the way that's comfortable. Hain't gotta be any particular way 'sides what's comfortable."

"How's this?" She switches to a kinda ridin' stance, legs wide apart. Knees a little bent.

"No. Regular-like. As if you's just standin' here talkin' to me. Forget that posture shit. You don't shoot nobody with your legs."

She changes how she's standin' to be more natural, legs just shoulder-width apart. Right foot a little in fronta the left. Raises her arms an' points the .32 at the silver beer can I set on the fencepost. Lines up her sights. Pulls the trigger slow like I told her. The pistol gives a loud pop an' jumps in her hand. She yelps, shakes her head, an' looks at me.

"My ears are ringin', Jer," she says, flushin' red in the face. "I forgot how loud it is."

"I wanted you to hear it again one time, so it wouldn't scare you none if you gotta use it."

I give her some earplugs an' put some of my own in. She cusses when she looks back at the can on the post. Hain't moved.

We're a coupl'a miles up the road from Grandma's house. It's startin' to look like rain. I step up 'hind her. Gotta talk close to her ear now.

"Now just try pointin'," I say. "Don't worry 'bout the sights so much. Point."

She looks back at me. Then raises her arms again. I get her hands placed good on the black rubber grip. Right one holdin', left one supportin' underneath it. She squeezes the trigger again, an' this time, with my hand on her waist, I can feel her body shake when the muzzle flashes. I pat her shoulder so she'll do it again.

She squeezes the trigger a third time an' sends the can flyin' over the fence. She looks at me with a big smile on her face. I give it right back.

I walk out to get the can. Set it on the fence post. Come up close to her ear again.

"How you gonna keep it on you?"

"Purse okay?"

"Sure thing," I say, an' walk down in the ditch to the patrol car. Open the door an' get her purse from the front seat. Walk back up to the road an' hand it to her. "Show me."

"Didn't know you were from Missouri," she laughs.

"Funny. Now show me how you gonna keep it. An' how you gonna pull it out."

She unzips her small black-an'-tan leather bag. The large one she left back at the house. The smaller one fit inside that'n an' will work just fine for most things. Puts the gun in the openin' an' finds she has too much in there. She looks up at me again, wrinkled forehead. Pulls out her wallet. Her checkbook. Her little clear plastic pouch a makeup. Then fits the gun inside the bag. Hands me all a the stuff she took out. Zips up the bag. Then unzips it an' draws out the pistol. Points it at the can on the post with her right hand, tryin' to hold onto her purse with her left hand an' still support her right. Finally she decides on tuckin' the bag under her left arm.

"How's that?" she asks.

I slip my finger in the waistband near the small a her back an' give it a snap. The slacks she's wearin' now we just picked up at the Walmart. Also her shoes, them flat-soled canvas ones. They work better for shootin' than her heels. I picked up another box of shells for her gun, an' a target poster.

"That'd work a lot better. Keepin' it back behind you like that. I can get you a holster that'd work good for the thirty-two. That way you don't gotta worry 'bout dirtyin' up your purse none. An' it's right on hand."

"Wouldn't that show up if somebody looked?"

"What's that gonna matter? I got a soft fabric holster that'll fit you great."

"Okay. Can I try yours? Isn't that one a bigger caliber?" she asks.

"If'n you want. But I want you to get the feel of the thirty-two. An' your hands are smaller. That's why I gave you this'n. Fits your hands perfect."

"What about the safety? Don't you need to show me how to take off the safety if I'm gonna be carryin' it around?"

"From now on," I say, "it's just draw an' shoot. No safety required. It'll take up time we don't have. Just be careful how you set."

I turn an' head back to the patrol car for the target poster. Walk over to a oak tree just 'hind the fence. Take out my 'lectric tape an' put it up on the trunk so the feller on the paper's right 'bout six foot. Walk back up to Maggie on the road.

"Go on an' see what you can do. Empty it out," I say, gettin' in close to her ear.

"Okay. Does it matter which part I aim for?" she asks.

"You're the doc, hon. You oughtta know that better'n me."

It's mistin' at four. Don't take long to find the car. Unmarked cop car, but Tom told me what to look for. Gray Mercury Sable, early 2000s. Maggie's in the back now, like I asked her to do. Under the blanket. I park in a space along the north side a the town square, watchin' the car right outside the sheriff's station. Five after four. Mist is turnin' to light rain. He oughtta be comin' out now. I look back at Maggie through the wire mesh, an' she's peekin' at me from under the blanket. I can see some of her red curls. Schnitzel's in the floor of the back, watchin' me. Then the station door opens, an' I see him come out in his cheap gray suit an' lift up his umbrella. I send the text message to Freddie.

I follow the Sable through town down Main Street, then onto Highway 412. He's stayin' at Shawnee's motel, too. Right when he gets past the city limits, right near the highway intersection, I put the patrol car's lights on. Get right up on his ass. After 'bout ten seconds, he pulls over onto the shoulder. I park behind him. Grab the laptop in the front seat. Wrap it in a black trash bag so's it don't get wet. Grab the denim sack. Tell Maggie to stay put. An' don't look nowheres.

Get outta the patrol car an' shut the door. Approach on the passenger side of the Sable. Door ain't locked, so I just open it an' slide on in. Shut it an' shake some of the rain offa my head.

"What the hell?" he says when he realizes who just got in his car. "This is highly inappropriate, Deputy Bowden. I have to ask you to step out of the car. Right now."

I just look at him for a second. I fish one of my cigarettes outta the pack in my shirt pocket. Light it an' crack the window.

"You can't smoke in here, Mr. Bowden. Shit. You can't even be in here. I'm afraid I'm going to have to inform your superiors of this. You need to get out before this gets any worse for you. Do you have any idea how much trouble you're getting yourself into right now, Mr. Bowden?"

"Call me Jerry," I say, an' toss the denim sack into his lap.

"What the hell is this?" he says. Opens it.

State Police Detective Michael MacKennon, white male, 39, 6'0", 175 lbs, grayin' brown hair, brown eyes, lookin' into a bag that got twenty-five bundles of hundreds makin' up ten grand each.

"Quarter mil," I say.

"Deputy Bowden, don't insult me. Did you think I'd actually consider taking this from you? I mean, I'd heard about the way business is done in the backwoods, sure. But come on. You can't seriously expect me to just drop the case because you throw some money my way. For starters, I don't want to. I've got you cold on this. You and Sheriff Haskell, and you both know that. And after today, after this—this bribery attempt—Deputy Bowden, it's a slam dunk."

I tap my ash on the window. Breathe the smoke up at the crack into the rain.

"When I was a kid," I say, "I always heard my grandma say *the carrot or the stick*. You heard that expression afore? I guess probably you have. You're a educated man."

"Jerry. Might I ask you just what the fuck you think you're doing?"

"Don't get testy. Not yet. Just listen," I say. "Like I was sayin', my grandma said it one way. An' then when I got to school, I heard my teachers, an' all my other classmates, say it *the carrot an' the stick*, or even *the carrot on a stick*. Now this confused me, Mike. You mind if I call you Mike? Don't answer. I don't really give a fuck."

I drag on the cigarette again an' tap the ash on the sleeve of his suit.

"When I got older an' knew how to look in a dictionary—an' not just any dictionary, but one the school librarian showed me when I asked the question—it said that the phrase was just like my grandma had said. *The carrot* or *the stick*. You see, Mike, folks never dangled carrots from sticks to get a mule movin'. No sirree. The carrot was a reward for the mule. The stick was punishment if it misbehaved. It'd get beat if it didn't do as it was told. The thing everybody else was sayin', that whole *carrot* on *a stick* thing, that was just a corruption—that's what that dictionary said—a *corruption* of the original."

I take the laptop outta the bag. Aircard's already plugged in. I open it up to the black screen an' move my finger on the mouse pad. Blow away the ash flakes that fall on the keys. The screen comes to life.

"West Eleventh Street. Forest Hills, just outside Little Rock."

"What the fuck are you talking about—" He starts to cuss at me, but the screen kills that. The two-story light-blue house with the red door an' a fat linden tree near the front walk comes up. Hangin' from the linden tree's a tire swing. Knots up the rope.

"Karen, Christina, Victoria, an' Michael Junior are all hopin' right now that you take the carrot. But *you* gotta tell me if it's gonna be the carrot or the stick."

"You unbelievable bastard," he says.

"'Cause there's a man inside the car there, just a waitin' out on the street, to go on in an' meet 'em all for dinner. What's Karen cookin' tonight? Want me to make a call an' have him find out?"

"You can't be fucking serious, Jerry. This isn't real, you aren't really saying this."

"An' he's lookin' at pictures of them. Spread out 'cross his lap. An' he's thinkin' right now, should I go from oldest to youngest, or youngest to oldest? Hell of a thing to decide."

Mike looks up at me an' is almost as white as Maggie was the other night. Shudders. Then does it again. Then has to open the driver's-side door to vomit onto the highway shoulder.

"Hain't got all day for it. Carrot or the stick?"

I get back in the patrol car an' tell Maggie it's safe to come out from under the blanket. But she's still gotta stay down for a minute or so, till this other feller pulls away. She puts her hand up to the wire mesh near my shoulder an' slips her fingers through. First I touch her pink little fingertips with my hand. My own fingers is wet from the rain. Then I turn an' kiss hers right through the metal. I can taste the paint, an' metal where it's chipped away, an' I know some of the nasty sons of bitches that had their fingers there 'fore now. An' I don't care nothin' for it. Right now her little pink fingertips is all I care 'bout.

CHAPTER ELEVEN:

The little end of nothin'.

WE ALL WATCH Tom as he walks up to the lane, ball in hand, steadyin' himself on the return. I'm holdin' onto his cane right now. Maggie's next to me, Bobby's on her other side, an' Conrad's over on the bench at the scoreboard. Last night to practice 'fore the league tournament begins. They delayed it by a coupl'a weeks for Tom to get outta the hospital. Wouldn't do that for most folks.

He steps through the swing slow an' steady, like he always rolls. Winces as his knee gives a little bit, releasin' the ball a little off. It clunks down hard on the boards, goes right into the gutter.

"Holy shit, Tom," I say, "stayin' in the hospital improved your game."

Bobby an' Conrad laugh. Maggie bumps my knee with hers, but she's holdin' in the laugh, too. Tom turns 'round an' gives me the finger. Limps back to the ball return.

"All you'ns can kiss it," he says. He rolls again an' gets eight pins.

Bobby gets up to roll an' slaps Tom on the behind when he walks past. Tom sets down next to Conrad on the bench.

"So who's the best one on the team?" Maggie asks to either Tom or Conrad. "Or am I not supposed to ask that?"

"Well," Tom says, leanin' over 'round Conrad to give her eye contact. "I'd say it comes down to these two young bucks right here." He's pointin' back an' forth from me an' Conrad. "But don't tell Bobby up there I said that."

"I heard you, dumb-ass," Bobby says, pickin' up his ball. "That's okay, I can't hold them that's ignorant accountable for they mistakes."

Them that's ignorant, Maggie mouths to me. "I like how that sounds," she laughs.

"So how'd Jerry drag you back out here into the hills?" Conrad asks Maggie, strokin' on his bird's-nest beard that reaches his shirt collar. Bobby releases his ball down the lane. Seven pins.

"Just my natural charm, buddy-boy," I say. Bobby don't say nothin' of his roll, just waits up at the ball return so's he can redeem himself.

"I'm only here for a quick trip," she says to him. "They need me back at work in a few days." She sips her beer. I sip mine. Conrad marks Bobby's first roll.

"Get that spare, hoss," I say. Bobby picks up his ball an' steps up to roll again. He lets it loose an' gets all them three. Grins real big an' points to Conrad.

"Mark that for me, would ya?" he says. "Ribs of the *spare* variety."

"You're up, Jer," Conrad says. I pat Maggie on the knee an' stand up. Walk up to the ball return an' take up mine. Wiggle my hips a little an' tap my heels to the side in a quick two-step for luck, which makes Maggie laugh.

"What're you doin'?" she says.

"He's got these little dances he does," Conrad says. "Lord knows why."

"It's called style, mi amigo," I say, not lookin' back.

"More like," Bobby says, "called bein' a fairy. Did you know you was datin' yourself a fairy, Maggie? Real closet case."

When I let go the roll, she yells, "Jerry, don't trip!" So I mess it up, an' the ball goes in the gutter. All of them bust out laughin' over it. I hunch over an' slap my knees 'fore headin' back to the return. Point over at Maggie.

"Wicked woman!" I say. "Wicked, wicked woman. Damn Jezebel right over there."

She just smiles at me all innocent-like an' sips her beer. Next roll I get nine. Don't believe I'm ever gonna live this'n down. I'm a little surprised when I set back in my chair, Maggie lets me put my arm 'round her. She don't lean into me, but don't shrug me off neither.

Conrad gets up for his turn an' walks on over. Grabs the ball an' stands 'fore the lane a minute, like he always does. Conrad Mills, white male, 30, 5'10", 150 lbs, brown hair, brown eyes, rolls himself a strike.

When the game's done, we head over to the lounge to have a coupl'a more drinks. Tom says he's gotta get back over to the station, an' everybody says good-bye. Bobby starts tryin' to talk Conrad up enough to go an' talk to one a the waitresses. That'n with the pink stripe in her blonde hair. Conrad don't say nothin'. Maggie's grinnin', shakin' her head, an' pourin' from the pitcher. Tom motions for me to follow him to the door. We walk on out to his patrol car.

"How'd it go with Mike today?" he asks. He takes the box of cigarettes from my shirt pocket. Lights him one an' hands one to me 'fore puttin' it back. It's still rainin' a bit, an' I don't care to have my uniform soaked.

"Hain't gonna be no trouble," I say.

"You sure of that?" he asks, lookin' me up'n down.

"Pretty damn sure. Boy likes carrots."

"What the hell you talkin' about, Jer?" he says, spittin' back on the concrete. "Long as you sure. An' what 'bout Jose? Whatta his boys?"

"Found out where Stevie went to. Gonna drive up an' talk to him tomorrow. It's in Missouri. But I got a question for you, boss."

"What's that?" he says, draggin' on the butt.

"'Bout that Jimmy kid. I mean Tony, or whatever the hell his name was. Who sent him over? He come from Fayetteville, right? Whose recommendation you hire him on?"

"Marcus sent him. But I wouldn't go lookin' there," he says.

"How come? What if I just wanna ask him some questions? Like how much he checks his references."

"Best not go sniffin' in that direction, Jer. That's Sanhedrin home turf, 'member? Big Cal's in charge of that. We don't deal with Marcus, 'cause he's Cal's responsibility. An' we don't never wanna break ranks on this deal. That shit gets you dead fast."

"I just go where the wind blows me, boss," I say. "Cain't help that."

After a pitcher in the lounge, we quit the bowlin' alley an' head down to Tree-Dog Willie's. Me an' Maggie an' Bobby an' Con all take turns on the pool table. Just like them old times. We have another pitcher, an' Maggie orders herself a Bloody Mary. Then the rest of us fellers go for that too, an' it's Bloody Marys all 'round. After a hour, I'm just settin' with Con watchin' Maggie hustle Fat Bobby at the table.

"'Member that kid on the baseball team?" Conrad asks me. "Ben Schafer. Skinny Benny. That'n got you kicked off? 'Member him?"

"Sure. That's way back in the day," I say. I must'a been fifteen. Con'd been fourteen. He grew up in Fayetteville but spent his summers at his great uncle's place just outside Huntsville. Me an' him was on the little league baseball team a few summers.

"I seen him in the paper the other day," Con says. He's got that hangdog look on his face. Been up here in the hills four years now, since his wife left him. I just assume she left him, though, 'cause he never says shit 'bout it. He was married when we was in Guards, an' in Afghanistan. Then maybe a year after we got back, he moved up to his great-uncle's old place.

"What's he doin' in the paper?" I ask. Con drains his Bloody Mary. One time he showed me a picture of his wife. I reckon I know why he ain't got over it.

"Hung hisself. Skinny Benny took one of them fifty-foot extension cords an' wrapped it over a rafter in his parents' cabin. His parents was rich, so's they could afford that cabin on a lake somewhere."

"Sure. Maggie's family got one of them."

"An' anyhow, he stood up on a barstool. Tipped it an' hung hisself. Skinny Benny stretched his own neck," Con says.

"How come?" I ask.

Raises his glass to me almost like a toast.

"Wife left him."

Now Bobby an' Conrad are arguin' whether or not it was a scratch 'cause it touched another ball. Bobby's gonna win, just like he always does ever' argument he has with Con. Maggie's settin' next to me in the booth. Sippin' another Bloody Mary. Leanin' on me a little. That damn dog, Willie the sixteenth, he come out a minute ago an' started sniffin' at all the folks 'round. I had Maggie come 'round the table an' set on my side, so's she'd be 'tween me an' that mutt when he come by. She gave a laugh an' said she didn't mind none.

Rests her head on my shoulder. Her hair got some cigarette smoke in it. But it also still smells some like the shampoo I got in my shower.

"You know what I said was true back there," she says.

"Hmm?" I ask.

"'Bout goin' back. It's true. I gotta go back in a few days. Just as soon as you get all this sorted out."

"Cain't stay no more'n that?"

"Can't do it, Jer. I'm glad you're gonna clean up the mess. An' I'd be lyin' if I said I didn't enjoy your company," she says. "But I can't stay with you after this is done. An' I don't mean this to be cruel. But I do endanger my own life every minute I stay with you, an' you know that." Sets up an' turns to look at me. Her eyes waterin'.

"You ain't forgiven me yet," I say.

"Nothin' to forgive, Jer. Can't blame a snake for bein' a snake."

"You think I'm a snake, then?" I ask her. My ears is gettin' warm.

"I think you're a cold killer, Jerry. A snake is a snake,
an' by stayin' with you, every day my chances of gettin' bit
increase."

I'm comin' back from the bathroom when Tom calls. Says
there's a accident over on Highway 73. It's near one in the
mornin'. I ask him what the fuck that has to do with me.
He says the folks that called it in gave the make, model, an'
color. Tom knew right away from that. When he says who it
is, I liketa shit. Said the ambulance's at another accident up
on the 412, an' won't be en route for another twenty minutes. Said I might wanna have first crack at this'n. I don't
wanna take Maggie with me for this right now, but I hain't
leavin' her here with Heckle an' Jeckle. I don't have to park
right next to the accident. I can park up the way a bit. She
don't have to know who it is for a while.

A lotta the docs at Huntsville Memorial drive Oldsmobiles.
Some LeBarons an' a few Cadillacs. No Saabs now that
Maggie don't work there. A coupl'a BMWs. Only Mercedes-
Benz I know 'bout belongs to Maggie's big brother, Dr. John
Kavanagh, psychiatrist extraordinaire an' all-'round pain in
the ass. His Benz is turned up on its side in the ditch on the
right side of the road.

I stop about fifty yards back, so's Maggie cain't tell
whose car it is. She's in the front seat with me. Drunker'n
I seen her in a long time. She'd switched to Jack'n Coke by
the time we left. Had to walk with her to the patrol car an'
help her inside. That's when I decided against my no-safety

policy an' switched hers on. Then thought better of the whole thing an' put the .32 in the glove box. Right now she's hummin' some country song I cain't recognize. Eyes shut. Slumped on the window. Had to put her seat belt on for her. She'll raise up her head ever' minute or so an' look over at me.

I step outta the patrol car. Put on my slicker for the rain. Walk on up to the wreck. Click on my flashlight. The Benz is settin' on its right side, but I don't reckon that's how it first landed. There's glass in the road that shines up at my flashlight as I walk past. Fuck knows what made him swerve. Or how many times it rolled. But it ended up mostly in the ditch turned up on its passenger side. I look back at the patrol car quick. Left the door open, so the dome light's on inside. Little bitta Maggie's red hair's all I can see. I walk closer to the car, 'round the undercarriage.

Can't smell no gas leakin'. I can hear somethin', though. A gruntin'. I walk 'round the vertical front bumper an' shine the light inside the busted windshield. Two bodies. John's belted into the driver's seat, strainin' to get out. Face flushed red from the struggle. Cut an' bleedin' in his hair an' on his clothes. Coughin'. Groanin'. I shine the light down to the passenger seat. Other'n is some woman I recognize from the hospital. One of the nurses. Small frame, short black hair. Midtwenties at most. Pale skin with freckles like Maggie. Only with all them cuts an' smears, you cain't see freckles no more. Legs is up on the dash. No breath. Way her head's twisted 'round it ain't no secret what happened. Didn't wear no seat belt an' got her neck broke bouncin' on the inside of the car.

"Hi, John," I say, shinin' the light on my own face.

He moans an' wrestles with his belt a little more. I watch him for a minute. He's bleedin', but I hain't sure how much. Looks mostly like shallow glass cuts. John's tryin' to get his belt unbuckled, but cain't get his arms 'round to hit the button. Wonder if maybe one of them's broken an' that's how come he cain't get it done.

"Why the Christ are you here?" he yells, but it sounds more like a whinin' kid, cryin' an' drippin' snot. Wouldn't be hard to get him outta there. Not a bit.

"Just dumb fuckin' luck, buddy, that's how come."

He goes back to tryin' to work his arm on the buckle. Slaps at it an' grimaces after. Somethin's broken anyhow. I clack out my expandin' steel rod. Reach it up through the hole in the windshield. Try not to get no glass on my uniform. Punch in the button with the end.

John falls on top of the dead girl. Screams when he lands. Starts kickin' at the windshield. Makin' these little wet sounds from his throat when his leg impacts the glass. Tries the left'n just one time an' howls from the pain.

"You know you got a girl in there, Doc? She ain't lookin' too hot, neither."

"Fuck you, Jerry," he screams. "I know about her. I fucking know."

Nod my head an' look at him, curled up in a ball right on top of her.

"Figure you got two ways to get outta that car, Doc," I say. "You can try to get through that windshield. An' that might work, but it'd take a awful long time to kick it out like that. An' you liketa get snagged on some of them glass chunks on your way through. Or, you might try goin' straight up. Through the driver's window. Go on an' try it."

John tries standin' up. Sets his foot on the armrest an' pushes himself up to grab the steerin' wheel. Pulls his body up to get his arm outside the door. Sucks air in through his teeth when he sets his right arm outside the window. Moves his right leg up to the edge of the seat an' gives himself another push up. Works his way out onto the side of the driver's door.

"Help me down," he says.

"Fuck a duck," I say.

John rolls himself offa the car, falls maybe six feet, an' slaps the wet grass an' mud in the ditch. Now he's cryin' like a little baby. Sobbin' from his arm an' his leg. I shine the light in his face from maybe five feet away. Looks up at me with them red eyes.

"What're you gonna do?" he asks me.

"Hain't figured it yet," I say. "Right now I'ma watch you crawl up to the road, an' I'm sure it'll come to me."

He starts movin' through the grass up the side of the ditch. 'Fore he can get more'n a few feet, I slap him on the back of the skull with the steel rod. He falls flat on the grass. I reach down an' get a fistful of his hair. Yank his head up. There's that Scotch strong on his breath.

"You wanna know how come I didn't string you up in a barn? Make you watch in a mirror whilst I gut you like a hog? Wanna know how come you're still breathin', fucker?"

He don't say nothin', just rolls his eyes up at me, then over to the car. Then up at the sky. I get him in a headlock an' pull him up offa the ground. Tilt him back an' let him fall down further into the ditch, facin' the other way. Let him splat in the mud. Grab his hair again an' shove his face down in the slop. Hold it for about twenty seconds. Starts fightin' me a little.

Yank his hair an' pull his face up outta the puddle.

"I can make this shit go away for you. You know that," I say. "She didn't have her seat belt on, so that means there's gonna be bits of her all over the inside of the car. Blood an' spit on the dash an' upholstery. Maybe a earring stuck on the ceilin'. An' if'n I say you was the passenger an' she was the driver, cain't nobody prove it wrong."

"What the fuck are you talking about?" he shouts, hoarse, coughin' some.

"You kill a girl from drivin' drunk. A nurse. If'n you don't go to jail, you lose your practice. How's that sound?"

After half a minute of wheezin', listenin' to the rain pick up, he says, "Okay. I'm listening, Jerry. What are you going to do?"

I put his face back in the mud.

"Hain't gonna do shit, now!" I yell. Grind his nose in the bottom of the puddle. Pull him out enough so's he can breathe. "Ask me how come you ain't already under six feet of dirt back in them woods somewheres. Go on an' ask me!"

"How come I'm not?" he chokes out.

"'Cause of your baby sister, fuckwad. That sweet thing's the only barrier 'tween you an' meetin' God. An' I hear He's one *mean* son of a bitch."

Let him breathe a minute more 'fore dunkin' his head back in the puddle. When his arms an' legs is flailin' pretty good, I take him out again.

"Jesus, Jerry, don't. Don't fucking do this."

"Wasn't gonna. But you know what, hoss? She went an' changed my mind for me. She's gettin' herself gone for good in a coupl'a days. An' I liketa never hear from her again. An' that's what put you in the mud."

"She's here?" he asks, gaspin' again. "What's she doing here, Jerry? What did you do to her? Jesus Christ, Jerry, tell me you didn't do anything."

"She come up here of her own will. Cain't get me offa her mind. Cep'n now, I think she's gonna try for real. An' that puts you up shit creek. It don't mean the little end of nothin' to me, leavin' you here with that Arkansas red clay-dirt settled in your lungs."

Back in the mud. Hold him for half a minute. Bring him up an' box his ears.

"One question for you. I'm gonna ask it an' you're answerin' quick, less'n you wanna find out what's at the bottom of that mud hole."

"What is it?" he dribbles out.

"What'd you cover up for Maggie when she worked in Fayetteville?" I ask, pullin' him next to the puddle. Turn him over on his back. Coughs brown water out his mouth. Stares up at me for fifteen seconds. That's all it takes him.

"You know what euthanasia is, Jerry?"

"Sure, that's when you—" Then I figure what he means. "Oh shit."

He nods at me. Coughs up some more.

"What do you call it when nobody asked for it? When there was no terminal case, even? You know what you call that, Jerry?"

"Most folks call that a homicide."

"She did it in April, four years back. Called it justifiable. Called it God-damn *charity work*."

Maggie's got her fingers laced 'round the back of her head, elbows closed over her ears. Knees up to her chest an' feet on the seat in the corner of the waitin' room. I'm watchin' her from 'cross the way, standin' up at the nurses' station. Coupl'a minutes ago Doc Simpson told me he was done with John. So I made a phone call, an' just now got done talkin' with Tom. Told him what I wanted said to Doc Adelson, the examiner. He an' Tom got a long-standin' relationship.

Maggie's still drunk, I can tell. But she's panicked now, an' scared for her big brother. Face gone pale under her freckles. Hair dark from the rain. I just look at her for a while.

Bring her over a blanket I got from a orderly. Some coffee. I didn't tell her 'bout John till the ambulance arrived. Then I gave the EMTs a story while they fastened that neck brace on him, loaded him on the stretcher. Followed the ambulance in the patrol car. She looked up at the flashin' red lights 'bout halfway there. What's that, she asked. Had to tell her. Soon as we parked outside the ER, she was outta the patrol car right by the door as they unloaded him. Knees buckled when she seen the blood on his head. I stood by her out in the rain a minute 'fore helpin' her up an' inside.

"Doc Simpson says he's gonna be all right," I say, settin' next to her.

"You talked to him?" she asks, lookin' at me. Them wide green eyes, whites turned red.

"Yup. They just finished. He's gonna be in a cast an' on crutches for a while, but there ain't nothin' too terrible. Nothin' that'd keep him from goin' back to work."

Didn't feel like mentionin' the woman in John's car.

Maggie reaches over an' grabs my hand. She don't look at me, just right on ahead down the hallway to surgery.

"I wanna see him," she says. Squeezes my hand.

"He's in recovery right now. Had to put him under to set his arm an' his ankle. We oughtta just come back in the mornin'," I say. "They won't move him to Fayetteville right away. You need to get some sleep, hon."

"You don't have to call me that," she says. Still lookin' down the hallway.

"Okay. Margaret. I'ma take you back to the house so you can get some sleep."

"I'm stayin' here tonight. I'll sleep in one of the rooms. You can go."

"Less'n you forget," I say. "Our problems ain't solved yet. There's still folks 'round to be worried 'bout."

She looks over at me now. Blinks.

By the time we get to the house, she's comin' down offa the adrenaline. Alcohol's hittin' her again. I park the patrol car in the drive an' help her inside. She's the stubbornest woman I ever met. Insisted on goin' into the recovery room to see John 'fore she left. Doc Simpson escorted her inside. John was still out, so he showed her what he'd done. I watched her noddin' as he pointed to different casts, to stitches on his face an' neck. Wouldn't leave till she known what antibiotics he was on. What pain meds. An' how mucha each.

I help her walk up the steps. One at a time. Schnitzel's on the foot of the bed when we come into my room. She seems crashed pretty good, so I lay her 'cross the bed an' head into the bathroom. Start the bath.

"That for you or me?" she calls out. Pop my head outta the bathroom door.

"You want it?"

"If you don't mind. Help me sleep."

I get Maggie up offa the bed an' walk her into the bathroom. She's wobbly now, so when I set her on the edge of the tub, she has to grab on to the toilet seat to keep from fallin' back in the water. Looks up at me with her eyes half-closed. Smiles.

"When was the last time you seen me naked, Jerry?" she asks.

"In my mind or in person?" I say. After a few seconds she laughs.

"I'ma crack my skull open if I try it without you," she says.

She kicks away the shoes. Off with the shirt. Puts her arms 'round my neck so I can pull her up off the tub an' work down the slacks an' her underwear. Shivers a little when she sets back on the cold porcelain. Right sock. Left. While I'm leanin' over, she puts her arms on my back an' rests her head on 'em. I move up a little an' let her get off her bra, turn her so her feet's in the hot water. Slide her down into the steamin' bath. She closes her eyes an' folds her arms over her stomach. I look down at her for just a minute 'fore closin' the shower curtain. Walk back into my bedroom.

"What're you doin'?" she calls to me when I set down at my desk.

"Gotta find this place in Missouri where we're goin' tomorrow."

"Still *we*, huh?"

I pull up the website for the *Arkansas Democrat-Gazette*. Go to the archives four years back.

"Hon, you're tied to me at the hip for now," I say.

"You behave yourself, Jerry, an' that might be all right," she says.

Look in the obituaries for April. Candice Johnson, mother of four. I click for the document to print. Go back to the main page for the newspaper. Find the search box an' put in the name of the departed. Nothin' comes up cep'n the obit an' a few entries in the public record. I look 'em over. A divorce. Coupl'a prostitution arrests. No convictions. I open my desk drawer, pull out a empty file folder, an' put in the printed obit. Set the folder under my keyboard.

I look at the time on my alarm clock. Almost three a.m. My teeth feel grimy so I get up an' go back in the bathroom to brush 'em. Schnitzel gets up an' follows me in. Props his paws up on the lip of the tub, peekin' through the curtain. I stand in fronta the mirror an' brush my teeth. Dark under my eyes.

"C'mon over here, Jerry," she says. I spit out the foam in my mouth.

"What is it?"

"His bruise ran from left shoulder to right hip. From the seat belt."

"Okay?" I say, then rinse out my mouth.

"Means he wore the driver's side belt. Means he was drivin'," she says.

"Think so?" I ask. Put my toothbrush back in the cup on the sink an' set down on the toilet seat. Schnitzel comes up to me. Scratch 'hind his ears. Under his chin.

"But the chart said he was on the passenger side. There was a specific note of it. You said somethin', didn't you?"

"Maybe I did." She pulls back the curtain a little to look over at me.

"Thank you," she says. Leaves the curtain open a bit. "I know you probably wanted to hurt him after what he did. Callin' you out like that. Musta taken some restraint."

"Well, you're not near as drunk as I thought you were," I say. "Thought you'da passed out 'fore now. Have to pull you out an' carry you to bed."

"Not that drunk. But just drunk enough to get into some trouble," she says. Slides her arm up, openin' the curtain some more so's she can put her hand on my leg. Skin's tuned kinda red from the hot water.

"You'll liketa cook in there. I doubt you want the water as hot as I keep it."

"Wanna come in?" she says. Pulls back the curtain some more. "Don't wanna get your uniform soaked. Better lose it."

I stand up, chucklin', undo my belt an' let it clack on the tile when I drop down my pants. She's watchin' me with that innocent-little-me smile she had at the bowlin' alley. Then she looks down at my shin while I'm unbuttonin' my shirt.

"Jesus, what happened to your leg? It's black an' blue. That's not from today, the scab's too thick. Looks pretty new, though."

"Compliments of my last office visit with Doc Maggie."

"Oh. Yeah, I forgot," she says. "I'd apologize, but you kinda deserved it. Scared the hell outta me. Bargin' in, grabbin' me like that. It's one thing to pretend in a game, but when it happens for real, Jesus Christ."

"Didn't wanna scare you. Wish I'd had a choice."

Cain't complain now, though. Not one bit. Maggie raises up her arms to welcome me as I step into the water. Kneel down over her. An' just like that, she's all mine again.

"What time are you settin' the alarm for?" I ask. She's settin' on the edge of the bed, messin' with the clock. Looks back at me an' sets the clock down on the table.

"Quarter of nine. Five hours' sleep. I still wanna see John 'fore we head out in the mornin'," she says. "How far a drive is it?"

"It's a far piece."

She shuts off the lamp an' curls up to me. Schnitzel's on the chair at my desk. I'm startin' to drift off when she says somethin'.

"This is just pretend right now, Jerry. You know that. We're just pretendin'."

Then, 'fore I can stop myself, "You oughtta know 'bout pretendin', baby."

"What're you talkin' about?"

Too late. Better let the cat out the bag. "Go'n see, then. Check under the keyboard. Some of your pro bono work. That there's a pretty good bitta pretendin'. If'n I ever seen it."

She gets outta bed an' walks over to the desk. I stare up at the ceilin' while listenin' to the sound of her liftin' up the keyboard. Clickin' on the desk lamp. Schnitzel's claws tappin' on the floor as he jumps down from the chair. Her fingers slidin' over the edges of the folder. Paper inside shifts when she opens it up. Her weight collapsin' in my chair. Folder's spine knocks the wood floor. Cryin' through her hands.

"A snake is a snake is a snake. That what you said, darlin'?"

"Jerry," she says. Tries to say more an' cain't. Cryin' again.

"If'n you ask me, I'd say takes one to know one."

CHAPTER TWELVE:

Cut your throat for two bits an' give fifteen cents back.

I SET OUT in the rented car while Maggie talks to her brother. Don't reckon she got much sleep last night. What with all her cryin'. Finally she come back to bed. Just lay beside me an' didn't say nothin'. We had to pick up breakfast at the MacDonald's 'cause Grandma'd cleaned up the kitchen by the time the alarm went off. Maggie was already in the shower when I rolled over to shut it off. Hadn't even heard her get outta bed.

I smoke an' watch folks comin' an' goin' from the hospital. Pet Schnitzel an' listen to the weather forecast. S'posed to be rainin' all 'round the area still. Got quite a downpour last night. Real goose-drownder. Still spittin' some this mornin' an' gonna pick up again tonight. Had me a dream last night 'bout Maggie's wet hair. She was on top of me in the dream. Settin' on my stomach an' leanin' over me. There was thunder from a storm, I 'member. An' my face was all wet from everythin' drippin' offa her hair. Wasn't no rain nowhere else, though. No clouds neither. An' then

I knew where the thunder come from. 'Cause her hair *was* the rain.

I flick the butt away when she comes a walkin' out the front doors. Tell Schnitzel to get in the backseat. She walks up to the passenger side, opens the door, an' gets in. Shuts it an' looks at me.

"How far is the drive there?" she asks. Cain't read nothin' in her face.

"Figure three or four hours. Four if I get lost."

"Then wake me up when you get there," she says, leanin' the seat back. She shuts her eyes an' lays down a little on her side. Facin' the door.

"How was John?" I ask, pullin' the car outta the space.

"Beat up. Weepy. High on Vicodin. Didn't wanna look at me."

"Well, he'll do all right," I say. She don't say nothin'.

A hour 'cross the Missouri line, just a ways south of Springfield, I stop at this little roadside café. Maggie's been asleep for two hours now. Or at least quiet for that long.

"I'ma get some lunch. Wanna come in with me, or should I just bring you somethin'?"

"Just bring it, if you would," she says.

She's surprised when I bring her out a club sandwich with fries an' tomato juice to drink. I set the Styrofoam boxes up on the dash an' squeeze them ketchup packets out on the folded-back lid for our fries.

"Not everyplace has tomato juice on the menu," she says, poppin' the tab open on the plastic lid a her cup.

"I made the gal go an' look."

"I don't need that much ketchup for my fries, Jerry," she says. "You know I like mustard better with 'em."

"Sure. But some of this is for Schnitzel. He don't like mustard with his so much."

She laughs, an' I start a glowin' warm in my stomach.

I eat my ham-an'-cheese sandwich an' listen to the music on the radio. All the country stations is playin' garbage right now, so I stop on the oldies an' find Chuck Berry. Fat Bobby'd be proud. Dip my fries in ketchup an' share 'em with Schnitzel in the backseat. What he wants is that ham, but he'll have to settle for now.

"Who's this person you need to see today?" she asks.

"Just a feller with some information I need," I say.

She swallows a bite of her sandwich an' warshes it down with a gulp.

"You think he'll part with it willingly?" she asks.

"Reckon so," I say. Give Schnitzel another fry.

"What are you waitin' for?" Maggie asks me. We're parked up the road a ways. Just drove past Stevie's cabin. When I passed by, his yellow Toyota was in the driveway. Couldn't see the family's minivan, though. Either they're out or it's in the garage.

"Gotta figure on what I'm gonna do if the wife'n kids is there," I say.

"You just need to ask him questions, right?" she says.

"Sure. But I don't want nobody gettin' panicked. He ain't got too many kind memories of me. An' if there's little'ns around, then that's a whole lotta wranglin' I don't wanna have to do. Cain't hardly make 'em set still. Don't wanna have to do no extra work if I hain't got to."

I can tell she don't wanna know what I meant with that last bit 'bout the extra work. If'n I go in the front door, just to talk, then nobody needs to panic. Gettin' everybody all panicked's a whole other animal.

Knock on Stevie's front door. Wait a minute. Wife answers. Tell her I'm a friend of Stevie's an' he asked me to come by to talk over some business. I'm not in uniform today, so she don't suspect nothin' right off. She looks tired. Bad skin an' rat-nest hair. She lets me right inside. I keep the tote bag tight under my arm.

It's a nice enough cabin. Big an' roomy. Logs panelin' the walls. Rough-sawn rafters, like the kind I imagine Skinny Benny swung from. Big ol' fireplace in the livin' room, with a round rug laid in front. When I look through the windows to the backyard, I see the three kids out playin' in the trees. An' just like that there's a gun muzzle pressed on the back of my scalp.

"Carol," Stevie says from 'hind me, "go on outside and see to the children."

"Just come to talk today, Stevie. No need to lose ya cool."

"I feel *very* fucking cool right now, Jerry. Drop that bag, huh?"

Carol leaves the livin' room right quick, an' I hear a patio door slide open an' shut. I drop my little tote bag on the floor.

"Move over here to the rug," Stevie says. He taps my head with the barrel. I walk over where he said. Picture frame reflects him. Looks like a revolver that he's got. A big'n, too. Cain't tell if'n it's cocked or not.

"Jerry, get on your knees," he says.

"Just wanna talk, Stevie," I say, an' he slaps my head again hard enough to break skin. No way he'd do that if it's cocked. Less'n he's a idiot.

That's when I hear the dog come into the livin' room.

"Skipper, get out," Stevie says. I turn to look at the big black lab boundin' over to me. He gets right up in my face an' starts a sniffin' an' lickin' me.

"Oh Jesus fuckin' Christ, Stevie, get this fucker offa me, huh?" I yell. "God-damn it, *please* get him the fuck away."

"He's not hurtin' you," Stevie says. "Skipper, get out."

I double over an' cover my face from the dog. "Oh shit fuck God-damn it, get him *outta here*, Stevie," I yell.

He kicks at the dog a little. When Stevie's leg is off the ground I spin my body on my knees. Hook out my right leg an' catch the other'n still on the ground. Sweeps him good an' he falls on his back, knockin' his head on the hardwood floor. Right quick I'm on top of him. Got the revolver by the barrel, looks like a damn .44 Magnum, an' first I slam the butt of the handle into Stevie's balls. Then another knock to his sternum.

While Stevie's coughin' an' curlin' up, I grab the dog real hard by the scruff of his neck, lift him back a little so's he cain't bite, an' drag him through the livin' room an' into the kitchen. Whines at me. Nails a scratchin' on the planks. Shove him in the pantry an' shut the door. My hands is a shakin' now, tinglin' like they gone to sleep from bein' set on. Heart's wantin' to jump outta my chest. Throat's gonna close up quick if I don't do somethin'.

I splash cold water on my face from the sink, an' it helps a little. Warsh that dog offa me. Least I can breathe regular again. Pick up that big silver revolver an' head back in to see Stevie. He's tryin' to get up from the floor now. I kick him in the ribs, an' back down he goes. Open the cylinder on the revolver an' let the bullets fall out on the floor. Kick 'em under the couch. Get out my 'lectric tape. Grab one of them sturdy chairs from his dinin' room table. Pick up Stevie by the hair.

Once I got him taped to the chair by his arms an' legs, I go on over to get my bag. Walk over to the window in the dinin' room that looks out into the backyard. Carol's playin' with the kids over by their little tractor barn, lookin' back at the house ever' few seconds. Ready to flinch. He musta told her what to do, what he was gonna do to me, when they seen me comin' up the walk. I unzip the bag.

"Surprised you wasn't more glad to see me, Stevie-boy," I say, settin' in a chair next to him. Set the bag on the table.

"Fucking eat shit, Jer," he says.

I look over at the patio door. They'll see him like this when they come in. I get up an' tip him back in the chair. Drag him 'round the table to set up at the head an' push him in close. That way nobody'll see the tape right off.

"That's just downright un-neighborly, Stevie."

I grab the bag an' set in the chair 'cross the corner from him. Reach inside an' pull out the black carpentry hammer with the orange rubber grip. Set it in fronta him. Pull out the big mason jar of sixteen-penny nails. Put it next to the hammer. I'd planned all this for Stevie, but I got me a better idea now.

"These is some damn nice chairs, Stevie," I say. "Real sturdy, but got that old-fashioned look to 'em. Almost like that kind Conrad makes. Ever seen his woodworkin's?"

"Fuck off," he says, coughin' some more.

"Cain't afford it, myself. Not yet, anyhow. Coupl'a years back he made me a gun rack for my birthday. Almost the nicest thing I own."

Pick up the jar of nails. Unscrew the lid slow. Take off the top ring then pry the lid with my fingernails. Set 'em down an' let the ring spin on its side a few seconds 'fore fallin' flat.

"What is it, huh, Jerry? What the Christ more do you need from me?"

"That's it. Get to the point," I say.

Dump the nails outta the jar all over the tabletop. Set down the jar.

"Just tell me what it is. I can't help you if you don't tell me nothin'."

"That's a nice-lookin' barn out there. You build it?"

"What?" he asks, lookin' dumb, like he don't get me.

"You build that barn or did it come with the place?" I ask.

"Came with the house. What the fuck does that have to do with anything?"

Pick up a handful of nails an' fling 'em in his face, hard enough to mark but not cut.

"I shouldn't have to tell you not to try my God-damn patience right now," I say. "'Cause you know better'n anybody, Stevie, I'll cut your throat for two bits an' give fifteen cents back. What you wanna do right now, buddy, is think good an' hard 'bout your position."

Get up an' walk over to the patio. Dog's whinin' in the pantry.

"I'ma hang one of your kids on the side of that big red barn for ever' question you don't answer. Or for ever' lie you tell."

Open the slidin' glass door. Call for Carol to bring the kids inside. She looks over at me, turns pale, an' I can tell she wants to bolt into the woods with her kids. I motion to her with my finger. Wait.

She comes walkin' up slow. Unsure. Stops 'bout twenty feet from me.

"Me an' Stevie got our differences worked out now. You can bring them kids inside."

"I'm not bringin' them anywhere near you," she says. Bites her lip an' wrinkles up her forehead. I nod at her.

"Your husband's forty-four's settin' on the table in there. You an' three kids is four. There's six in the cylinder, honey. Good view through that bay window. You think you can get through the yard an' into the woods 'fore I get to it? Wanna see what a forty-four'll do to them girls' pretty little dresses? I'm 'bout to lose my patience, sweetheart. An' I been real nice today so far."

She turns her head to yell somethin'.

"Don't disappoint me, now," I say, cuttin' in. "You leave me all alone here with Stevie an' I cain't vouch for what you gonna find stuck to your kitchen floor when you come back."

"Why are you here, Jerry?" she asks, lookin' back at me.

"Just havin' a conversation with your husband," I say. "An' I'll be on my way in just a moment. But you need to cooperate. Then I'll get gone."

She turns to look back at her kids. Three-year-old boy. Five-year-old girl. Six-year-old girl. Two older'ns tryin' to teach the young'n how to skip rope. He don't wanna learn.

"I'm goin' back inside now. You got half a minute to make up your mind. Know that I hain't gonna chase you. One way or another. Hain't givin' chase today."

I walk back inside an' keep my eye on her as I head to Stevie's end of the table. Grab a shawl offa the couch an' drape it 'cross his arms, so's the tape don't show. Stuff the .44 under the couch cushions. Then I reach my arm over the mess of nails an' hammer an' drag 'em a little further to the middle. Carol ain't moved a inch since I talked to her. She's started goin' pale so she's liketa fall over.

Carol Jeffries, white female, 33, 5'4", 120 lbs, black hair, hazel eyes, calls her kids to come on inside.

Stevie's sweatin' somethin' awful as his kids march in through the back patio door. Carol comes in behind 'em.

"What's a matter with Daddy?" the five-year-old asks. Mom tries to shush her, but I step in. Squat down 'side her.

"Well, sweetie," I say, "me an' your daddy was talkin', an' all the sudden he got awful cold. Like maybe he caught a draft. We was lookin' down in the garage for his tools, an' I think he caught a draft."

"Who're you?" she asks. The other two come up right next to me.

"I'm your daddy's friend, Ol' Deputy Jeremiah," I say. That's what I call myself when I'm visitin' them kids up at the hospital. Schnitzel's Deputy Dawg.

"Jerry," Stevie says through his teeth, "just ask me what you come to ask."

"Sure thing," I say, then look at the kids. "Know why I come here today?"

"How come?" the oldest one asks. She's got that curly red hair like Maggie.

"Me an' your daddy was gonna talk 'bout buildin' a dog house for you."

"Not for me," the girl laughs. "You mean for Skipper!" The others laugh, too.

"Well, I reckon we can build one for him, too," I say, an' pinch her cheek. She blushes.

"Where *is* Skipper?" she asks.

"We had to put him up for a minute," I say, "so's he wouldn't see his surprise. It's gotta be a secret for him." The girls laugh at that.

I stand up an' beckon for 'em all to come over an' set 'round the table. Pull the chairs out all along one side. The six-year-old tugs on my shirtsleeve.

"Mister, if you're a deputy, how's come you ain't got the clothes? I seen one in school this year an' he had a badge an' a gun an' everythin'."

"He did, huh?" I say. "Well, he must a been on the job. Deputies don't wear they uniforms when they offa work. An' I took offa work today to come up an' see your daddy."

They're lookin' at the nails spread 'cross the table.

"How's come you got them nails all over," the five-year-old asks, pointin' down at 'em.

"That's what we was gonna use to build the dog house," I say. "We was gonna try an' pick out the best ones of the lot. But your daddy, he said we should talk to you'ns first. Said you'd know which'ns was the strongest. You wanna do that for me? You wanna look through the pile here an' pick out the best ones?"

The two older'ns nod they heads an' start pickin' through the mess on the table. The three-year-old follows along, grabbin' at this'n an' that'n. I walk over to Stevie an' bend down by his ear.

"How many you reckon I oughtta use?" I ask. "Hain't quite sure."

"Just fucking get it over with," he hisses, never raisin' above a whisper. "Ask me what you need to and get the fuck outta here."

I'm not even gonna ask him any questions till I'm for certain he's got hisself a mortal terror for his family. No point askin' afore that.

"See, Stevie, my problem here is that I don't want any of them kids to slip off once I got 'em up on that barn. That'd be trouble I don't need. So I wanna put enough in so's they don't come free."

"I already told you I'd answer your question, Jerry. Just fucking out with it," he says.

"How many nails they put in Jesus?" I ask him. "Was it three or four?"

He turns to look at me, an' I can tell he wants to vomit.

"One for each arm an' leg, wasn't it? No, wait, it was one for each arm, an' one goin' through botha His feet. That's right. Now I 'member. So that'd be three."

"I'm gonna fucking kill you, Jerry," he says. Spit dribbles offa his lip a little.

I get up an' head back to the kids. Stand next to Carol. She's lookin' pretty faint, so I pull a chair out for her at the other end of the table.

"Now you can only choose three," I say to the kids, "so make sure you pick the best three you can find."

The five-year-old looks up at me, then points to the back of my head.

"What happened?" she asks. I touch the back of my scalp, an' it's wet. Look at my fingertips an' see a little blood.

"Oh, that?" I say, "That's from one of them widow-makers fell on me walkin' up the driveway just now. You know what a widow-maker is?"

"What?" the five- an' six-year-olds ask together.

I turn to look at Carol. Touch her chin with my hand so's she'll look up at me.

"Just one of them dead branches that falls offa trees. Only they got that name 'cause they'd liketa kill a feller if'n he wasn't lookin' out. Turn his wife into a widow lickety-split."

She shivers when I take my hand away from her chin. I can hear Stevie kickin' at the legs of his chair, tryin' to get the tape loosened, or maybe just puttin' up a fuss.

"So you'ns just pick out them three, like I told you, the best ones you can find."

I walk back on over to Stevie. Set on the corner of the table by him an' look over at the kids. The girls found all their nails an' are now helpin' the little boy pick his.

"First question," I say in Stevie's ear. "Who was it got you set up doctorin' paperwork an' tax returns for the field hands anyhow?"

"Tom. He got me into it," Stevie says. His eyes don't leave his kids.

"Second. When did Ronnie first talk to you 'bout findin' properties to set up cook-spots?"

"Two years back. Two years this June. He come to me and said I could make three times what I made workin' for Tom, and not to worry about gettin' caught, 'cause he'd taken care of everything. Said he had it fixed right. I swear to Christ, Jerry, I thought he had permission."

"From who?" I ask.

"Well, you know. From the board. From those guys down in Fayetteville."

"Third question," I say. "Who was Ronnie's contact from the board? Think real hard. Look at those precious little hands over there an' think real hard."

"Saw him one time only. Though my window. Just sat out in the car while Ronnie came into my office to talk to me. Kinda stocky. Dark curly hair. That's when Ronnie gave me some information on a feller he wanted me to forge some tax returns for. I figured it was that feller settin' out in the car. Wouldn't have thought anything of it, I'd done hundreds for Jose's boys, except for the fact that he didn't come inside. Usually they come in, so I can ask them a few questions. So I can match up place of birth with their accent. Stuff like that. But this guy just sat there and didn't move."

"What was the name? Was he the one you called when Ronnie died?"

"Yeah. I called him. Didn't know anybody else to call," Stevie says.

"What was the name on the fake tax returns? The feller's name?"

"James Howell," Stevie says.

I stand up an' walk to the window. "Shit," I say. Trail's gone cold now.

"What is it?" Stevie asks. I think of Jimmy's slick fingers grabbin' onto my hand when I put the .22 against his forehead.

"I put *him* in the ground already."

I tell the kids to hang onto them nails, 'cause Mommy an' Daddy's gonna buy that doghouse pretty soon. Take the .44 out from under the couch an' stuff it in my bag on my way to the door. Then walk down the long driveway, wipe it clean on my shirt, an' set it inside on top of his mail. Stevie was kept compartmentalized just like everybody else. I don't gotta worry 'bout him makin' no phone calls on me, 'cause there ain't no one left for him to call.

Maggie's smokin' a cigarette when I get to the rental car. She's settin' on the hood an' got Schnitzel on a leash. He's sniffin' somethin' in the ditch. They both look over at me when I come walkin' up.

"How'd it go? Get what you need?" she asks.

"Got some more calls to make," I say. Get back in the car an' light one of my own. Stare out the windshield. Watch the clouds movin' up from Arkansas.

I hain't yet figured what to say to her. Watchin' her takin' spoonfuls of her soup. Crushin' up crackers in they little packets. Tearin' the packets an' pourin' the crumbs over the soup. Some kinda vegetable beef somethin' or other. Watch her sip her water. She just looks out the window, or up at the counter. Don't never make eye contact. Don't say nothin'.

We're at this truck-stop diner in Springfield. Stopped for gas an' decided to have supper since it was gettin' on to five. It's rainin' outside the window right now. Weather said it's rainin' all the way down to Little Rock.

"You like livin' in Memphis?" I ask her. She looks right at me, like how I seen her look at patients on stretchers in the ER. Cold. Evaluatin'.

"Sure. It's all right," she says. Shrugs her shoulders. "Like Fayetteville better. That's my home. But I can't go back there."

Looks at me again with them cold, patient eyes.

"One time," I say, "a couple years back me an' Sam went over to Memphis for a gun show. Wasn't nothin' special there, so we took in a few sights 'fore headin' back. Saw Beale Street. Bobby was jealous of that when I told him."

She just nods. Sips her water. Crushes up some more crackers.

"Figure it's just gonna be a coupl'a more days. Thing's gonna get sorted out," I say.

"Good. I gotta get back to work, Jerry," she says. "I'm in dutch as is. The sooner I can get back the better." Looks down at my hands. Hain't hardly touched my ham steak. She moves her hands to grab mine.

"Well, hey there," I say. She smiles up at me. If she's fakin' I cain't tell.

"You wanna fuck me tonight, Jerry?" she asks. Smilin', but not grinnin'.

"I reckon."

"Then you need to buy me some flowers," she says. "Nothin' fancy, but a nice little bouquet. And write somethin' about how you love me on the card."

"You know I love you," I say. She nods, looks up at the counter again. Then back out the window.

"I know. But it's part of the game. We're gonna play a game, like none of this is goin' on right now. Like we're just a coupl'a people who love each other. An' we're young an' stupid, an' flowers are all I need to believe you'd never hurt me. That's the game we're gonna play."

"Jerry, what the fuck are you doin'?" Tom yells at me from his back porch. I look up from the rose bed an' wave at him with the clippers in my hand I took outta his tool shed. Tom's a gardener, he's even entered contests at the state fair. Never won, though. Too busy with the job to put the effort into it. His wife, Susan, she's won blue ribbons for her landscape paintin'. Tom says he's gonna bring in a few more of them once he finally retires an' can devote more of his day to the flowers.

"Hey, boss," I say. "Don't ask. I just need a few. The Walmart didn't have nothin' worthwhile." I clip another rose.

It's about seven thirty, an' Maggie's back in the car parked in the alley just beside Tom's back fence. She rolls down the window.

"Hey, Tom," she calls to him.

"Hey there, Doc," he says. Looks back at me. Then over at her again.

"Talked to Stevie today," I say. He closes his back door an' walks out 'cross the yard to the flower beds. Stands next to me. Watches me clip a rose.

"What'd he tell you?"

"Jimmy—or Anthony, I guess was his real name—was connected up with the Sanhedrin," I say, clippin' another rose.

"Damn it, Jer, how many you gonna take?"

"Need a dozen. So that's three more."

"Well, don't take all the big'ns. Susan likes 'em too."

"You got plenty here, boss," I say, clippin' another'n. "An' there's lots more to bloom yet."

"How was he connected? Stevie tell you that much?"

"I know that already," I say. Clip the next to last.

"Uh-huh. You better be damn sure 'fore you try anythin' like that. An' don't tell me nothin' about it. I don't wanna know what your crazy ass is doin'."

"I gotta talk to somebody else first. 'Fore I'm certain. I hain't stupid, boss."

"Sure. Just put them shears back in the shed when you're done, Jer."

I clip the last one.

When we get back to the house Maggie goes upstairs to my room while I set at the kitchen table an' write out the card. Grandma walks in an' opens up the fridge. Takes out the pitcher of lemonade an' pours herself a glass. Then one for me. Sets it in fronta me an' pats me on the head. Leaves for the porch. I can hear them chains squeakin' from the swing.

I walk on up the stairs an' knock on my own door. Got them dozen roses wrapped up in wax paper with the note taped to one of the stems.

"Enter," Maggie says. I walk on in, an' she's settin' on the bed. Hand her the bouquet. She takes it an' smiles real sweet to me.

"These here's for you, darlin'," I say.

She takes the card, holds it up in fronta her face, an' reads it out loud.

"*Dear Margaret. I know you got every reason to be mad at me. I hurt you awful, and I'm real sorry. I'm real mad at myself for hurting the only woman ever cared about me. It's real simple, I fucked it up awful bad and can't forgive myself for it. I love you like you was inside me, under my skin and living in my blood. I don't know what I'd do without you. Love, Jerry.*"

She sets the card down on the bed next to the flowers. With one hand she starts unbuttonin' her blouse. Pats the bed beside her with the other'n.

CHAPTER THIRTEEN:

Gettin' et up.

"SO WE'RE GOIN' out again tonight?" Maggie asks me with a mouthful of toothpaste. She's wrapped up in the bedsheet an' brushin' her teeth at the sink. It's near ten. I'm settin' at my desk, lookin' through some of the files Tom sent me some days back. Known associates of Jimmy, an' that'n I recognized from the car tailin' Maggie. Them other fellers that got buried down in that hole along with Jimmy, too. I open my file drawer an' look for a empty folder. Take one out an' slip the pages with all they photographs in it.

"Hey, Jer, I asked you a question," she says. Then sees me closin' up the folder, an' I can tell what she thinks it is by the way she stops in her tracks in the doorway. Foam still on her lip.

"Just some pictures I gotta show somebody. Jose from yesterday."

She just keeps lookin' at me. Then after a coupl'a seconds, she goes back to the sink an' spits. Warshes her mouth out. Wipes it on the towel.

"Were you gonna ask me about all that?" she says, leanin' in the doorway.

"You mean what you seen last night. I's gonna wait for you to bring it up. You had yourself quite a shock. No sense pushin' things when you ain't got to."

"Make a deal with you," she says. "You tell me how come you're 'fraid of big dogs, an' I'll tell you everythin' you wanna know about Candy Johnson."

"You might have to be the one to break the ice, there. I'm nowhere near high enough to tell it."

"Suit yourself."

Jose's out at Tree-Dog Willie's, 'cause it's Friday night. Hollis tried doin' that karaoke for a few hours, but not enough folks liked it. But Jose an' some other fellers convinced him to keep it for just a hour on Fridays. An' he had to promise he wouldn't sing no Spanish.

It's eleven now, so by the time we get there, Jose's done singin' for the night. I find him back by the pool table. Settin' with some of his white campesino foremen.

"Was it Bon Jovi tonight? Or more a Eagles kinda night?" I ask him. Outta the corner of my eye, I see Maggie get a stool up at the bar. Told her not to stand close to me till I went outside. Then she's to walk back out to the car an' get in the front seat.

"Hijo de puta," Jose says an' grins up at me. Extends his hand. "What you need here, Jerry? Just come for pleasantries, hombre?"

I shake his hand an' figure just how drunk he is when he nods off while I still got his hand 'cross the table. No good to me like this. I look over at Hollis, servin' Maggie a drink.

"You got a hose out back?" I ask.

"Vete a la chingada!" Jose yells at me when I spray his face with the cold water. He's on his back on the picnic table where I laid him down.

"I woulda, but your momma was all booked up for the night," I say.

"What the fuck, Jerry?" he yells, settin' up on the table. Says my name *Cherry*. Cain't pronounce the *J* when he's drunk. "La agua fria no es buena."

"Need you to sober up long enough to look at some pictures, caballero."

"You coulda fucking said so, rinche. Don't got to pull that shit!"

I help him up an' walk 'round to the fronta Willie's. Maggie's out on the porch by now. Waitin' at the top of the stairs. I nod to her, an' she starts walkin' to the car. I get Jose seated in the back of my rental car while she sets in the front passenger seat.

"You bringin' her in on this or something?" he asks, starin' right at her.

"Okay. Well, maybe you oughtta give us just a minute," I say to her. She steps outta the car without sayin' nothin'. Shuts the door an' lights a cigarette, leanin' on the car.

"Why you draggin' her into this shit, gringo?" he asks.

"Don't you mind her. Just look at the pictures. See if'n you recognize any folks here."

"You know, gringo, how strained my end is now? I can't hire nobody else till they find a new chew!"

"A new chew?"

"A chew. Fucking paperwork guy for the W-twos and tax return shit. A chew."

"Oh, sure, a Jew," I say. "Sorry to disappoint, but Stevie was Church of Christ."

"He was an accountant, man, same fucking thing."

I shove the pictures at him again.

"Es mierda, rinche," he says. I figure it's bullshit, too.

"Just look at 'em."

"You got a fucking woman like that, una mujer fabulosa, you don't pull her into this kind of thing," he says. "You gotta keep her far a-fucking-way as you can."

"That's real sweet of you," I say. I'm startin' to lose my patience. I grab his hair an' pull him in close to the open folder with the pictures. "I wouldn'ta never put her in any danger, hoss, but y'all fuckers done somethin' pretty damn awful. You'ns put that sweet little angel out there in harm's way."

"I ain't done nothing like that, Jerry! I ain't gonna hurt no women. Not without no good reason. No fucking way."

I let go his hair an' hand over the file to him. "Just look at 'em, puto."

He does. Nods. "Sure, I know him," he says, pointin' to Jimmy's photo. "These guys, too." He points down at some more I don't know from Adam. Then to the photo of one of the guys that got in the same hole as Jimmy. An' one more from the car in Memphis. "Yeah, sure, I seen these guys."

"Where? Think 'bout it good."

"No son mis campesinos. Not my fucking guys, Jerry."

"Whose guys?"

"Marcus. They work for him. Seen 'em when he brought me in to interview some new campesinos at his warehouse last year," he says. Then points down at Jimmy's picture. "This one the year before."

"An' what'd you see 'em do?"

"Just standing around with guns. Looking like badasses, you know? Like they was guarding the meeting or something. It was just to scare those kids. Marcus likes to do that."

I take the folder back from him an' close it up. Pull a plastic zip tie outta my back pocket. Get outta the car an' walk to the back door. Open it an' thread the tie through the handlebar on the ceilin'. Jose just watches me while I do it. Nothin' registers.

"What's that for, Jer?" he asks. I grab his hand by the wrist an' slip it into the hole. Then I zip it closed. Not too tight. "Hey, what the fuck, man?" he yells.

"Cain't trust you not to call nobody. So you're gonna spend a day in a cell. Don't worry. I'll tell your boys they can run it by themselves for a day 'cause you're sick."

"This ain't fucking right, rinche!" he yells at me through the bars of the drunk tank at the station. "You know that! I ain't gonna tip nobody off. No fucking way I'd rat out my buddy like that. Huh, Jerry?"

I give him his cigarettes through the bars.

"Rolled a coupl'a them myself, comprende?" I say. "So take a twenty-four-hour vacation. It's on me. An' don't worry. Nobody's gonna bother you. You're in the private drunk tank. Reserved for city councilmen who don't know when to quit the kill-devil."

"You ain't gonna let me out for twenty-four hours?" he asks.

"Oughtta be all I need. You'll get your meals. But not no phone calls. See you then."

Too late to go into Fayetteville tonight. Near midnight now. So I take Maggie back to Grandma's house an' check what's in the fridge. I set out the leftovers on the table. The roast is only a few days old. I cut some chunks off an' put 'em on two plates. Set the plates in the microwave for a coupl'a minutes. Maggie gets some water glasses set out. Some silver.

"The microwave looks new," she says.

"Coupl'a years old. Course I'm the only one uses it. Grandma won't touch it."

I call Sam in Fayetteville while we're waitin' for the roast to cook. Tell him to close up shop early tomorrow. Find a good spot in the hills on the other side a Fayetteville to go shootin' afore dusk. Says he wants to know what's goin' on. I tell him I'm gonna go huntin'. An' I'm gonna use his new Winchester.

When we set down to eat, Maggie eats maybe two bites. Then speaks up.

"Candy was a hooker," she says, not lookin' up. "Excuse me, stripper, but did tricks part time."

"Don't gotta tell me, Maggie," I say. "Not if you don't want to."

"You know the important stuff already. Just a matter of fillin' in the details. More for me than you. For vanity's sake, Jerry. I wouldn't have you think somethin' of me that wasn't true."

She takes another bite, an' I chew on mine. Swallows.

"My ex-husband was a pediatrician. I ever tell you that?"

"Nope. Hain't never even told me his name."

"Jacob. We got married once my residency was finished. Anyway, he'd treated a coupl'a her kids. Broken finger.

Bruises so bad the eye swelled shut. A few cigarette burns. Malnutrition. So Jacob reported it right off. Only the judge, he'd seen her show at the club where she worked. Turned out he was a fan."

"So he wanted a taste of the real thing?" I ask. She nods.

"That was the rumor goin' 'round after the trial ended. So 'bout a month after, she came into the ER. A john worked her over pretty bad. Or *good*, if you ask me."

I chuckle, then catch myself quick. She don't look in too jokey a mood. I toss a piece of my roast down to Schnitzel, waitin' with a pity-me look. I watch Maggie's face an' listen to his jaws chomp into the dry meat.

"Wasn't even conscious. Head trauma. Broken ribs. The damage probably woulda kept her off the pole for quite a while."

I wait a second for her to say somethin' else, an' when she don't, I say, "Baby, look here. You already know this, but takin' her out was a favor to them kids. Odds are they'll fare better with they other relations, or even state-raised, than with that whore."

"I didn't expect you to be like this, Jerry," she says. "I've only ever told this to one other person. An' he couldn't stop preachin' at me."

"I'm not one for all that religion, darlin'," I say. "How'd you get it done, then?"

"Insulin," she says with that same coldness from afore. "Once I saw her on that gurney. Had her chart in my hand. I knew what was gonna happen. I knew I was gonna order a drip IV. Keep her sedated. Order enough units of insulin, though do *that* for another patient, a diabetic that came in that night."

"So you put it into her IV? Didn't leave no marks. That's damn smart of you," I say.

"Smart enough to squeak my way through med school," she shrugs.

She looks back down at her plate. Starts cuttin' up some more of her roast. Her appetite seems to've come back.

"You know they keep it cold?" she asks.

"The insulin?"

"Uh-huh. An' when I drew it from the little bottle down into the hypo, I 'member thinkin' how strange it felt. That cold hypodermic."

I nod an' give Schnitzel some more roast. Maggie takes a coupl'a bites of hers. I just watch her for a minute while she chews. She looks down at the floor an' smiles at my dog.

"I almost dropped it," she laughs, then covers her mouth with her hand an' looks up at me, then back down at Schnitzel. "The nurse pulled back the curtain an' I knew I had maybe two minutes 'fore she came back. Took the hypo outta the pocket on my lab coat an' stuck it right into the cannula," she looks back up at me, "that's the neck that attaches the line to the bag, an' pushed the plunger down slow an' steady."

"Know what it was that clicked?" I ask. "I mean, you know the trigger? That's what you call it, ain't it? The thing set you to think serious 'bout doin' it in the first place?"

"Sure. The kids were the first thing I thought of when I saw the patient's name on the chart. Didn't even recognize her. Just knew the name, thought of the kids an' the trial. An' Jacob, too. How angry he was after. Knowin' those kids were goin' right back to that woman. An' I knew. She wasn't gonna hurt anybody. Not ever. Wasn't a decision, even. Just like an autopilot took over. It was scary, but the actions felt routine. Like just another part of my day that was s'posed to be there."

"So how'd you get caught?" I ask.

"Pathologist reported hypoglycemia during the autopsy. With no diabetic history. He didn't think that was the cause of death, though. For him it was only peripheral to her head trauma. But when my boss, chief of emergency medicine, when he saw that, an' he knew I'd treated her. An' he knew Jacob treated her kids. 'Membered the trial. He figured it right off. Gave me the option to pack up an' leave town, never come back, or face legal consequences."

"Why'd he give you the choice?" I ask.

"Happened on his watch. In his ER. Unacceptable. Didn't wanna see what the board would do to him when Candy's family sued the hospital for wrongful death. Or what'd happen in a criminal trial. So he let me run with my tail tucked 'tween my legs. Jacob put two an' two together. Never said a word to me about it. Just asked me to sign the divorce papers. Didn't blame him. John got me the job here in Huntsville right after."

She pushes her plate away. Mostly finished. Raises her arms up to stretch. Shakes her head an' looks at me.

"It feels different talkin' to you 'bout this," she says. "But talkin' to you's always been a little different. Ever since you pulled me out of my car. I guess I was emotionally fragile. Impressionable. Like how a just-hatched chick will think the first thing it sees is its mother. Believe it for the rest of its life. Follow it around."

She leans back in her chair a little. Grins at me. Eyes narrow.

"But you got some of that, too," she says. "An' I reckon I'm partly responsible."

"How'd you mean?" I ask.

"I mean your *treatment*, Jerry. How I cured your impotency. *Took the cuss off* as you like to say. You probably know by now that I really didn't help you get over your fear. You're still afraid of sexual infection, right?"

I nod. "Now that you mention it."

"Jacob cheated on me, Jer," she says. "So I saw in you an opportunity. *Fidelity*, Jerry. Faithfulness. I never wanted you to get over your fear, generally. Just with me. Encouraged you to trust me while neglectin' to work on the phobia overall. I wanted to be your only option."

"Why're you tellin' me this?" I ask her.

"So you'll know why you're in love with me. So you'll understand that it comes from your illness more than anythin' else. Animals love their owners because they feed them."

She pushes her chair back an' stands up. Half past midnight now. She walks over to the stairs, an' I gather up the plates an' rinse 'em off. She waits for me, an' I follow her up the stairs.

In the mornin' there's the rental car thing. It's been out for a coupl'a weeks now. That's no problem, cause I put it on one of Tom's emergency credit cards. Don't gotta worry 'bout them leadin' back to him. He's got it set up. Uses the names of cons servin' life sentences, but pays the bills himself with money orders. Uses a fake name for them too, but nobody cares 'cause cash is cash. The card bills go to a box in a Fayetteville post office. He's probably gonna have to set up another card after this.

We drive into Fayetteville early in the afternoon. Maggie's got this nice pleated skirt on she picked up at the Walmart this mornin'. Kicks off her flat-soled shoes in the car an' puts her feet up on the dash. Got her a pair of sunglasses. She puts 'em up on top of her head when we're almost there an' says to me she's glad she told me what she did last night. Slept a lot better, she said. She's not sure why, exactly.

Drop off the rental car an' pay up with Tom's card. Call for a cab an' have 'em drop us off at another car rental lot. After rentin' another car, I drive to Sam's Surplus Shop. Park in the lot an' wait. It's five of three now, an' he said he'd close up at three.

Maggie's just quiet, watchin' the door, like me. Got her shoes off again. I reach over an' stroke her bare ankle an' up her calf a little. She glances at me.

"Always loved them legs," I say. She don't say nothin'. Goes back to watchin' Sam's front door. Don't move her legs down, but after a few seconds, I take my hand away.

At ten after three, Sam flips the sign around to CLOSED. Me an' Maggie get outta the car an' head on over.

"No, God-damn it, Jerry, you can't saw off the barrel," Sam says to me. Gettin' red in the face. Squirmin' in his wheelchair. Lookin' over at Maggie ever' minute or so. She's settin' up at the counter, workin' on the project I give her. Showed her how to clean her .32. Said when she's done I'd help her put it back together.

"I'll pay you for it, Sam," I say. "Not just for the barrel, but for the whole gun."

"It ain't 'cause it's a thousand-dollar gun, Jerry, it's that you just can't. What you wanna do won't work. An' you can't saw off the stock neither. This ain't never gonna be a hand-grip weapon. Not ever, got it?"

"What'd you mean?" I ask him. "I done that with shot-guns 'fore. Works just fine."

Me an' Sam is settin' at the table in the middle a his shop. The Winchester SX-3 layin' out 'cross the table 'tween us. Settin' next to it's a box of shells I brought. Got another'n in the car. Sam shakes his head when he looks up at me.

"I mean, Jer, that you can't control it. Sure, on a pump-action, you can do somethin' like that. But the speed you gonna fire this'n here, it'll jump right outta your hands. Pull the trigger that fast an' you won't keep the grip. Need to brace it against your shoulder. Got it?"

"Okay, sure. How come I cain't saw the barrel though?"

"Extendin' tube. That's how come it can fit twelve rounds 'steada five. Excuse me, four-plus-one."

He points down the SX-3. Black metal, wood stock, an' forearm grip. Don't look no different from a regular pump-action, cep'n the extendin' tube that runs under the full length of the barrel.

"First off, that tube there's attached to the barrel. See that clamp? Nothin'd support it if you took that barrel away. Second, then there's the issue of scatter. You cut that bar-rel far enough back, the widened scatter'd wreck the tube, 'cause it'd be stickin' right out in the way. Probably pop the whole damn thing right off, an' then you got no shells 'steada twelve. This is the Flanigan Model, which means longer barrel, an' that's what allows for a tube that'll fit seven more in it. So no, physically, you can't cut *this* gun down. If you wanna use it, you'd better figure out how to make it work as is."

I set back an' glance over at Maggie. She's lookin' at us. Listenin' in.

"Maybe another gun. I could sell you a little H-and-K submachine gun with a shoulder strap, that MP-five up on the wall there. Fix the receiver right here for you so's it's full-auto. 'Course you'd have to remember where you *didn't* get it from. But I figure that may be the case with this'n here already."

"I need the spread," I say. "Full-auto's a whole other animal. A bullet hits or it don't. With a shotgun, you get a spread, an' that's what I need. To absolutely cover a area quick as I can. Gotta saturate it."

Sam nods. "Then you'll need to be farther back."

Maggie empties the .32 into the target poster on the tree further down the holler. Not rapid, but careful, no faster'n one per second. Make her count off Mississippis as she pulls the trigger. Eight of ten on the body from twenty-five feet.

"Gettin' better," I say. She takes the plug outta her ear an' looks back at me.

"What?"

"Improvin'," I say. She nods an' puts back the foam plug.

We're a ways into the woods, back on a gravel road. I don't know the area, so Sam had to show us. Drove us here in his van that got the wheelchair ramp on the side so's he can get in. He's settin' out by the van just a ways offa the road on the edge of the clearin'. Got his ear protection on, too. That plastic kind looks like orange earmuffs.

"Now you," Maggie mouths to me.

I got eight sticks planted in the ground 'bout forty feet from where we're standin'. Plastic milk jugs fitted on the ends of each'n. Tops are right at shoulder level. Spaced a few feet apart. Spread out over maybe twenty feet. I raise the Winchester to my shoulder.

Start from right an' go to left. Squeeze off twelve rounds an' blow apart eight milk jugs. Takes four seconds. Gotta get it closer to two.

Sun sets behind us as we're headin' back to Huntsville, an' I'm glad it ain't in my eyes. Maggie's shiftin' in her seat, tryin' to get comfortable with that .32 in the small of her back. Someone we gotta pick up 'fore headin' back into Fayetteville.

"I'm gonna set in the back with him on the way there, okay? So you gonna drive."

"Okay. Sure," she says.

"He's a doper, so he's liable to say some crazy shit, but don't listen to him. I mean for you to pretend he ain't even there. Just tune him out."

"I know how to do that," she says.

When we're 'bout halfway back, I get antsy in the driver's seat. I pull over on the shoulder. Best let her start drivin' now, if'n I'm gonna be nervous. Put the car in park. Unclick my seat belt an' open the door. Then I shut the door. She looks over at me.

"I was out in them woods for three days tied to that tree. First an' second night it rained."

"Who did it? Who tied you?" she asks.

"Momma done it," I say. "She was all jittery an' high on somethin'. Showed up at Grandma's house an' said she was gonna take me up to Silver Dollar City in Branson. Grandma weren't there, so Momma just put me in the back-seat an' drove off. She started talkin' all weird up near the Missouri line, an' I guess I got scared, 'cause I started cryin'. She wouldn't stand for none of that. Shakin' her head an' a pullin' at her hair. Nossir. Nossirree. Walked me down one of the hikin' trails at a rest stop off the side of the highway. Then walked me a ways back into the brush so's the trail was long outta sight."

"Jesus," Maggie says. She moves to put her hand on my shoulder, but pulls it back.

"I thought the Wowzer was gonna get me. Ever' night an' ever' day, too. Wowzer don't just come 'round in the dark. Some folks seen him in broad daylight."

"What did you do?" she asks. Clenchin' her hands into fists like she wants to do somethin' she cain't.

"I prayed to Jesus. Like Momma taught me. Like I did ever' night 'fore bed. I's so afraid I'd get et up by the Wowzer. I prayed to Jesus Christ in Heaven for three days an' nights. Screamed it out at first. Like He was gonna hear me better. Save me from gettin' et up."

"How'd you get away? What happened?"

"Then I *did* get et up. Coupl'a stray dogs found me. Tied up like that. Weak. They was awful hungry. I could count they ribs pretty good. Started sniffin' me at first. I tried to scream, but I'd lost my voice after prayin' all the first day. Whisperin' only kept 'em away for a minute. One of them started in on my leg. That left'n. 'Member when you asked me how's come I got no hair a growin' on that calf or shin? Weren't no fireworks burn, like I said."

She shakes her head an' looks out the windshield into woods on the hillside up ahead.

"The first'n, the bigger, he started right in, like I's a side of ham. The other'n, he joined in, too, an' that only lasted for a minute 'fore they got to fightin' over the meat I had on me. It was they fightin'. Barkin' an' a growlin'. Whinin' an' a yelpin'. All that noise. Coupl'a hikers come down from the trail to see 'bout it. Come through the briars an' found me."

"That makes sense," she says. "That'd make anybody scared of big dogs."

"An' the thing is, they wasn't big. Just medium-size mutts, I reckon. Nothin' like a lab or a shepherd. But when you six, medium-sized mutts seem a whole fuck lot bigger."

She looks back at me. Face still got that icy look again, like a hypo full of insulin.

"I don't know what to say to you, Jerry."

"You'd better drive now. Reckon I'm a bit shaky."

"Jesus, Freddie," I say, "you look like you been sortin' wildcats."

Settin' on the floor in fronta his TV. Blood on his arms an' neck an' face. A little crusted in his dreads. But it ain't fresh. Then I see it. Glass tabletop got busted an' scattered over the floor. Musta fell on it.

"Had a accident, Jerry," he says. Mosta that blood's dried black, now, so it probably happened yesterday. Maggie peeks in the door from outside.

"Should we clean him up first?" she asks.

"Nope," I say. "It's better if he looks like this. Don't even wanna change his shirt."

I go into the room a little further an' start lookin'. Check the drawers in the nightstand. Nothin'. The counter in the bathroom. Under the bed. The drawers in the dresser. Then I grab Freddie by his dreads an' make him stand up. Move him over to set on the edge of the bed.

"Where'd you put the rest of it?" I ask him. Shakes his head like he don't know.

I kick a few empty beer cans outta the way walkin' to the head of the bed. Pick up the pillows. Shake 'em with the open end of the case facin' down. Then it drops out. What's left of the weed. Freddie musta smoked half. I'm surprised there's that much left.

"Why don't you start the car," I say to Maggie. Freddie's a little wobbly when he stands up, so I get under his arm an' help steady him. Somethin' don't look quite right on him, though.

He needs some fresh.

On the way outta the room, I knock his face into the doorframe. He yells an' falls to the floor, grabbin' his nose. Bright red blood drippin' through his fingers.

"Fuck was that, Jer!" he yells up at me.

"Oh, shit, I thought you was watchin' where you's goin'. Sorry 'bout that."

I walk back to the bathroom an' find a towel. Tip his head back an' hold the towel on it. Walk him out to the car an' get him in the backseat. Climb on in an' set next to him.

Maggie looks at the fresh blood in the rearview mirror. She don't ask.

Turn on the radio for Freddie. Remind him to keep his head tilted back. Nobody really talks mucha the way back to Fayetteville. He asks me one time who the chick behind the wheel is, an' I slap the back of his scalp. Tell him not to worry 'bout it.

"But I just wanna know who she is, Jer," he whines.

"Don't aggervex me boy," I say, twistin' his ear. "Hain't in the mood for it."

The road's dark. Usually most the traffic is headed the other way, but this is a Saturday night, so everybody's comin' into the big city for fun. I give Maggie directions, an' she follows 'em just fine. Then I have her pull over at a gas station on Lafayette, three blocks south from where we headin', an' drive into the alley. We both get out.

"See where that diner was, 'cross the street?" I say. "You wait there."

"Thought we were attached at the hip," she says.

"Not no more. Hain't takin' you in there with me. For starters, they'd never *let* you in. An' second, in 'bout ten, fifteen minutes, you ain't gonna need no protection no more. No matter what, you get me?"

"No matter what. You mean whether you come outta there or not?"

"That's exactly what I mean. I figure on comin' out, but you never know. Either way, you're in the clear after I get done."

She looks at me for a few seconds. Opens her mouth to say somethin' an' shuts it quick. Then opens it again.

"Thanks. For doin' this. For protectin' me," she says. "I keep thinkin' that maybe I oughtta say somethin' else."

"Tell me later," I say.

"What if there *is* no later?" she asks.

"Then what would it matter?" I say.

She nods, turns, an' heads down the alley toward the diner. Looks back just the once.

I reach into the car, under the front seat, an' pop the trunk. Walk 'round behind the car an' look inside. Check the little mat on the bottom that's s'posed to cover the well for the spare tire. Check the long bump under it. Make sure the tape's still holdin' the mat in place. I step 'round to the side of the car an' open the back door for Freddie. Maggie's outta the alley now, an' I just catch her crossin' to the other side of the street 'fore she's outta view. Don't need to think 'bout all that right now. Cain't help but muck things up.

"How's come you got the trunk open?" Freddie asks.

"Shut up'n get in," I say. Help him climb inside. Then I take out my 'lectric tape.

"Don't need that, do you?" he asks.

"'Fraid so, buddy. Don't worry. We'll be done lickety-whoop, an' you'll have more money than Carter has oats."

"Who's Carter?" Freddie asks.

"Damned if I know. Grandma always used to say that."

Tape his wrists an' ankles. Rag goes in the mouth, an' tape over that. Run a strip over his eyes. Don't fight me none, just moves his head 'round, wantin' to know what's goin' on.

Shut the trunk.

CHAPTER FOURTEEN:

Thick as crows at a hog-killin'.

IT'S NOT THE biggest warehouse he's got. Maybe a hundred by two hundred feet. Right on Highway 71, settin' on a half lot of woods, elsewise surrounded by a run-down neighborhood. But Marcus likes this'n 'cause it has a fence 'round it an' a guard at the gate. This is the same damn buildin' I worked at when I's nineteen an' twenty. Carried 'round a flashlight, a .38 on my belt, an' a walkie-talkie, walkin' through all them rows of old crates. Readin' shippin' manifests an' mostly just tryin' to look busy. When there were shipments to unload, he'd keep up to six of us guards 'round at a time. Not countin' that'n at the gate.

The guard wants to know what I'm doin' here when I drive up. He recognizes me. Little fucker. Probably eighteen. Cuts under his chin from shavin'. I tell him to get Marcus on the phone for me. While the kid's callin' up the boss, I look up at them cameras. Hain't changed one bit in eleven years since I started as a deputy. Outta all the warehouses they got 'round here, all the video surveillance gets recorded on them machines in Marcus's office.

"He says to go on in," the kid at the gate says, pushin' the button to open the ten-foot chain-link fence gate. I pull into the gravel parkin' lot. It's pretty big, on accounta the semis they have comin' in an' out. Enough room for 'em to turn 'round in. Drive up to the big aluminum overhead door. Get outta the car an' head over to the small door beside. Head in an' wave to one of the security guards to open up the big door. He turns to look over at Marcus's office, an' there the man is, standin' right outside his door. Marcus nods his head, an' the guard presses the button to raise the overhead door. I head back out an' get back in my rental car. Drive it on inside the buildin' as the door gets halfway up. Park just inside the door.

"What brings you up to these parts, Jer?" Marcus says, walkin' on up as I get outta the rental. I slam the door shut an' bring him on 'round to the back bumper.

"I need you to do me a favor. An', really, I'm doin' you a favor."

"How's that?" he asks.

I watch the guard bring down the door. They've replaced it since I worked here, so I watch for where the button is. When the guard heads back over to the crates, I look at Marcus.

"I better show you what's in the trunk," I say. Walk 'round to the front driver's-side door an' open it. Reach down an' pull the lever to pop the trunk.

"Fuck me, Jer," Marcus says. "That who I think it is?"

"The very one. An' I'll give him to you if'n you want him. But I need some information first."

"What kinda information? I'll help you if I can," he says as I walk back 'round to the open trunk. Look down inside at Nappy Freddie, movin' his head 'round like he's tryin' to see through the tape on his eyes. Blood an' snot slicked all over the 'lectric tape on his mouth. Rattlin' comin' from his nostrils.

"Not from you," I say. "From Freddie there. He knows somethin' I wanna get figured out. An' I bet you'll wanna know, too."

"What the Christ does this little fucker know? Thought he was just another perma-fry."

"You been hearin' 'bout all this trouble we been havin' up in Madison County, I reckon," I say. "Well, this little peckerwood here, he knows where it come from."

"How you figure that?" Marcus asks, lookin' up at me.

"Ronnie was tryin' to start up a meth operation on our turf. You know that. An' Freddie here was still workin' with him when it happened, 'fore he went an' put them holes all through his wife. Matter of fact, where you think we found Freddie last month?"

Marcus steps away from the trunk, still lookin' at me. Takes a slim cigar outta his shirt pocket. Unwraps it an' fits it 'tween his lips.

"You mean Ronnie took him in?" he asks, shakin' his head, fishin' his lighter outta his pocket. "That little fucker. Now I'm doubly glad you done that Ronnie in."

"An' Freddie can identify Ronnie's connection. Said it was a feller from your office, too. That's how come I'm here."

"That's fuckin' bullshit, Jer."

"How well you screen your employees?" I ask. "'Cause there might be a bad apple in the barrel somewheres. Or maybe Freddie's full of shit. But I just wanna have a look."

"Well, Jer, you can look at everybody you need to."

"Nope, it's Freddie that I wanna have a look. He needs to see some faces from here."

"How you wanna do that?"

"Bring 'em in by your office window," I say. "Just have everybody workin' today come in an' have a seat in your office. If I drive the car 'round an' back a little down that aisle, I can see 'em through that big window, nice an' framed. Go call a meetin'. Then I'll shut the lights off out here while you keep 'em on in there. I'll pull Freddie's head outta the trunk far enough for him to see who's there. That oughtta be all we need. Then we'll know."

"He didn't say who it was?" Marcus asks, backin' away from Freddie.

"Nope. Just said he worked here under a false name."

Marcus nods his head. "So what if he's not here, then?"

"Then Nappy Freddie's gonna get his ass beat for wastin' both our time. Probably I'll lose track of him after that. He'll go right back into the woods an' stay there."

"'Bout fuckin' time," Marcus laughs. Turns to go to his office. Looks back at me. "I'll call the meetin'."

I look down in at Freddie. Close the trunk lid shut. Get back in the driver's seat an' wait. Light me a cigarette an' roll down the window. One hundred feet to the other side of the warehouse from here, an' Marcus's office is against the wall, forty feet to my right. From his office, lookin' out the window's the main freight aisle that runs two hundred feet to the back side of the buildin'. Them crates is everywhere. Textiles, foodstuffs, kitchen appliances, all boxed up in wood. White plastic-coated manifests stapled to all they sides. Marcus's voice comes on over the intercom. All staff, he says, come to the office for a meetin'. I drive the car down the front area to park it in the main aisle, trunk facin' the office window. Make sure it's at least fifty feet back from the window. Get out an' lean on the side of the car, finishin' my cigarette.

There's the question of what Marcus is gonna do. Seemed kinda paranoid. S'posin' he don't wanna be in the room to be looked at by Freddie. S'posin' he thinks he's at risk for bein' identified, too. I got my Sig Sauer 226 in my pocket. Picked it up at a show in Springfield last year with Sam for three-fifty. Just like that M9 I had back in Memphis, it holds fifteen-plus-one 9 mm rounds. If Marcus don't show in the office, then I'm gonna have to get him with that.

I count four security guards. One janitor. One clerk. They all come walkin' from different directions. File on into the office. Take seats on the couches. Two on the couch against the wall facin' me through the window. Two with the backs of they heads to me. Two at the far left edge, facin' Marcus's desk. Hain't see Marcus yet, though. I leave the car an' walk back to the big door where I 'member the light switches was. Click off all the ones out on the floor. Back goes dark. Middle. Then front right outside the office. Some of them inside the office turn they heads to look, but then just look back at the desk. Office door opens, an' I can see in the dark Marcus walk on in.

Walk 'round to the driver's side, lean in the window, an' pop the trunk. Drop my cigarette in the ashtray. Head back down to the trunk. Reach in an' shove Freddie back a little bit. He wiggles, tryin' to say somethin' through his gag. Shove him just far enough to reach the bump along the inside under the taped-down carpet. Pull up the tape. Get the little bag first.

Earplugs come first. Then the yellow dishwarshin' gloves get taped on. Look up at the lighted window again. Marcus is standin' 'hind his desk. I can see his arms wavin', like he's yellin' somethin' to the staff, but I cain't see his body. Reach back in an' pull the carpet all the way back. Pick up the Winchester SX-3. Click off the safety.

From the left side of the car I can get his arms, but there's them two 'cross from him that'd be outta the line of sight. I don't like that. Move on 'round to the right side of the car an' I can see 'em both settin' there, but nothin' of Marcus at all. If'n I get his arms, probably he'd bleed out from it quick, but then I'd have them other two fellers to deal with. From the right side of the car, there's only Marcus left.

In the dark, the muzzle flash blinds me a little, like I figured, but not too bad. First five shots goin' from right, Marcus's side, to left. Each'ns a jackhammer in my shoulder. First feller by the window bursts blood out all over the shattered an' fallin' glass. Second an' third an' fourth shots are for the fellers on the couch facin' me. An' I see the taupe paint on the wall 'hind 'em turn red in giant spots, an' white drywall dust rolls like kids clappin' erasers. After that I lose count an' fire whatever else I got in the gun. Coupl'a fellers try an' get up from they couches an' get caught with more shots, openin' up stomachs an' bladders to spill all kinda mess down they legs. One of them on the couch facin' Marcus's desk gets up an' tries to duck, but I still catch his shoulder with a shot an' flip him 'round. Then the shotgun clicks empty.

My eyes are a glarin' as I throw the Winchester in the trunk, shut it, an' walk on up to office. Pull out my Sig Sauer. Had the safety off already. Walk up to the window an' look inside. Five bodies. Some spread 'cross couches, some on the floor. Marcus is shakin' right 'hind his desk. He's covered by it pretty good. Gotta wait for him to come outta the office. I walk back from the window an' wait up against the wall, still peerin' in. He starts comin' out from 'hind his desk. I can just see him from where I'm standin'. Take aim on his fat belly as he crawls to the door.

Then the door on the outside of the buildin' opens an' a feller comes runnin' inside. The guard from the gate. Musta heard the noise an' come to see. Got his .38 out. Look back down at Marcus, an' he's already right by the door, outta my field of vision. I switch my aim over to the gate guard an' see he's already drawn his. Starts firin' at me from thirty feet, just when the door to Marcus's office swings open wide, right 'tween me an' the kid. Marcus walks out, pistol in hand. Holes poppin' through the door from the other side. I start firin' through both Marcus an' the door from my side.

I'm caught by one of the .38s in my right side. Throws me on the ground, an' all I can see is white for half a second. Force my head to look up again. Kid's almost on top of me now, an' I point an' fire 'bout six times. From the light in the office, I can see a coupl'a holes open up in him. One in the neck, an' another'n in the stomach. He's on the ground an' squirmin'. I try gettin' on my feet, but the pain gets worse when I move. Blocks out everything else, an' I feel kinda like I'm floatin'. I know I need to check it. But I cain't look down at it. Cain't.

You know what I do? That pain's startin' to change the way I feel. There's this other feller under my skin that's gotta get out. That Wowzer. Gotta claw his way right through. I can feel him movin 'round under there. Wantin' to tear his way out. Feel his claws pryin' at that hole in my ribs, from on the inside. I'm gonna lay back an' pass out if'n I don't do somethin'.

I jam my thumb into the hole an' twist it. That rubber glove squeaks on the blood an' bone. Help him to pry it open. As I dig my thumb in, the pain tears strips of my skin away. His black fur is under it. That pain peels me away like peelin' a apple. All that's left is that Wowzer. Breathin' heavy. Smellin' blood everywhere. He gets up from the floor, an' I just watch. Then after a moment, I realize I'm lookin' through his eyes. Look down at where the paws are, an' just see yellow gloves. My own skin on the arms where there should be black fur. His breath is my breath. That saliva on his teeth is on mine. His motion is my motion. Cain't worry over it, 'cause there ain't no way to tell no difference no more.

I'm on my feet, but leaned way over to the right. I'm leakin', I can see. Not quick, no drops on the floor yet, but my jacket's soakin' through. Breathin' hurts somethin' horrible. I walk over to where Marcus is layin' on the floor. His legs is holdin' the door open, an' I see the holes through the steel-wrapped wood-core door. Some from my side. Some from the kid's.

Marcus is breathin'. He's got blood comin' from his gut. Coughs up some dark mess as I walk up. Winces, an' then strains his muscles to try an' reach his gun. The .38 he had in his hand as he was walkin' out. Dropped it, an' now is layin' on it. Coughs again.

Get up close an' take his .38. Throw it down the aisle. Put my Sig Sauer to his left thigh, an' pull the trigger. Blows a hole through it, an' he screams an' cries. Watch for it. Bright red blood starts squirtin' out an' then beads on the wax-sealed concrete floor. I take the plugs outta my ears an' stick 'em in my pocket. Look the fat man over. Me an' Marcus was real tight awhile back. Thick as crows at a hog-killin'.

"That's it there, buddy," I say. "Femoral artery. Maybe got a minute 'fore you black out. Probably less."

"Call a ambulance, Jerry," he wheezes. Looks up at me, goin' pale. Wide eyes.

"No time for that. You dog meat, buddy," I say. "Tell me who it was got you killed. You do this on your own, or did somebody put you in it?"

Coughs some more, spittin' out more of the dark blood. That bright kind from his leg's gettin' less now. Slowin' up.

"Neither of us got all day, hoss," I say. "Tell me if there was some other'n got you in on it. I gotta know."

Closes his eyes. Coughs again, forcin' that dark blood out his nose.

"Just done what I was told," he says. "All I done was what I was told."

Cain't hardly walk, but I gotta get it done. Go into his office an' grab his laptop from the bottom desk drawer. Then back in the adjoined room where the computers is. 'Bout twenty monitors in all, each hooked up to the central hard drive that records all the surveillance video from all the warehouses. I'm gonna hear the cops pretty soon. I unplug the main unit from the monitors an' the power strips an' tuck it under my arm. Then I head back out to the warehouse floor an' walk down the aisle to my rental. Toss the laptop an' hard drive in the trunk. Bounces offa Freddie's body, an' he moans an' wiggles some. Drive up to the big door. Gettin' out 'bout kills me. Notice my pants are startin' to feel wet from the soakin'. Open the big overhead door. Drive up to the gate. Startin' to get a little dizzy again. Don't know if that's from pain or blood loss.

Stop at the gate an' get out again. Have to brace myself on the door frame as I go inside the guard shack. Hit the button to open the fence. Stumble back to the car an' get in. Peel outta the gravel an' offa the property. Vision's goin' white ever' five seconds or so. Cain't see to drive.

I make it the three blocks down to Lafayette an' park outside the diner I sent Maggie to. Move over to the passenger seat, gettin' blood on the gearshift, my side burnin' an' a searin' the whole time. Pull my cell phone outta the glove compartment. Open it an' find her number. Press send.

Told her walk, don't run, outta the diner. Pay the check an' leave, don't hurry. Said I just needed her to drive me someplace. Then she's done. She can take a plane back to Memphis or wherever. For right now, I said, need her to drive 'cause I'm blackin' out some.

"Fuck, Jerry," she says, openin' up the driver's-side door an' lookin' inside. Sees the blood on the gearshift an' armrest. Right away she leans in an' makes me open up my light jacket so's she can see.

While she was payin' the check I called Tom. Said I needed somebody to fix up a Gee-Ess-Dubya, but I couldn't go to the hospital. Tom said he'd call back in two minutes.

"What kinda weapon an' from how far away," she asks, lookin' up at me. "Handgun?"

"A thirty-eight, an' from maybe twenty-five feet."

"Bullshit. Not enough damage," she says. "From twenty-five feet, you'd be bleedin' out both sides."

"Went through a solid wood door on its way to me."

Phone rings an' I open it up right away. Maggie takes off her jacket an' rolls it up into a ball. Presses it on the hole in my ribs an' my sight gets fuzzy from the pain.

"You need to get to the hospital, Jerry," she says. "There's no fuckin' around with this, you know?"

"The thirty-eight'll place me at the scene, honey," I say, "an' I left my blood back there. I go to a hospital, then I go to prison or worse. Got it?"

I put the phone to my ear.

"Guy I knew from back when I's on narco," Tom says, "he done work for a coupl'a Big Cal's boys awhile back. Still has a clinic. Wants you to come in the back-alley entrance. You got a pen for the address?"

Dig 'round in the glove box an' find a ballpoint. Write it down on my hand. Still got the gloves on, so it's blue ink on yellow rubber.

"You're not holdin' it right," Maggie says after I hang up. First she takes my phone. Sets it on the dash. Then she leans in an' takes the jacket offa the wound.

"See, it's still bleedin' pretty good," she says. "I might could make somethin' work if you got one of those zip ties you put on that Jose last night."

"In my bag on the floor in the back," I say. She nods an' leans over the seat. I watch the gap 'tween her blouse an' skirt. She unzips the bag. Roots 'round in it for a bit. Comes back over the seat with the plastic tie in her hand.

"I'll come 'round to the other side," she says. "Get a better angle to work with." She opens the door an' gets out.

Shuts it. Walks 'round in front an' comes to the other side. Rubbin' her temples on the way. Opens my door an' squats down by me. Sees my gun stickin' outta my pocket. Takes it out an' sets it in the bottom of the door frame.

"Why isn't your seat belt on?" she asks me.

"'Cause I just moved over," I say. She reaches up an' takes the top part of the buckle an' stretches it 'cross me. Leans over me an' grabs the bottom part. Struggles with it for just a minute while my sight's goin' fuzzy again.

Then I hear the zip tie.

Maggie gets up an' moves back, grabbin' the phone offa the dash on her way out the door. Picks up the gun from the bottom of the door frame. Moves a few feet back an' just looks at me a second.

"What'd you do?" I ask. She just shakes her head. Don't say nothin'. I look down at the seat belt buckle. She took the top end an' zip-tied it through the belt to the bottom end below where the buckle is. So now I'm stuck in the seat.

"How come you done that?" I ask her. "All you gotta do is drive me to that clinic. Then you can go. How's come you done that?"

"And then what, Jer?" she says, lookin' right at me. "After that. If you live. Then what? You'll just come an' find me. Said so yourself the other night. That's why you were willin' to put me on that bus. 'Cause you knew you'd just come an' find me."

"What're you doin', baby?" I ask her. "Gee-Ess-Dubya in my side that's still bleedin' pretty good. You want me to die, huh?"

She just looks down at the concrete parkin' lot. Shakes her head. I struggle a little against the belt, but it hurts so damn bad, I come to tears an' just 'bout piss myself.

"Jesus fuckin' Christ, Maggie," I say. "You're gonna fuckin' kill me? Right fuckin' here?"

She don't look up at me no more. Just rocks a little on her heels, a huggin' her knees. I watch her move for a minute. Startin' to feel a little lighter.

Here it is, then. She fixed it so's I cain't move an' I'm gonna bleed out here in my seat. What's this mean? She's killin' me, an' I oughtta be pissed. But I hain't, much.

"Okay, hon. Then listen up," I say. "You'll wanna cut away that zip tie. Prints. An' then there's whatever you touched on your side. Mine, too, 'cause you also rode on this side today."

She looks up at me. Her eyes are red now, too.

"You gonna wanna wipe it all down. I mean everythin', baby. The steerin' wheel. Gear shift. Panels inside the doors. Window control buttons. Radio. Blinker. Buckles on both seat belts. AC knobs. Whole instrument panel, I'd recommend."

"Shut up, Jerry," she says. "Or I'll close the door an' leave you alone."

"Don't forget that bag in the back. Prints on the zipper. An' you already got my gun. Wipe that down an' get ridda that pretty quick. Throw it in a dumpster or somethin'. Also the thirty-two. That'd be a good idea."

"I said shut up, Jer."

"I don't want you to get caught, baby. I love you, get it? Hain't mad at you. Too fuckin' tired for that. Feelin' too light. Just don't get caught's all. 'Cause it sucks."

She stands up an' comes to the door. Puts her hand on the top edge to shut it.

"An' the phone. Take out the battery. That's important. When I don't call Tom back, he'll try an' get holda me. When he cain't, he'll have somebody he knows run my number through they computer an' locate it. They can do that even if it's turned off. But not when the battery's taken out. So 'member the battery."

She slams the door shut. I watch her stick my Sig Sauer in her purse an' walk back toward the diner. She don't go inside, though. 'Cause of the way I'm slumped, I can see her in the side-view mirror. She sets on the edge of the brick flower bed. Takes her cigarettes outta her purse an' lights one up. Has to flick it several times. Hands must be shaky.

I have a minute to set an' think for the first time today. She looks at her watch. I like that she still wears a watch. Lotsa folks don't do that now, 'cause of cell phones. But she does to take folks' pulse. Part of her job. She don't wanna understand that this mess is part of *my* job. This is the shit that happens when people don't wanna take direction. When folks wanna run they own show an' don't respect nobody's authority. You end up tied to your car, leakin' out a hole in your side, your girl just settin' over there watchin you, waitin' for you to die so's she can get on with her day.

You probably knew I'd end up thisaway. Gettin' light again. Eyes cain't focus. After what I seen today, I don't even know what'll happen now. I seen the Wowzer come out, an' I seen him take my own place, right where I's standin'. 'Memberin' what I done when I's a kid. How I'd walk back through them woods. Lookin' for him. Lookin' for that Wowzer.

Eyes come back into focus in time to see Maggie puttin' her cigarette butt out in the flower bed an' look at her watch again. Crosses her legs. Then uncrosses 'em. Folds her arms up under her breasts. Unfolds 'em an' rubs her temples.

Slips off one shoe an' scratches the sole of her foot with the toe of her other shoe. Crosses her legs another time. I'm fadin' out again. Think of Puerto Vallarta. Rubbin' sunblock on her shoulders. Slippin' my fingers under the straps of her one-piece bathin' suit. Seein' that iguana sunnin' hisself. Watchin' seaweed get carried up the beach with the tide. Tequila still on my lips. Grain of salt under my tongue.

She thought it'd be funny to bury me in the sand. Somethin' fun to do after drinkin' a couple too many margaritas. So that's where I am now. Down in the sand. Weight on me. Givin' a little burden to breathe. Lookin' right up into the sky. Her face comin' into view now'n then. Feels nice an' cool inside the sand. Maggie laughin' at me while she piles more sand on top. Some gets in my face, but I don't care. I just like hearin' her laugh while she does it.

Just stay here.

"Where's the address?" Maggie asks. She's opened the door an' is leanin' over me from the driver's side.

"Mmm. Writ on my glove," I say. Hold up my arm a little, but it don't stay where I want it. She looks down at the address. Don't need no directions 'cause Fayetteville's her home. Closes the driver's door. Starts up the car. Puts the car in reverse an' backs outta the space.

"What's happening now, Jerry," she says, "is that your body has gone into shock from the wound. You're not gettin' enough oxygen to the tissues an' organs. You've got some blood loss, but the bleedin' looks to have slowed down. But you can die from the lack of oxygen. So I need you to stay awake. Try an' take deep breaths, okay? Do not, Jerry, do not take them fast or you'll hyperventilate. Just long an' slow breaths. Got it?"

I tell her okay. Watch her drive through the city. Down Lafayette an' cut over to Dickson Street by takin' St. Charles Avenue.

"Talk to me, Jerry," she raises her voice a little. "You need to stay awake."

"Okay," I say. "I's thinkin' of that time you covered me up in sand."

"What else?" she asks. Tryin' to keep me at talkin'.

"An' how much I wanna go back to that beach."

"Uh-huh. An' what else, Jerry?"

"How come you came back? To the car I mean."

"Shut up," she says. "Just talk on somethin' else for now."

"Okay," I say, tryin' to keep my eyes open. "You know that bullet I said went through the door first? That one that got me?"

"Uh-huh. What about it?"

"I think it went through another feller first. Maybe just his arm. The upper part. Cain't get that outta my mind, though. Punched through the door, then Marcus. Then into me."

South on Locust Avenue. Don't hurt as much anymore when she takes them sharp turns.

"An' you gotta take that turn half a block 'fore Spring street, so right up here," I say.

She pulls the car into the alley, an' I tell her to keep goin' till the fourth door down the block. She stops an' gets out. Knocks on the door. Feller opens it right up.

Doc Elias McKinley, white male, 75, 5'8", 155 lbs, white hair, blue eyes, steps out into the alley, shakes Maggie's hand, an' waves at me as he walks up to the car. Got his lab coat on already. Maggie gets the door an' helps him carry me out. She's got my legs an' I watch her wrestle with trippin' up the back step to his clinic. Then when we get inside, I see her eyes get real wide. There's the sound of dogs barkin' everywhere.

"What's your blood type, Jerry?" Doc McKinley asks me, after they set me on the steel table in the operatin' room. 'Course it ain't all that long, an' my legs dangle off the edge.

"No, you're not gonna do this," Maggie says.

"My dear, it's perfectly fine. I've done favors just like this many times."

"But on a gunshot wound?" she yells.

"What's your blood type, Jerry?" he asks, pickin' up the phone on the wall.

"O-Neg," Maggie answers for me. "But neither the blood bank or the hospital will deliver human blood to a veterinary clinic."

"The great thing about undergraduate interns is, they all know each other from their classes, whether general biology or organic chemistry. One of mine will just run two blocks up to the campus health center and ask a friend a favor. As I said, Doctor Gordon, I've done this many times before. Have the blood units here in thirty minutes. He's not in too dire a condition. Look, dear, it's simple biology, whatever the species. Just put this blanket over him to help with the circulation. Looks as if he's gone into shock."

"Yes, Doctor," Maggie says, "I know how to treat shock. But I'm not going to let you operate on a *Homo sapien*. For Christ sake."

"What's your field?" he asks.

"Emergency medicine," she says.

"Well, if you'd like do it yourself, you're more than welcome. I'll assist."

He hands her the blanket to put on me. I can hear them dogs a barkin' in the kennel in the back, an' I don't even care none. Maggie spreads the blanket over me.

She goes over to look at the tray of instruments he's got set out. Scratches her head. Goes to warsh her hands. I hear her snap on her gloves.

"How much does he weigh?" Doc McKinley asks. "For the anesthesia."

"About one-sixty or so," she says. "I think."

"It'll have to do. I don't think he'll fit on the scale."

I grab Maggie's wrist from under the blanket. She moves over toward my head an' looks down at me. Hasn't pulled up her face mask yet.

"Cain't gas me," I say. Squeeze her wrist.

"What?" she says, wrinklin' up her forehead. "Why not?"

"I'm not done workin'. Tonight, I mean."

"What the hell do you mean, not done workin'?" she asks me.

"One last fucker to get tonight," I say. "An' it has to be tonight."

"Jerry, you can't go out again tonight. It's not possible."

"If'n I don't," I say. "Then I'm dead by mornin'. He's gonna kill me an' Tom both less'n we get him first. I got no time to be knocked out by gas. Just dig the little fucker out, an' we'll leave it at that."

"I'm not operatin' on you without anesthesia, Jerry," she says.

"Nobody's puttin' me under tonight," I say. "Not gonna happen. Need to be out findin' somebody in two hours. Cain't be groggy."

Maggie just shakes her head. She pulls back the blanket. Cuts open my shirt with scissors. Reaches for a bottle of alcohol. Unscrews the cap.

"No anesthesia, then," she says. "Gotta sterilize it, though."

She dumps the bottle over on the wound. I clench ever' muscle in my body. Grit my teeth an' shut my eyes. Kick my legs an' make fists with my fingers an' toes.

Then it's just black.

CHAPTER FIFTEEN:

Tom an' Jerry burn out the crowded bottom.

"YOU AWAKE YET?" Maggie asks. I can smell coffee. Hear her sippin' at it. Hear Tom talkin' with Doc McKinley out in the hall.

"How's come I feel so weird?" I ask.

"Let's see. That could be from the bullet that was lodged just under your shattered rib. The shock you went into. The fact that I was just diggin' around inside you with instruments unfamiliar to me. Or it could be the amphetamine I just gave you."

"What's Tom doin' here?" I ask.

"He left right after you called him, apparently." Sips her coffee.

I try to set up, an' wince a little. Maggie helps me get swung over on the edge.

"You're lucky," she says. "You said the bullet went through a door. Maybe someone else. An' if it was his upper arm like you said, it could also have hit the humerus. Must have slowed it down enough to reduce impact damage. Very low energy. Minor wound. Only needed the one unit of blood. But we need to watch the bleedin', Jerry, you understand me?"

"What'd you give me? What kinda amphetamine?"

"Better'n Sudafed, but not quite meth," she says. "Had to improvise with what was here in the animal clinic. S'posed to be a mood stabilizer for dogs. How funny is that?" she laughs. "Elias knows his shit. The amount I gave you should get you through whatever you have left to do tonight. Probably start to crash hard in about four to six hours. Till then you won't really notice the pain."

"Thanks," I say.

"I'm worried about the stitches, though. You move around too much an' they'll tear. You'll start up bleedin' again. An' amped up like that, you probably won't notice it either."

"You didn't answer me 'fore when I asked you why you come back," I say. "I mean, you had me cold. Why'd you come back?"

She rests a arm on my shoulder an' leans a little on the side that ain't got a hole in it. Sips her coffee. Leans in to smell my neck.

"'Cause I'm not quite like you, Jer," she says. "I couldn't just not feel anything."

"Did you feel somethin' with that Candice?"

"Different. That's what I didn't count on. With her, I just did it an' didn't think about it till after it was done. With you, I had to set an' wait."

"So it'd been different if'n you'd done it quick."

"I don't think so. With her, I didn't feel hardly anything. Like I didn't even blink. She got exactly what the fuck she deserved. All I did was a little charity work."

"An' with me?"

"I couldn't stop thinkin' about the little boy tied up to that tree in the rain. Prayin' to Jesus to make it stop," she says. "An' I kept thinkin' about how you said you'd never let the Wowzer get me, an' how you probably meant it to the best of your ability. An' it wasn't your intent that failed when you put your hands on me, just your ability."

She leans her head on mine.

"At first I thought I could go through with it," she says. "But I didn't figure how different it'd be with someone I knew."

"Hey there, hoss," Tom says, comin' in through the door. "Doc Maggie here get ya all fixed up good?"

"She fixed me good, all right," I say.

"Wanna give us a minute to talk shop, dear?" Tom says to her. She nods an' pats me on the shoulder on her way out, but don't look back.

"So what the doin's?" Tom asks once the door closes.

"We're gonna kill Big Cal tonight," I say.

"What the *fuck* are you talkin' about, Jer?" he yells.

"He done it," I say. "He done it all. Set the whole thing in motion. Give orders to everybody. Marcus an' then on down the line to Ronnie. He had me followed an' Maggie staked out. He was gonna take her if'n I didn't do what they wanted. But I got to 'em first, 'fore they had the chance to do nothin'."

"Slow down, Jer. First off, *I* told Cal to have you followed. You can understand my decision on that, given how you's actin' then."

"But did he tell you 'bout them stayin' behind to keep watch on her?"

"No, he did not. But then we don't even know what all that mess was 'bout. None of them ever connected to Cal, no matter how many known associates I tried. None of them knew anybody he knew. Cal's a dead end, Jer."

"Marcus said so. He told me right 'fore. Said he done what he's told."

"That don't mean shit, Jer. You know that. You been followin' tattoos 'round like there was some meanin' to it, Jer. You ask that fuckin' kid Freddie where he got his?"

"He didn't know what he's talkin' 'bout," I say, shakin' my head. "Just gibberish."

"See, that's what I mean, Jer. These kids get high an' do stupid shit. No reason for it. Freddie got that tattoo probably with the rest of them."

"Then how's come he had the same tattoo as Jimmy?" I say. Tom gives me a serious look. "Wanna go out to the trunk an' ask him? Probably he'll just give more gibberish."

"Didn't know Jimmy had that same tattoo," he says. Backs away from me. "That puts a whole other light on it. You said you got Freddie in your trunk right now? Ain't shittin' me?"

"Nossir. He's out there right this very minute."

"May have to pull him out an' ask a coupl'a questions. What kinda gibberish you say he gave you?"

"Revelation stuff," I say. "From the Bible. No, wait. Weren't the Revelation. It was Isaiah. 'Member 'cause I looked it up later. Chapter six of Isaiah. Seraphims an' burnin' lips with a live coal. Thine iniquity. Trippy shit."

Tom backs away from the table I'm settin' on. Leans back on the metal sinks an' makes 'em creak. Stares right at me cold. Plucks at his beard.

"What did you say, Jerry?" he asks.

"I said—"

"I heard what the fuck you said. Just can't believe it," he says.

"What's that mean?"

"Means we're killin' Big Cal tonight," Tom says, lookin' down at the floor.

"Cal marked all his snitches when we worked narco together. Like brandin' cattle so there's no question whose property they is. When I worked with him last, he was givin' 'em all snake tattoos on they shoulders. But they was all the same. Guess he's changed the symbol. But he ain't changed the ritual."

"How's that? What ritual?"

"Cal was serious 'bout workin' with his snitches. I mean he *worked* 'em. But he rewarded 'em in return. They got holda some power. Let 'em hurt other folks. Even up scores. Take over rivals' territories. Shit that made 'em loyal as hell. That's part of how we got offered the jobs we ended up gettin'. Sanhedrin saw these two boys gettin' fellers in line an' decided to recruit us. Cal for the Fayetteville work, an' me for this end. But Cal, back in the day, he had a whole initiation ritual he'd make a perp go through to be his snitch."

"When he tattooed 'em?"

"After. First, he showed up at they house in the middle of the night. Put a sack over they heads. Took 'em to some basement somewhere. I only know this 'cause I had to help him with it once. An' only once."

"What'd he do?"

"Made 'em swear on they families that they's givin' themselves over fully. The perp'd be tied up in a chair.

Hood taken off. Head taped to a board or a beam 'hind 'em. Then one of Cal's helpers'd get the perp to open his mouth. Get his tongue pinched into a pair of cloth-wrapped pliers. Pull it out just far enough. Then Cal'd take a piece of metal he'd heated. Straightened clothes-hanger was what I seen. Walk up slow an' recite them verses from Isaiah. 'Bout the Seraphim. Coal on the lips. Then he'd burn the perp's tongue."

"Fuck."

"You're tellin' me, kid. He didn't burn it for long. Didn't want it to swell up too much. Just enough to make 'em squirm an' cry a little. Told me he tried the lips at first, like in the Bible verse, but them lips scarred. Mighta drawn too much attention. Tongues heal like nothin' else. An' he said that he liked the symbol. Tongue seemed more appropriate for snitches."

"So these guys I been seein'. They was all Big Cal's snitches at one time or another?"

"Reckon so. But he probably recast 'em when he got a new crop of kids. Fucker's been tryin' to run his own side-show. I won't abide that. Neither'll the Sanhedrin."

"But them fellers followin' Maggie in Memphis didn't look like no snitches," I say. "They don't usually look like cops. More like Freddie mosta the time."

"Probably them fellers was from the security company Cal uses to guard the warehouses. The same'n you used to work for back then."

"So, then," I say, "sounds like we got a crawded bottom. All filled up with dead trees an' just rottin' away. Too many standin' in one place for any others to grow."

"Sounds like."

"Reckon we gonna have to burn it out," I say.

"Reckon so, Jerry."

I open up the trunk an' help Nappy Freddie MacDonald out. Pull the tape away from his eyes an' mouth quick so it don't hurt too much. Walk him in through the back door an' into the room where they done the surgery.

"Ready to get paid, buddy?" I ask him. He looks over at me an' just nods, blinkin'.

I grab the trimmer an' click it on. He backs away from me. Puts up his hands to block.

"What you need that for?"

"Your hair gotta come off," I say. "Nobody can recognize you. Cal sees them dreads an' he's gonna know who's come for him. Don't think he'll have time to see 'em, but still, you never can be sure."

"How much money you talkin' about?" Freddie asks.

"Right around a quarter mil," I say.

He nods. Puts his arms down by his sides. Looks down at the slick tile floor. I grab a handful of his blond dreads an' lift 'em up to run the trimmer near his scalp.

"How's come I heard all them gunshots back there?" he asks.

"Folks gettin' restless nowadays," I say. Pull off the first handful of dreads an' let 'em drop on the floor. Grab another'n an' get to shearin'. "We gonna set things back in order."

Freddie's got a clean scalp now. Settin' in the front seat of the rental car out in the alley. Got him buckled in an' the radio turned to the station he likes. Some kinda surfer-alt-rock shit. Light a joint for him, just a little'n, an' let him set in the car an' bob his head for a coupl'a minutes. Back inside the animal clinic, I find Maggie.

"What the hell do you think you're doin'?" I ask. She's got a bag that she's puttin' some of Doc McKinley's instruments in. An' she's got a little blue-an'-white cooler under her arm 'bout the size of my school lunchbox when I's a kid.

"Tom said you were goin' outside of town. Out in the woods a ways."

"Sure. An' you're stayin' here. Or better yet, hon, you're gettin' on a bus to Memphis."

Shakes her head.

"You can't keep at this, Jer," she says. "What you don't understand is that if you tear those stitches, you'll bleed slow, but not as slow as before. The wound only gets bigger. An' doped up like you are, you won't feel it till you're bled out."

"So you wanna be right there to sew it up," I say. She nods. "What's in the cooler?"

"One unit of O-Neg."

Afore we headed out, Tom went on a errand. I'd asked him what he knew 'bout Big Cal's house. Said Cal'd just moved last year, an' he'd only been to the new place one time. Maybe fifteen miles southeast of Fayetteville. Just north of Highway 16, old Huntsville Road, an' right 'cross White River. Nice little acreage, only not a farm. Right out in the middle of the God-damn woods. Wonder if he thought he'd be safe there.

Tom's errand was to go in his car to two different Walmarts. Pick up four ten-gallon gas jugs at one, an' a insecticide sprayer at the other'n. When he got back, he honked the horn, an' we followed him outta downtown. He calls me while Maggie's drivin' an' I'm in the backseat.

"You got a scanner with you?" he asks.

"Nossir," I say. "What, they talkin' 'bout Marcus's warehouse already?"

"Not a fuckin' word, Jer. You check what time the night shift comes in?" he asks.

"That was the night shift. They'd just got there. Far's I 'member, the only person that wasn't gonna be there all night was the janitor. Mornin' shift don't come in till six a.m."

"Well, there's nothin' on the band 'bout it. Either nobody heard the shots, or nobody cared. Point is, Jer, Cal probably don't know we're comin'. Nothin' to tip him off."

We follow Tom offa Highway 16 onto 74, then onto Hummingbird Road right quick. Drive north, an' Tom pulls onto unmarked blacktop just past General Road. We drive down it for near a mile. Pass a couple houses near the highway, but no more as we get further back in the woods. On the left, the side that goes on down to the riverbank, a clearin' opens up. Tom shuts off his headlamps. Maggie does the same. At the edge of the clearin', where the road turns north an' heads back into woods, Tom stops his car. Right in the middle of the road. Maggie stops a little behind him.

He gets out an' opens his trunk. I tell Freddie to stay in the front seat for now. Maggie gets out with me, but she don't go over to Tom. Just stays put, settin' on the hood watchin' us.

"It's gonna take a little longer," he says, "'Cause we gotta be careful 'bout the whole thing. We go into the woods here, an' head past his house an' up the ridge a bit, then back so's we can come in from behind. Got it?"

"I think I get it," I say. "You bring your Benelli?"

"Fuck yeah, I did," he says, pickin' it up outta the trunk. "What'd you use for Marcus?"

"Nothin' I wanna take into that house with me. Barrel's too damn long, an' it'd be hell to maneuver. What else you got in the trunk there?"

"You ain't got nothin' else?" he asks.

"There's that Sig Sauer that Maggie took offa me, but I don't wanna use that'n, just in case the Fayetteville cops find the warehouse 'fore we got a chance to clean it up. They'd match this'n here with that'n there."

"Jesus Christ, Jerry, *that's* what you're worried about? How 'bout worryin' how many *guards* he got up there."

"Or how we gonna deal with his family," I say.

"No, he sent the kids to camp an' his wife to stay with her mother right when them two fellers went missin' in Memphis an' Jimmy didn't report nothin' back. I couldn't figure how come he done it then, but it makes sense now."

"So it's just him an' whoever he got with him."

Tom reaches into the trunk again an' up under the spare tire. "There's my spare," he says. Hand comes out holdin' a Beretta 9 mm.

"That the ninety-two?" I ask, an' he nods. "Give that'n to Freddie."

"You know you gotta wait until I call," I say. "Then you can move the rental here up the drive to the house. But stay in the car, don't get out."

"Okay. How long do you think it's gonna be?" Maggie asks me. I take her purse outta the front seat an' pull the Sig Sauer out. Set down on the seat an' eject the clip. Hand the Beretta over to Freddie an' nod to the door. He takes it an' gets outta the rental. Reach back to the glove box an' open it up, take out the box of 9 mm rounds. Then gloves I peeled off earlier. Dig the tape outta my pocket. Dizzy ain't quite the word for what I am now. Kinda like them clay-animal cartoons. Stop motion where you can just see how jerky it is. Little in-between bits missin'. My side don't hurt none. Throbs, but don't give no pain. Hands a tinglin'. Startin' to feel antsy from the drug Maggie gave me. Like tappin' your feet in class when you gotta go to the bathroom. I look back over at Maggie, blink, an' give her a answer.

"It's gonna take probably twenty minutes to walk 'round there, then who the fuck knows how long to figure exactly what we gonna do. Then a coupl'a minutes to do it. So I'd say if'n you ain't heard from nobody in forty minutes, get back in the car an' go."

"All right," she says. "I don't wanna, but I know you're serious."

Walkin' up through the woods, I think about her. Tom's behind on my left. Freddie's on my right. An' lucky me gets to be on point. Trudgin' through the bushes an' briars an' steppin' over rotted logs. She took my hands 'fore I left.

"Do you know why I'm helpin' you, Jerry?"

"I think so. 'Cause you know that them'ns bad folks an' got to be put down."

"Sure. Maybe. But why I'm helpin' you tonight's got nothin' to do with good or bad, deservin' or not. It's that they're aimin' to put you down. An' the more I think on it, the more I figure that just won't do."

I smiled to her an' turned to leave, but she held my hands tight. I turned back to look at her.

"I couldn't have done it," she said. "Not even if it'd been quick. I couldn't have."

"Truth be told," I said, squeezin' her hands back. "It'da been the easy way out for me."

"What do you mean?" she asks.

"I mean, Maggie," I said, lettin' go her hands. "Plain an' simple, it'd been a hell of a lot easier to die in the car like that than to never see you again."

She nodded. "Yeah. I figured as much."

We're settin' 'bout ten feet back from the tree line on the north side of Big Cal's property. We circled 'round to get a view from all sides an' came back up here, watchin' the back porch. Seen a feller out on the porch, smokin' with a automatic rifle in his lap. Looked like same kinda Chinese AK-47 that Jose has, with the stock folded up. Feller on the back porch has a shotgun. Cain't tell what kind. It's a hundred feet from the tree line to the house. Short grass on a manicured lawn. No cover. Just a tool shed 'hind the house.

"How's your accuracy at a hundred feet?" Tom whispers to me.

"We gotta know what's comin' next, though. Once we start, we better damn well get it done right off."

I whisper my plan into Tom's ear. He nods an' hands the shotgun to Freddie, takes back the Beretta.

Freddie starts runnin' from the tree line an' heads for the back porch. I watch him from 'bout a hundred an' fifty feet further down toward the fronta the house. Cain't see what that feller on the back porch does, but I figure he raises up his shotgun pretty quick an' points it. Soon's he does that, I reckon, Tom starts in on him with the Beretta.

When I hear Tom's shots, I watch the feller on the front porch stand up an' bring his assault rifle up into position. So I start on him. Hundred feet's a good ways off for a pistol, an' I miss the first two shots. No rush. I squeeze 'em off ever' coupl'a seconds. Third shot gets him in the left thigh as he's turnin' 'round to aim at me in the trees. He lunges forward a little but don't fall, don't lose the rifle. Opens up holes in the front lawn. My fourth shot gets him in the gut, an' that puts him down. I come outta the tree line an' head for the porch.

When I get there, hop up on the porch. My vision gets them glowin' little spots on the edges. I look down at the feller, an' he's still movin', tryin' to raise his rifle. He's lyin' flat on the floor, so I stomp on his throat hard an' quick. Pick up his rifle as he's gaggin' on blood an' reachin' his arms up. I put the Sig Sauer in my pocket. Move over to the front door, crouch down, an' wait. Hard to hear inside right after that gunfire. Couldn't wear earplugs 'cause we had to time it.

Listen. Sounds on the stairs. Shades come up, an' I can see a shadow cast out 'cross the painted boards. The shadow disappears as the sound I been waitin' for gets loud enough to hear. Freddie's kickin' at the back door. Just like we said.

I move back from the front door an' over to the railin'. Peek into the front bay window, rifle up. Right off I see movement, but it's gone 'fore I can aim. I can see the staircase. The back of the couch by the window. Can see through the livin' room into the hallway. That's where he went, through the hallway an' turned the corner. Tom said it was the kitchen that led to the back porch, so that's where he'd be now. Freddie's still kickin' away.

I cain't kick in the front door 'cause it looks like the solid oak kind. I *can* pick up that porch swing, though, an' toss it through the bay window. I move over an' start unhookin' them chains. Freddie give another kick on the back door. Pick up the swing by one end.

Then I hear the blast from inside the house. Toss the swing through the window. My vision goes white for half a second after throwin' it. There's another shot from the kitchen as the swing crashes through the glass an' tumbles on the livin' room floor. When I'm sure my vision's back, I jump in through the bay window an' roll in the glass on the carpet. Check the hallway. Look up the stairs. Then when I look back, Big Cal's comin' down the hallway in boxers an' a white T-shirt. He's holdin' a gun, but I don't see what kind 'cause them spots in my eyes is comin' back. I point the rifle over, an' he leaps back as I squeeze the trigger. All I hit is the corner by the kitchen.

Get up offa the floor an' move 'hind the corner of the hallway. If he goes outside, Tom's got him cold. If he comes down the hall, I'll drop him. Rub at my eyes an' the spots get worse for a second an' then clear up.

There's another pop, an' I get dust an' paint chips in my right ear. Came from up the stairs. I swing 'round an' point the rifle up at a white female, 19 or 20, 5'8", 110 lbs, long blonde hair, in a blue satin bathrobe holdin' a shaky .38 revolver. I fire a coupl'a short bursts up the stairs at her that rip her legs from under her an' throw blood all over the wallpaper an' banister. Then the corner beside me explodes from Cal's shot, an' now I reckon it's probably a shotgun. I swing back 'round an' level the rifle at the entry to the hallway. Nothin'.

Cain't hear shit now. I'll hear it if'n Tom fires, but he's not firin'. There's just the ringin' in my ears. Little pinpoint spots pulsin' on my vision. Fingers tinglin' like a motherfucker. He's gotta be watchin' the hallway. Fuck this. I walk back to the mirror on the stair closet above the antique wood warshstand. Throw it on the floor an' watch it shatter. Pick up one big shard an' head back to the corner. Look back up the stairs at the woman. Blood on the walls an' streaked down the spindles, creepin' down the steps through the carpet, but no movement. I slide my back down the wall into a crouch. Hold the mirror out just 'round the corner. Nothin'. Fuck.

I crawl slow 'round the corner, waitin' for the shotgun blast. Still nothin'. I get up an' move slow up to the corner leadin' into the kitchen. I look at the back door an' see the big hole through the top panel, right 'bout head level where Freddie woulda been. Look at the door to the garage. Cain't tell nothin'. Then I notice the door on the other side of the kitchen's just a hair open. That's gotta be the one to the basement. Didn't go into the garage 'cause he ain't got no keys.

Walk over to the basement door an' get ready to open it from the knob side. Think of all he could have down there.

Whether the rifle I got now coulda come from down there on a rack with several others. Catch the knob an' push it to open up quiet, 'cause it ain't latched. Wait for the poppin' from down the stairs. Nothin'. Drop down into a crouch an' get up to the top of the stairs just inside the door. Light's off. Switch's right there next to the wood handrail over on the other side of the little landin'. Probably he didn't hear the door open. Turn that light on an' he knows right where I am. But he'da seen the light from the kitchen anyhow. Shit. I hain't goin' down there in the dark.

Unfold the stock on the rifle an' stick it out butt first to click the light, then draw it back. Wait a second. I can hear somethin' down there, but cain't tell from the ringin' what it is. Then the sides of two steps 'bout five feet from me blow up an' splinter on me. I jump back through the door frame an' get back against the wall. One more shot from down the stairs that gets the doorjamb an' blows a piece of moldin' off onto the linoleum floor. There's that peppered look on the edge of the moldin'. Look over at the back door, an' the hole's 'bout twice the size of my head. Two shots at Freddie through the door. One at me in the hall. Two more on the stairs just now. It's a shotgun, an' probably got a four-plus-one load. Shit. I cain't know that. Maybe he reloaded. Or picked up another'n. I cain't know what the fuck he got down there.

I move back through the door an' empty the resta the magazine in the direction the blasts come from. Some cardboard boxes burst pieces of plastic toys on the concrete, an' a rack of old clothes spits rags out the other side. I drop the rifle on the steps an' take out the Sig Sauer from my pocket. Walk down the steps, pistol movin' here an' there. Lookin' for Big Cal's wide face.

Then I see the open window above a empty bookcase. Run over an' get up on the case, peek out the window just in time to see him runnin' away from the house an' go outta sight 'hind the turn in the driveway. I try crawlin' up through the window. Get halfway out when I notice Tom comin' over to me.

"You see where he's headed?" he asks. Reaches his hand down to pull me on through. As my side scrapes on the window frame, my stomach twist up a little. Like maybe I oughtta feel somethin' else that don't register.

"Looks like he's just runnin' down the driveway," I say. "I'll get the fucker. Hain't even got shoes on."

"Maggie's down that way, hoss," he says. He looks down at my side an' says, "Jesus Christ, Jer."

I hain't interested in lookin'. Take to runnin' down the driveway after Big Cal like I'm cuttin' mud.

"Is there anybody else in there?" he yells after me.

"Just a dead woman," I say over my shoulder. "Girlfriend or hooker."

"Not his wife?" he shouts.

"Not less'n he married last year's prom queen. Quit lally-gaggin' me an' get to burnin' it out!" I shout an' take the turn in the drive.

My eyes ain't adjusted to the dark yet, an' I'm runnin' blind. Probably he's goin' down the drive to the clearin'. If he can get 'cross the clearin', then he can wade the river an' come up on the highway an' maybe stop a car. An' Maggie's 'tween him an' the river. He'll see her an' take the car if he even thinks to stop. 'Cause of the curve of the drive, I cain't see him up ahead. This concrete's hell on my ankles, an' it's all downhill so it's hard not to trip. My eyes are gettin' used to the dark. No moon tonight. Rain clouds blockin' everything out. I pull out my cell phone an' punch Maggie's number.

I'm gettin' close to the end of the drive where it opens up from the woods. Her phone's ringin'. Picks up her voice mail after four rings. I press end an' try again after damn near droppin' the phone. Rings once. Then there's gunshots up ahead.

I count five or six pops from where the cars are up ahead. When I get outta the trees an' into the clearin', I see Maggie standin' on the shoulder of the road, pointin' her .32 at the trees to my right. I slip on the gravel shoulder, take a spill, an' slam my head right into the passenger door panel of Tom's car. Dent it pretty good, too.

Maggie comes over to me. She got wide eyes.

"I got him, Jer," she says.

"Where'd he go?" I ask. She points over to the trees.

"I know I got him at least once. I saw him grab at his hip an' limp. So he probably won't be too fast on foot. Saw him go in there."

Woods. Just gray trunks an' a black canopy tonight. I get up to my feet, an' my head feels funny right now. I liketa fall over. Steady myself on the hood of Tom's car.

"Pop the trunk to the rental," I say. She nods an' moves 'round to the driver's side while I head to the back bumper. She pulls the lever, an' the lid goes up. I reach in an' consider takin' the SX-3. Too God-damn bulky. Still.

I have Maggie get the box of shells outta the glove box. She brings 'em 'round to me at the back bumper. In the light comin' from the inside of the trunk, she sees my side.

"Fuck, Jerry. You seen how much you're bleedin'?"

I look, an' from the busted rib on down to my knee, it's a red slick.

"He gets away, I'm dead anyhow," I say. "An' since he seen *you*, it means your ass too, darlin'."

I take the shells an' load 'em in. Chamber a round. Then load the last'n. Dump out the roadside emergency kit on the carpet of the trunk that's got spots of Freddie's blood on it.

"You're not gonna last another ten minutes, bleedin' like that. You'll lose consciousness, Jerry. You're gonna just drop dead out there in the woods," she says. "An' Jerry, I saw a gun in his hand. He has a pistol."

'Course he does. Musta got it from the basement on his way out. I grab what I need from the emergency kit an' stick it in my back pocket. Then stuff a few more shells in my front pockets.

"I'ma kill him 'fore I bleed out," I say. "That's gettin' done tonight."

"Jerry, you don't—" she says. Stops. It's her ass, too, like I said. She cain't argue.

"Just 'member I done that," I say, an' take off a runnin' into the woods.

Ears ain't ringin' so much, now. It's all comin' out, the adrenaline from the shootin' back in the house. The amphetamine she give me a bit ago's spikin'. Runnin' down that drive forced up my heart rate, an' that's makin' me see things. Spots comin' out in my eyes, fadin' away just as fast. My feet are carryin' me over rocks an' mud, dirt an' rotted tree stumps. I cain't hardly feel my legs. Like I hain't doin' the runnin' at all.

Stop an' listen for him. Heart's poundin' in my ears. Take a coupl'a slow breaths an' try to get it under control. Listen for his steps. Cain't hear well enough yet. I look 'round me an' don't see nothin' cep'n tree trunks an' bushes on the ground. Then I catch it.

I take off runnin' to the west. He's movin' through the underbrush up ahead, an' I heard him trip. Maybe it's a hundred feet. Hundred an' fifty. My ears are back, an' I could probably hear him from 'cross the county. I bring up the shotgun to a ready position. Don't wanna fire yet or my ears'll be gone again. Cain't fire until I can see him.

I can feel the Wowzer again. This time he ain't under my skin, like afore. It's like he's all 'round me. I'm under his skin. He's carryin' me along right now. Four feet on the ground 'steada two. I think of Jonah an' the whale, from Sunday School.

I know I'm in the belly of the Wowzer.

My feet are on the ground again, an' I'm tearin' through bushes an' briars an' kudzu. I crush brittle felled branches under my shoes as I run over 'em. I can hear my heartbeat in my ears, an' it's slowed down to a *thump-bump* that's nothin' like what I had back there. I can smell rain in the air an' feel that cool humidity on my skin, collectin' on them little hairs. The way I can see now, it ain't even like it's dark out. Everythin's bright. There's them spots still, but they don't block nothin' out. More like they light it up. Ears pick up Cal's scramblin' through the vines an' bushes. Jump over a log stickin' up outta the ground. Land an' notice the little bitta pain in my side. Just a trifle. Nothin' to make a fuss over.

Look down at the red an' see Jerry leakin' out.

Comin' up on Cal now. Big plump fucker in his white boxers an' T-shirt. Hain't even a challenge. That white T-shirt's
almost too bright to look at in the dark. Hear his breathin'.
Moanin' little bitch at thirty feet. Wheezin' an' gaspin' an' a
coughin'. Limpin' so bad he liketa fall flat. Drop down into
a crouch an' raise up the SX-3. Pull the trigger an' the noise
an' bright flash hurt somethin' awful. Watch Big Cal's body
go tumblin' up ahead.

Get up an' head after him. Just barely hear the screamin'
through ringin' ears. His leg's gone under the right knee.
Watch him as, for a second, he tries crawlin' away. Stops an'
vomits out on the dry leaves. He turns an' points the gun.

Fire again at Cal's right arm an' watch it burst red in
ever' direction an' the pistol get thrown back into the briars. Listen to his screams a moment longer. Stand right over
the bleedin' sweaty fuck an' pass the barrel over his face,
over them fork-tine scars, put it to his lips. Steam sizzles offa
his mouth, an' he twists his head away.

"An' thine iniquity is taken away. Thy sin is purged." But
he cain't hear nothin' through his screams. Don't matter
none. Put the barrel under his chin, right down on his neck.

Pull the trigger twice more. Watch his head roll away
into the briars.

I walk over an' set down by the trunk of the tree nearest
Big Cal's body. Hold the shotgun 'cross my lap. I dig out my
phone an' punch Maggie's number. This time she picks up.

"Jerry? Where are you? Tell me an' I'll come an' get
you," she says.

"Drive up to the house. When we's checkin' it out earlier,
I seen a path that oughtta run near where I am. Probably

there's a four-wheeler in the garage. Seen parts for it in the basement. Bring it down the path an' look for me. You gotta load me an' Cal both up to cart back to the house."

"How will I know what to look for?"

"Be shinin' bright for you, darlin'."

I take the flare from the roadside emergency kit outta my back pocket. Twist off the cap an' set it over to the side. Watch the shadows movin' back in them woods.

While I'm waitin', the rain starts. Like when I's a kid. Couldn't move then 'cause of them ropes. Now I cain't move 'cause there ain't nothin' left in me. My eyes is gettin' dark. Feelin' rain on my skin', but ain't neither cold nor wet.

I can see the Wowzer walkin' back 'tween them trees. That bright red light from the flare's keepin' him at a distance. He weaves in an' outta them trunks, turnin' to look at me ever' now'n then. Little shinin' red spots reflect in his eyes. Circles one way, then back the other, never leavin' my vision completely.

I can hear the four-wheeler comin' down the path. Grumbles like I imagine he would. In a minute I hear Maggie comin' through the undergrowth.

The Wowzer steps back into the trees an' waits.

CHAPTER SIXTEEN:

The Wowzer.

"Tom's sayin' he's gonna call me Jeremiah 'Forklift' Bowden from now on," I say.

"How come?" Maggie asks, then goes back to sippin' her tomato juice.

"'Cause he had to *use* one to move all them bodies when he got back to Marcus's warehouse. Took the ones outta the trunk you helped him load up. Then lined 'em up an' went an' got the forklift they use for them crates. Took a empty crate, lifted up them bodies over it, an' had to get a ladder to go up an' pull 'em down into it."

Maggie just stares at me for a second.

"How many were there?" she asks.

"Um, well. Marcus an' the boys was five. Then them two other fellers an' the gate guard. So that's eight. Then he brought with him Big Cal, Freddie, them two guards, an' that whore in the trunk an' under a blanket in the backseat. So that's five more. Lucky thirteen."

"They find his head, yet?" she asks.

"Hain't been nothin' on the news 'bout it. Reckon some animal come an' took it away."

We're at the lunch counter in a diner 'cross the street from the hospital in Memphis. Same place I watched her from my car a month back. Right now it ain't yet lunch, an' the place is mostly empty. I look down at Maggie's club sandwich an' fries. Hardly touched it.

She's in her scrubs. These'ns is blue. Got her hair tied back in a ponytail, just like she always does at work. She's lookin' down at the counter now, fidgetin' with the silver. Then she reaches up an' plays with her necklace. It's that'n I give her awhile back. That'n with the diamonds. What I seen in her hand through that telescope.

"I know it was hard," I say, "for what you had to get done."

She nods.

"Disorientin', more like," she says. "Wasn't anythin' I hadn't seen before. You know I've handled gunshot wounds. Just never this many at once. Nor never fired at someone. An' I'd never put someone in a trunk, neither. That was the most difficult thing about it, I think. Closin' the trunk over top of that girl. Never done anythin' like that. Just a kid."

Looks up at me again. I count the freckles on the end of her nose.

"What surprised me," she says, "is how easy most of it came. There were some tough spots, sure. Pickin' that girl up off the carpet an' watchin' half her leg go clunkin' down the stairs. But overall, it didn't affect me that much. An' later, not at all. I 'member wantin' to feel somethin'. Like guilt. Sadness. Anythin'. An' I couldn't."

"You got nothin' to regret," I say. "You just done what you had to. Tom couldn't'ta got everybody outta the house an' spread the gas through it in the time we needed it to get done."

"You know what Tom did with the crate?" she asks.

"Took it back in a U-Haul. Then got a backhoe from a construction site 'round Huntsville. Drove 'em out on a flatbed. Dug a pit somewhere back in them woods. Pushed it in with the backhoe. Filled in the dirt. That's what he told me anyhow."

"An' nobody ever showed up at the warehouse?"

"Dayshift janitor showed about twenty minutes after he nailed up the crate. Told him there'd been a bad accident. Paid him extra to clean up all the blood, enough for the guy to bring his wife over from Mexico. Promised not to call immigration if'n he kept his mouth shut."

Maggie sips from outta her water glass. Sets it back down on the counter. Watch her suck the water offa her bottom lip. Ponytail bounces as she turns to face me again.

"Lemme see, huh?" she asks. "I wanna see my work, Jer."

I chuckle an' lift up my shirt. She leans over to inspect.

"Not bad," she says. "You been cleanin' it every day like I said?"

"Mornin' an' night."

"Well, almost to where the scab's startin' to resolve. Stitches give you any trouble?"

"No, ma'am. Come out last week just like you said. Mostly in the shower."

"An' you been stayin' off your feet? Takin' the antibiotics?"

"Until this very week," I say, "cep'n some paltry efforts at the alley on league nights. An' thank you much for them nasty pills. They give me diarrhea somethin' terrible."

"So don't get shot no more," she says, an' I see her smile for the first time today.

"Workin' on that," I say.

She starts on her fries. Dabs 'em in mustard a few at a time. Checks her watch.

"Oh, hey, how's it goin' with John?" she asks. "He said you were comin' into town to see him. Said you were his newest client."

"He needs more work'n I do."

"Surprised the hell outta me when he told me."

"Well. He offered pro bono. Says he wants me to work on impulse control. Says he can help me with that. Truth be told, I can always use some work on that. Don't want nothin' to get away from me. Mostly I think he just wants to do it so's *he* can sleep at night. Like maybe he's keepin' you safe somehow. He needn'ta bothered."

"Yeah, but it's funny," she laughs, "I'm tryin' to count up all the different ways it's unethical for him to do this. An' he used to chide me for that."

I slip my finger into the waistband on her scrubs an' pull it out a little bit. She turns to me an' slaps at my hand.

"Stop it, Jer," she says.

"What color are they?"

"Stop it," she says, slappin' at my hand again. "They're purple, now stop it."

"Just curious," I say. She shakes her head.

"So much for impulse control."

She chews her fries. I sip my coffee an' look down at them little orange hairs on the back of her neck that get my blood feelin' warm. After a minute she starts makin' a noise in the back of her throat. She's tryin' to swallow an' cain't. Coughs. She reaches for her water. Chokes down a few gulps.

"You okay?" I say, rubbin' her back.

"Wrong pipe," she wheezes. I can tell by the way she moves into me that she wants me to keep right on rubbin'.

"Take it easy, darlin'," I say. "I don't wanna have to carry you into another ER again."

She laughs at that an' spills her water as she's tryin' to sip it. The waitress peeks her head outta the kitchen to see 'bout the noise, an' I wave to her that it's okay.

"I guess I'm a little nervous, Jer. Little shaky, you know?"

"What ya nervous for?" I ask.

She puts her hand up over her mouth for a second. Not like she's gonna laugh. But like she cain't believe I just said what I did. I reckon I know what it's over.

"I'm not gonna hurt you, Maggie," I say. She nods.

"I know you wouldn't mean to. I know that. Truth is, Jer, what bothers me more is why I didn't let you bleed out in that car."

"Okay. How come you didn't? Said you was helpin' me 'cause it wouldn't do that they wanted to put me down. You didn't say how come."

"'Cause scared as I was, fuckin' terrified as I was," she says, "I knew how alone I'd be. I know I don't have to hide anythin' from you. You'll never judge me for what I done. For what I am. You'll never even tell me not to be."

"This 'bout that snake business?"

She nods again. "I've been thinkin'. Those kids. Candy's kids. You said I helped them. I agree with you a hundred percent there. An' I've wondered what I'd do if that situation happened to me again. Always frightened me." She looks back at me for a second. "But what if, Jerry, what if I didn't have to be afraid 'cause someone was lookin' out for me?"

"You already got that, honey," I say.

"I know it. You can help me not to be afraid to do what's right. An' that throws the whole snake business into a mess of confusion."

"Gonna have to let me in on that'n."

"You hurt others outta unconcern for their humanity. But if that enables you to protect me, then how can I argue it? Even if it's only on my behalf, I consider it a kinda service."

"Peas in a pod, then?" I ask her, movin' my hand up to rub her shoulder.

"An' do you know how God-damn scary that is, bein' in the same pod as you?" she says, meltin' a little to the pressure I give her shoulder. "Somethin' John said to me last week, or maybe the week before, was interestin'."

"What's that?" I ask. Her eyes is closed, an' she gives herself over to it as I bring my other arm 'round to rub both shoulders.

"Fourth decade of life," she says.

"Pardon?"

"Not a doubt in my mind you fit a psychopath's profile. Nor in John's. But there's a trend in folks with antisocial personality disorder, or psychopathy. They tend to stabilize in the fourth decade of life. It's not that they can learn somethin' like a conscience. They don't ever feel guilt. But it's like John said about impulse control. They can learn not to do the things that get 'em in trouble. *If* they live to the fourth decade of life, that's when it happens. Like accumulated experience finally starts fillin' in for what didn't develop as a child."

Her eyes is still closed. It's real nice lookin' at her that-away. She breathes deep a coupl'a times. Sets up straight an' turns to look at me.

"An' I know somethin' else, too," she says.

"Tell me," I say.

"Scared as I may be, Jerry," she says. "I reckon you're even more afraid of me."

"How'd you figure that?"

She leans in an' kisses me for the first time since I cut them roses for her. My ears get warm, an' my hands tingle a little bit. She pulls back, but only a inch or so.

"'Cause of what I can *take* from you," she says into my ear, slidin' her hand up my thigh. "You're afraid of what you might lack if somethin' happens to me."

I don't say nothin' at first. Just sip my own water. Look back at her watchin' me intently. I chuckle a bit. When she's right, God-damn it, she's right.

She goes back to her plate. Eats, an' neither of us say anythin' for a minute.

"I wanna know what's goin' on with Tom," she says. "Gonna keep workin' for him?"

"We got that figured out," I say. "He's gonna let me retire. Set it up with the bank in Zurich to transfer the money from my account to another'n that only I got the numbers to. Set it to happen in six months. Five an' a half now, I guess."

"Why that long?" she asks.

"Got a lotta work to do settin' up Fayetteville's end of operations again. We pretty much fucked 'em over good. Plus, Tom's gotta find another replacement for me."

"Another?" she asks.

"Anyway. He reckons the whole thing'll take that long," I say. "You think I oughtta look into Memphis properties?"

Maggie busts out laughin' again, a lot louder this time. Covers her mouth again.

"No, Jerry," she says. "You're not movin' here. No way."

"How come? God-damn it, I've missed you, darlin'. Didn't you say a piece back that you wanted to have a kid with me? What happened to that?"

"You're not movin' here. You're not movin' in with me. We're not havin' a kid, Jerry."

"Say *yet*."

"What?"

"It'd make me feel a lot better if'n you'd say *yet* at the end of all that."

She just shakes her head no an' goes back to her club sandwich. I look down at my food for the first time since the waitress set it in fronta me. Ham steak. Runny eggs.

"How 'bout you think of movin' back to Fayetteville, then?" I ask. "It's closer."

"Can't. I told you that."

"Yeah, but your old boss, I checked it out, he died about a year back. Had hisself a stroke out on the twelfth hole of Paradise Valley golf course. There's nothin' keepin' you away now. Nobody else knows. Didn't you say Fayetteville was your home?"

"It is. But it's not just my old boss at the hospital in the ER. The nurse charged with Candy found out, too. John's been payin' her off for years. If I went back, she might get greedier. Or who knows what."

"So maybe I'll pay her a visit. Then you can come home."

Maggie laughs again. Takes another bite of fries. Then she looks up at me again. Knows I'm serious. Swallows.

"No, Jerry," she says. "I don't want you to do that."

She looks up into the kitchen. Then down at her plate. Back at the door. Reckon she figures this is just what we was talkin' 'bout only a minute ago.

Then back up at me, an' I get the pleasure of them big green eyes.

She says, "At least not yet."

Drivin' back into Arkansas on I-40, I'm thinkin' of what I seen back in them woods outside Big Cal's house. 'Bout how I seen the Wowzer. An' before in the warehouse. How he just come right through me when I's shot. Waitin' under my skin to claw his way out.

I 'member waitin' for him when I's a kid. Thinkin' he's gonna find me on that tree. That's when I started talkin' to You for real. At first I just wanted You to protect me. But that didn't happen. You wasn't takin' no calls. Them damn beasts found me all the same.

I 'member gettin' home from the hospital. Openin' up my Bible an' turnin' the pages to Your picture. You were smilin', hands raised up an' a talkin' to Your heavenly Father. I knew then that You were nothin' but a pretty picture.

Call up Tom as I get nearer to Huntsville. It's gettin' on to the end of August, an' the sun's still settin' late.

"Hey, you'll think this is funny," he says. "Jose called earlier. Wants to meet the new accountant. Says he'll come by when you ain't around."

"Guess he's still pissed 'bout forgettin' him in the drunk tank," I chuckle.

"He'll get over it. How's that Maggie doin'?"

"Still kinda shook up. Never done the wet-work like that afore."

I'm comin' up on the turnoff of Interstate 40 onto Highway 23. Still on the floodplain, just south of the Boston Mountains. I can see a little bitta them to my right side.

"How long you been usin' this phone?" he asks.

"Had it a coupl'a days. Used it once 'fore now."

"Okay. Then I wanna tell you somethin'."

"Shoot," I say. He don't say nothin' for a minute. I just listen to him suck on a cigarette on the other end of the line. Hear the hum of my tires on asphalt.

"Been thinkin' on it, Jer," he says. "An' I don't reckon Big Cal could'a done it all by hisself. It don't add up thataway."

"You mean he had orders to run that little show?"

"Not from the Sanhedrin, Jerry. No way. All they care 'bout is runnin' a tight ship an' keepin' close to the willows. But somebody *on* the Sanhedrin mighta got greedy. Mighta decided to break into the new market on his lonesome usin' *they* resources."

"What'd they say when you spoke to 'em?" I ask.

"No. They was unanimous on it. Said we done the right thing. 'Course if'n it was somebody in the group, they *would* say that, now that they plans is all shot to hell."

"Well, fuck."

"Uh-huh. Listen, we don't gotta worry 'bout it now," he says.

"You know, Tom," I say. "They gonna have to kill they own snakes."

I don't even see him standin' outside with that big shoulder bag when I walk into Fat Bobby's diner just after six. Bobby waves to me from the window to the kitchen an' points to a empty stool at the counter. Pretty crowded right now. Mouths that he gonna have words with me. Bobby walks outta the swingin' kitchen doors in a apron that got his big flour handprints on it. Takes the cigarette box outta his shirtsleeve an' comes up to the spot at the counter where I'm settin' down.

He's 'bout to light his cigarette when there's a yelp from some woman behind me. Bobby looks over my shoulder an' goes ashy. I turn 'round to look. There's this feller, white male, 30 to 35, 5'10", 160 lbs, black hair, gray eyes, thick beard, an' a green baseball cap on, cockin' back the hammers on a old-style double-barrel shotgun. Standin' in the middle of the diner. Fifteen feet away an' lookin' right at me. I go for the little .22 in my front pocket. This'n is about the size of my wallet an's too small for a holster. Fall offa the stool at the counter tryin' twist 'round so's I can get my hand into my jeans. Folks clear away from the counter pretty quick. The feller raises the scattergun so I'm lookin' right into them twin black eyes on the end of the barrels.

Bobby throws the metal napkin dispenser offa the counter an' hits the feller in the left shoulder. He moves the barrels over on Bobby, an' that gives me a half a second to get my hand down inside an' grab out the .22. The feller puts it back on me quick. I start to pullin' the trigger on him at center mass. Loud as all hell.

He staggers back an' collapses onto his right knee, fires the shotgun. The blast sends chunks of the counter an' cash register back into the kitchen. I empty the rest of my .22, an' the feller falls onto his back.

Crawl up to him an' pull the shotgun outta his hand. Call back to see if'n Fat Bobby's all right. Couldn't hear him if he answered anyhow. Look down at the feller. He's got a dirty yellow T-shirt on that's got white paint stains. I count the holes where red's comin' out in a coupl'a different shades. Three in the stomach, four in the chest, one in the left shoulder, an' one just at the base of the throat.

He's clenchin' up the muscles in his arms an' legs pretty tight. Eyes closed an' face a strainin'. Harder he strains the quicker he'll bleed out. I pull up his shirtsleeve on the left side. Then on the right side. Nothin'.

Watch the last folks go runnin' outta the diner. Bobby comes up an' gets down beside me. When I look at him, he's got some specks of blood on his face an' forearms. Musta been glass or maybe plastic offa the register. I say into his ear to call 911.

"God-damn, Jer," the chief of police says to me. Rob Murch, white male, 44, 6'1", 185 lbs, blond hair, blue eyes, standin' over me an' the body. Sippin' himself some coffee. Tom's standin' next to him, but since it's within city limits, city police has jurisdiction. I'm still settin' by the body. Hadn't felt the desire to move one bit. Rob reaches down an' holds out a ballpoint pen. I take my .22 an' fit it over the pen by the trigger guard. Rob takes it up an' looks at it.

"What model is this'n?" he asks.

"J-22 LR," I say. "Got it at a show in Ft. Smith a coupl'a years back."

"How many this little thing take?"

"Eight-plus-one," I say. I watch Tom move over to the counter an' set on the left side of Fat Bobby. On Bobby's right side is a paramedic with a pair of tweezers pullin' a sliver of somethin' outta his cheek.

Rob counts the holes in the body.

"Uh-huh," he says. "Say, would you mind bein' on my shootin' team next year?"

"I already got claim to him," Tom says.

"Figures," Rob says. Then he looks down at the body again. "You know who this is?"

"Nossir," I say.

"This here's Andy Shaw. Works—*worked*—the graveyard shift with a minin' crew."

"Shit," I say. "Andy was two years ahead of me in high school."

"Yup. You know he was probably messed up on somethin'. Had a kid of his go missin' several weeks back. Fourteen-year-old boy. Just up an' gone. Right 'round the time you an' Tom come outta the woods with all that birdshot under your skin."

Tom looks up at us. Then down at the body. Back at Rob.

Rob grins. Extends his hand to me to help me up off the floor.

Stop at the Walmart on the way outta town an' pick up a case of beer. Me an' Uncle Ray's goin' froggin' late tonight. It's 'bout ten now, after all the paperwork they had me fill out at the city police station. Told Ray I'd pick him up at midnight, 'cause them big bullfrogs don't really start comin' out till then. Gotta pick up my flashlight from home, an' the spears. Make sure the tines is still sharp enough. If you miss an' plunge it into the bank, they can get dulled pretty quick on them rocks hidden in the sand.

Schnitzel greets me as I'm walkin' up the steps to the house. Bend down to scratch 'hind his ears for a second. Walk into the door to the kitchen an' open the fridge. Take out a big bright red tomato from them'ns Grandma put in there. Shut the fridge door an' head to the stairs. I can hear Grandma's television upstairs.

I walk on up the stairs an' peek in through the crack. She's settin' up in her rockin' chair, doin' needlepoint. Watchin' her comedy show. I open the door an' come inside. She don't look up at me. Walk over to the nightstand by the bed. Check her pillbox to make sure she's taken everythin'. Schnitzel stays at the door.

I go over an' kiss her on top of her head. Tell her good night. My hand's restin' on her shoulder, an' she reaches up an' pats it without lookin' at me.

Take a bite of my tomato as I start headin' back into them woods. Walk down the old path to Grandma's still. Schnitzel follows me the whole way. I check the boiler an' the connections to the mash pot. Check the valves. Look over the condenser coil for any leaks. Then I decide to take my shoes off. Tie the laces together an' hang 'em over my shoulder. Take another bite of my tomato an' walk further behind the still into the woods. The moss an' dry leaves feel real nice under my feet.

At first I thought that feller come shootin' was somebody sent by whichever one of the Sanhedrin went off the reservation. Till Rob identified him. Now I reckon I know for sure who sent him. Detective Michael MacKennon of the state police got awful scared when we last met. That was the idea, though. Probably he figured he could take what evidence he got against me an' show it to one of them boys' fathers. An' that'd be enough. He'da had to pick somebody near breakin', though. Which means he gave it a whole lotta thought. So now he's gotta be runnin' scared. I may have to give chase.

Follow the curve of the hill down to the creek. Set on a rock on the bank. Drop my feet in the water. Take another bite of my tomato. Them wet seeds is runnin' onto my wrist. I spot Schnitzel sniffin' along the bank.

There's other things to consider. Like if it wasn't just Andy that Detective MacKennon talked to. There was four boys. He might coulda talked to all four fathers. Or even if he didn't, Andy surely told the others. So that's three more.

Dig my toes into the moss an' mud on the creek bottom. Slurp another bite offa my tomato. Look up through the gap in the trees at the clear night. Moon's little now, so there's them stars out everywhere.

What about the wives? Could be each of the four dads told they wives. Probably none of them'd do anythin' as direct as Andy. But I hain't stupid enough to think women ever forget. So that's another four, there.

Take the last bite of tomato. Look down at my toes in the water an' think about Maggie. How she paints her toenails red. Watchin' her set on the edge of the bed wrapped up in a sheet, bent over, concentratin' with that little brush that come with the bottle. Movin' her head ever' minute or so to get some hair outta her face.

I know the Wowzer's movin' back in them woods. He don't like a bright moon. The darker the night the better.

He's the reason I talk to You. 'Cause of him we have some-thin' in common. I figured it awhile after I come back from the hospital. Awhile after I got et up.

I'd go out into the woods, these same woods here, a lookin' for him. It took me the longest time to figure how come I never found him. Thought he'd come an' find me so's he could get done what them dogs started at the tree. One night I come down to this creek here an' went walkin' right up the middle. Water up to my knees. Wobblin' on loose bed stones.

An' I figured it. He never come for me 'cause he *was* me. Like maybe he gets born into the world, I thought, like God gettin' born as You. I learnt in Sunday School that You an' God was the same, but You was also separate. One thing. Different folks. An' I figured that's how it is for me an' the Wowzer. An' that's when I knew who my father was, my *real* father, for the very first time.

I've talked to You ever' day since. I know You're dead. Dead as them boys I put in the ground. But if there's one thing I learnt from the job, it's that dead folk don't say shit. I can tell You everythin' 'cause I know it don't never go nowheres. An' I know if'n You could hear me, You'd under-stand, our situations bein' so similar an' all.

I get up from the rock an' start headin' upstream. Water's only to my shins now. Schnitzel follows me along the bank. Pretty soon I'ma have to head back so's I can get what I need from the shed for froggin' with Ray. I know Schnitzel wants a fried-frog-leg breakfast, too. But for right now, I like the flow of the cool water all 'round my feet an' ankles. Them sharp stones don't even bother me none when I step on 'em.

Reckon I'm gonna wait'n see on that list of folks I been buildin'. Keep close to the willows. Probably most folks'll back off for fear of losin' they skin. Them that don't can be handled as they poke they heads out.

In a few days I'ma go'n see Maggie again. Spend the night at her place. Needs to know she got no cause to be afraid of me or any other'n. When I'm with her I'm just plain old Jerry. Elsewise I'm the Wowzer.

ABOUT THE AUTHOR

Frank Wheeler Jr. was born in Memphis, Tennessee, the son of a preacher. Just thirty-three years old, he has lived in Minnesota, Texas, New Mexico, Colorado, Maryland, and Nebraska, where he earned his BA and MA in English studies from the University of Nebraska–Lincoln. He and his wife, Marie, do their best to stay in one place these days, living in Nebraska where Frank teaches at a community college in Lincoln. Inspired by the stories his Arkansas uncles used to tell, *The Wowzer* is Frank Wheeler Jr.'s first novel.